LAST HARVEST

By
G. M. Barnard

Last Harvest

by G. M. Barnard

ISBN-9781700132352

Editing and Design by Rosalyn Newhouse

Published in the United States of America

Cover Art: Paul Ranson, *Apple Tree with Red Fruit*, courtesy of The Museum of Fine Arts, Houston, gift of Audrey Jones Beck

E2

This book is dedicated in loving memory of

Teddy E. Mayfield.

Acknowledgements

Special shout out to the following people without whom this book would not be possible:

Huge thanks to Rosalyn Newhouse, my editor, who ensured I understood that *all* sentences *must* have a verb and that the word "because" is *not* a verb. This woman has the patience of Job.

Linda Ferguson, my writing instructor who gave me encouragement when I felt I couldn't and shouldn't continue writing.

To my two daughters who gave me the idea and outline for this story. To my son who gave me the ending. And to my husband for just being there.

Prologue

The figure of a young barefoot woman in a gray house dress moved through the old farmhouse on Rock Creek Road. With no one at home she could have the place to herself. Being alone felt good. The quiet felt good. The dark felt good.

She stopped at the kitchen table and looked over the newspaper articles spread out, going through each one carefully, taking her time. The picture of herself as a young girl in a cowboy hat flooded her beingness with fond memories and for a moment she almost felt whole. But that faded away as fast as it came.

Rest is what I need, she thought to herself.

Chapter One

Tuesday, September 30, 2014

Melody Marie Corbbet, age 33

She knew she shouldn't be driving. She could barely see the road. Not only was it raining so hard the drops appeared to be jumping up off the pavement, but she was raining as well. Crying and driving, wasn't that the name of some punk rock band from the '80s?

Once Melody faced the fact that she couldn't continue on to her Dad's place she began to calm down a bit and started looking for a place she could spend the night. *Motel 6 is okay,* she reasoned, *just beware of anything that looks like it could turn out to be a Bates Motel out of the movie Psycho.*

She settled on a Best Western, pulled in to the brightly lit parking lot, and sighed heavily. Yes, she was tired, more than she had realized. Interstate 5 going north up out of the Los Angeles area can be boring until you get around Stockton. Too dry and brown. It's true, you must watch what you are doing, avoid the big trucks and the crazy drivers in their speedy German cars. That will keep you occupied for a while but all too soon the monotony gets to you and the ride drones on.

This time it wasn't a boring ride. The phone call from her sister, Sammy, had come at mid-morning.

"Oh Mel," Sammy's voice had cracked and Melody knew something awful had happened. "It's Dad... he's gone, Mellie," and then long hard sobs.

"Nooooo," then Melody was sobbing breath for breath with her baby sister.

Mel and Sammy cried in tandem for what seemed like an hour but was only a few minutes.

"What happened? How can this be? Last time I talked to Dad he sounded just fine. Like his old self," Mel managed to get out before another wave of grief hit her.

"He got hit by a car, Mellie! Of all things. He ran across the road in front of his house to get his mail out of the mail box and he was hit by a damned pickup going about fifty on that main stretch of Rock Creek Road." Most of this was spilled out in fits and starts with crying jags in between.

"Well shit, Sam. You mean to tell me Dad died out there on the road by himself? Damn it! Sam!" Mel saw the picture in her mind, her aging father lying on the blacktop bleeding to death, afraid and alone.

"Oh, for God's sake no!" Sam crooked back. "The guy in the truck stopped, called the EMTs and the police. He tried to help Dad, held him in his arms until everyone arrived, but it was no use. The Yamhill County Deputy that called me said Dad was killed instantly, probably never even knew what hit him. The way to go I guess."

"The poor sucker that hit him was crying and calling Dad's name and wouldn't let the EMTs take Dad's body away, he was holding him so tight. Finally, they got him to turn loose after they let him kiss Dad goodbye. I mean, shit, Mel, this is just so fucked." Then Sam was back down the rabbit hole of her sorrow.

"Okay, I'm on my way," Mel sobbed into the phone. "I'll book a flight out of Burbank and should be up there by mid-afternoon." Melody checked the calendar on her desk at the Glendale car dealership where she worked. Tuesday, September 30, 2014. *Now there's a date that will stick in my mind,* she said to herself.

"No, Mel, pack up and come to stay. Drive up. Fill up your car with your shit and drive up."

That is exactly what Melody Marie Corbbet did, in between trips to the bathroom. She called it her nervous stomach but a medical professional would have called it IBS. It was something that she should have looked into but she put it off not wanting to have to deal with getting a colonoscopy or tell her troubles to a stranger.

She pulled out every suitcase she had, threw her clothes, makeup, shoes, books, and even a lamp from her bedroom into her 2012 Ford Focus and hit the road within an hour of receiving the call from Sammy.

Mel took the key handed to her from the night clerk and headed straight to her room and the bathroom. Once inside she burst into tears all over again. This time she cried hard and it took about an hour to gather herself enough to call Sammy to tell her she was safe and where she had stopped for the night. Melody figured she should be in Oregon and out at Dad's place in Sheridan around 6:00 pm if she got on the road by 8.00 am the following morning. There could be no fooling around, only stopping for gas, eating from drive-throughs and holding back on the coffee. Too much coffee would mean she would have to stop at rest stops to pee or whatever all the way up I-5. She had done this drive many times and knew the ropes.

****

Samantha Susan Corbbet was grateful her older sister called to check in and would be home the next day. She let Melody know Dad's house was a complete mess. She told her sister that she loved her and hung up the phone.

What Sammy didn't tell Melody was that staying alone in the old run-down farmhouse made her skin crawl. Several times she had felt like she was being watched as she moved from room to filthy room. Coming and going through the back door was the worst. A sense of alarm would wash over her, and she'd shiver nervously and look around to see who might be there.

Sammy was no stranger to this extra sense. Friends told her it was the artist in her that drew disembodied spirits to impress their turmoil upon her. This opinion gave her no comfort.

Whatever or whomever was now trying to get her attention was *not* Dad. She concluded she must have known them in the past but she pushed this out of her mind. Right now, she only had time for the flood of sadness that swirled around her from the loss of her father.

She flipped on every light in the house, turned the radio on to the local country western station, and continued cleaning and crying. She would try sleeping when it was daylight.

****

Melody turned on the TV, took off her clothes and got into bed. She was out like a light in no time. Her sleep was deep and full of dreams. It was morning in Dad's kitchen. Dad chatting happily about local small-town folks as he served her bacon and eggs. Sammy complaining about her toast being too dark. Mel offers to trade toast. She feels safe, the room is warm as sunlight comes in the window over the sink. She looks up at the ceiling and it is white. *White? No, that's not right.* She looks to the right. *Oh no, it is the motel room.* Melody is back in Stockton at a Best Western, hundreds of miles away from her dead father's farm.

Chapter Two

Wednesday, October 1, 2014

Melody Corbbet

Although it rained off and on all the way to her father's house, Melody made great time and arrived as promised close to 6:00 pm. Sammy came running out the backdoor as Melody splashed into the driveway, pulling in all the way to the back of the house close to the ramshackle barn. The two sisters embraced, sobbing in each other's arms, the sky dark, rain pouring down.

Mellie and Sammy, arms still around each other, walked into the house through the backdoor of the old farmhouse. The back porch was piled high with cans, bottles, stinky clothes and moldy towels, old shoes, and muddy boots. It smelled like an old toothless wet dog.

The rest of the house wasn't any better. Melody could see that Sammy had wiped down the kitchen counters and had moved off to the side years of stacked up junk mail, empty frozen food boxes, socks, old farming magazines, receipts, and other unexplainable items. But the table was still piled high with papers, the floor was dirty and sticky, a curtain hung off to one side on a broken rod showing part of the dirty window. The stove looked unusable, with burnt, caked-on food and layers of grease.

Melody moved through the house taking in each room as she went. The front room was dark from decades-old curtains. Still she could see years' worth of dirt on the carpet, sofa, and chairs. Thick dust on the coffee and end tables. A bookshelf overflowing with books, newspapers, and ancient photographs of family members long forgotten. A lamp with a broken shade leaned sadly to one side.

In the bedrooms upstairs there were light fixtures with burnt-out light bulbs, cobwebs clinging to doorways, and peeling wall paper. Posters of childhood heroes clung to the walls with curling edges.

"My God, Sammy! This place is a total disaster! What the hell? How did this get like this? I thought you were checking in on Dad regularly. Did you stop coming to visit?" Melody was in despair.

"Hey Mel, I live in Seattle. Give me a break. I've been here since yesterday, by myself! I had to ID Dad's body. He was smashed, Mel." Sammy was crying again.

Melody moved to hug her sister who was shaking as she cried.

"It's a messed-up deal, Mel! After that I got the number for Dad's attorney from Pastor Bob and called to let him know about the accident. You think the house is a rat's nest? You should hear about Dad's finances."

"Okay, okay. I'm here, Sammy. We are going to be just fine. We just need to eat some dinner. My treat. What's still open around here?"

Melody drove as Sammy sat quietly. It was still raining. When they got to the Chinese food restaurant, they tried to slip in without notice but that didn't work. Throughout their entire dinner well-meaning friends of their father came over to their table to offer good wishes and sympathies. News travels fast in small towns and news of a death travels even faster.

"Earl was a good man; he would always lend a hand when asked and never said no," seemed to be what most people said about Earl Jackson Corbbet. Lived his whole life, all fifty-six years of it, right here in this small town with these nice people, Melody thought to herself. She had lived here all her life too, up until she left for college. She never looked back and never came back. Sure, she could have stayed, married some log truck driver or mill worker, raised a few kids and maybe had even been happy. But it didn't sound good at the time and it didn't sound good now.

"Sammy, what exactly did the attorney say about Dad's estate? Is there any life insurance? Did Dad have anything in savings?" Melody asked in between interruptions from the locals and bites of pork fried rice.

"We are surely screwed, sister girl," said Sammy with a mouthful of spicy chicken. "You know Dad, did everything the hard way. Wrote his will himself to 'save money'." She paused, shook her head, then poured more tea for both of them.

"How do you know we're in trouble here? Can't we just sell the property and go home?"

"All I know is that the attorney said we needed to come to his office to read through the will. There's a letter from Dad as well which lays out his last wishes. Dad wanted us to stay in the house, keep the orchard. You know, run the place. I... just can't. Something about it gives me the creeps."

"You hearing voices or feeling ghosts again, little sis?"

"I can't go in or out the back door without the hair on my arms standing up!" Sammy choked out, "It's not Dad trying to talk to me, if that's what you're thinking." She sat staring at her plate, then pushed it away.

Melody felt sorry for her sister and reached over to hold Sammy's hand. They both looked out the window of the restaurant in silence for a time, watching it rain.

Melody thought about her mom. It was a very blurry thought. One that she seldom allowed herself. All she could remember was her mom and dad fighting. Lots of fights, yelling, screaming, throwing things. Melody would lie in bed at night and hear it all from upstairs in her little room. Then one day, when she came down for breakfast Mom was gone and Dad was fixing scrambled eggs and burnt toast. He told the girls their mom had run off with an old boyfriend from her younger days and that they were all on their own now, so eat your breakfast and it's off to school with you. *Can you believe it, just as if it was a common everyday thing that happened?*

And now Dad had left them. *What does he expect us to do? Farm the place, grow vegetables, raise chickens or something. The orchard is totally overgrown! When was the last time anyone got an apple or a pear out of it? The barn is going to fall down this winter for sure.*

"We are going to need help," was all Melody could say to Sammy.

Chapter Three

Melody Corbbet

That night Melody lay in her bed, the bed she had lain in as a girl being raised on this farm. The lamp she had brought with her was barely able to light up her old bedroom beyond her nightstand where she'd put it, as if it was unable to push back the darkness which hung over the house. She held a book in her hand but found she couldn't read. She couldn't sleep either.

Sammy had washed the bedding, even the pillows, but the room was still dusty. The old yellowed curtains, the same ones from when she was in high school, hung limply but stirred each time the wind blew. Melody was glad she had brought her favorite comforter.

Her mind raced with questions trying to figure out what to do first. They needed to go to the funeral home and iron out what to do with Dad's body. Cremation? Then there was the service. And a visit to that attorney's office. What was his name? Craig? Greg? Something or other Patterson, no, Patmore, no, Peanut Brain. What kind of bullshit will had he allowed Dad to write on his own? Yes, old Peanut Brain was going to get a piece of her mind, that was for certain.

She could hear Sammy in her bedroom softly crying.

Sammy was a gifted artist. Oil painting, beautiful landscapes and fairy lands. She lived in Seattle with a couple of roommates in the trendy Queen Anne district. It was great that she could make a living doing her art even if it was only a modest one.

Being an artist made her sensitive and caring with attention to small details, letting the bigger parts of life flow over her without notice. Her easy style attracted other artists and people with kind hearts and large pocket books. She was single and enjoyed her freedom. She dated when she wanted, worked most of the time, and now and then taught art at a local community college.

Melody was a bit jealous of Sammy's sweet life. Everything was harder for Mel. She worked in the accounting department of a large car dealership spending the entire day staring at a computer screen. She too was single, but lived without roommates. She wasn't as social as Sammy, often staying home to read or do some small craft project.

She sure as hell didn't miss this farm, that was for damned sure. Living with Dad had been okay. They had some good times and worked hard taking care of whatever animals Dad brought in. There was always a crop or two of something or other. And the apple and pear orchard, of course.

Like all farm girls Mel and Sammy learned to sew and cook, mostly from the mothers of their friends and the odd class at school. They even did some jam making and canning.

That's what made Mel fall asleep, dreaming of picking blackberries with Dad and Sammy in the hot sun. She could smell the berries, the dirt, and the hay. Dad was such a card, making jokes about the neighbors.

Chapter Four

Thursday, October 2, 2014

Melody and Sammy

Matters went as well as they could possibly go at West Valley Funeral Home, considering the girls were planning their father's funeral service. The business was owned by long-time Sheridan resident Andy Stokes. He was a kind older man. Overweight but dressed nice. Mel had always thought of him as Sheridan's own Pillsbury Dough Boy not only because of his roly-poly appearance but because it was a well-known fact the man loved pastries. Dad's body had been taken to the coroners in McMinnville because it had been an accident, and it wouldn't be released until the accident report was fully written up and the autopsy completed. So for now, there was no date set for the funeral.

Mel and Sam agreed that they weren't going to press charges on the driver of the pickup that had hit their Dad. They figured that poor guy had paid enough with this thing likely to be forever haunting him. Andy filled them in on the guy. Andy said his name but it didn't sound familiar and the girls decided they didn't know him. He was a young man in his early thirties, had a wife and three kids, and worked at one of the local mills.

Andy reassured the sisters that their Dad had lived a good and full life, was well liked and a productive member of the community. They should be proud of Earl and Andy would do whatever they wanted regarding his service.

The girls wanted a simple service. The minister from the First Methodist Church could do the eulogy. Pastor Bob had known Dad for years. Mel wondered to herself what sort of secrets Pastor Bob might know about her father. He was trusted and loved by many families in Sheridan. And wasn't above having a drink or two if the occasion called for it.

Mel and Sammy thanked Andy for his help and asked him to let Pastor Bob know they had chosen him to do the service. No open casket, no viewing times, no graveside ceremony. Just cookies and coffee before the service and a get-together back at Dad's place after. As for the music, *Amazing Grace* was off the list and no bagpipes at all, end of story. They'd work out the other details once they had Dad's body and could set a date for the service.

The idea of cremation was talked about. Andy let them know he was able to do that sort of thing onsite. He was willing to take them to the basement and show them the oven but the girls declined.

Next stop, the Coroner's office in McMinnville, same building as the Sheriff's department. Mel was allowed to view her father's body. She wished she hadn't; he was smashed up something awful. She and Sammy cried. The coroner was really sorry, the Sergeant on duty was really sorry, the gal at the front desk was really sorry. It was turning into a really sorry morning.

"At this point cremation really could be the way to go," Sammy whispered to her sister.

The sisters told the Sergeant that they weren't pressing charges against the fellow who had hit and killed their father. He said he already knew because he had gotten a call from Andy Stokes before they arrived. The Sergeant thought they had made the right choice. It was just a bad accident and the poor guy that hit Earl was the one really suffering at this point.

"You know, we don't need this guy coming over to the house to apologize. Really, we aren't pressing charges but that doesn't mean we want to sit and listen to the guy explain what happened over a cup of coffee," offered Melody.

"I understand" said the Sergeant, "but he is still going to be cited for speeding. You know, he said an interesting thing when I was asking him what happened. He said he didn't see your Dad crossing the road until the very last minute. Sort of like he appeared out of nowhere. Running like someone was after him. "

"I bet they all say that," whispered Sammy to Mel.

They left the Sheriff's office and went to the attorney's place. It was an old house turned into offices. Plain white with a nice green yard and a few flowering bushes. The receptionist was young and cute and told them to wait a minute; Greg would be with them very soon.

Melody made an effort to ensure she remembered his name. Greg Peterman. That name was just asking for trouble. Melody altered his last name several times in her mind. Peterman, Poodleman, Poodlehead, Poodlenuts. She almost laughed out loud.

Soon a tall, gray-haired older man stood before the sisters and introduced himself. *So, this is Dad's attorney,* thought Melody. *Seems nice but he is going to get a piece of my mind anyway.*

No sooner had the women taken their seats in the attorney's office than Melody let him know what she thought of him letting their father write his own will. She didn't hold back at all.

Peterman appeared unruffled. He sat, listened, then handed Mel and Sammy each a copy of the will. They sat in silence as they read the documents given to them.

"Earl was a man who prided himself on saving a penny anywhere he could. Rather than having an attorney draw up a will for him he went to an office supply store and picked up a kit and wrote it himself. He also wrote a letter detailing out his last wishes.

"You don't have to live on the farm if you don't want to," Peterman began to explain. "Your father, God rest his soul, figured you'd keep it, sell it, or walk away. If you walk away the property will go to the county and it will be their problem. There are taxes owing, both income and property. And there is a loan on the farm he took out as well. Earl was just living there on his Social Security. At one point he raised chickens for eggs which he sold to the neighbors, but wasn't working to make real money. For a while he let people pick apples or pears out of the orchard but it wasn't kept up so it didn't produce like it could have. He didn't have the money or the willpower to get out there and work the place. He didn't want to hire anyone and near the end he didn't want anyone on the property."

"Well, that's odd," chimed in Sammy. "He always used to get extra help whenever he needed it. Had no trouble with doing that at all. Why would he change after all these years?"

"He told me he just didn't want to be bothered, didn't want to have to deal with people, didn't like strangers poking around the place. Made him feel uneasy. Said people are nosy and asked personal questions he didn't like," offered Peterman. "He was only fifty-six years old but life had taken its toll on him. He was exhausted."

"Still seems odd to us," Melody said pointedly. "Was he feeling bad, was he sick? I mean, he ran right out in front of a pickup you could hear and see coming a mile off. Did he have something on his mind, something bugging him? Is there something about Dad you need to be telling us?"

"Ill? No. Your father was a private man. He loved his daughters. He loved you both very much but as he got older, he didn't care much for others," Peterman replied.

"Whatever you decide to do with the property is up to you but you'll both have to agree. He left it to the both of you, as stated in the will. But he didn't leave you any money. No life insurance. No savings.

"You girls might want to work out selling the place. I have no idea how much you could get for it. You just need to be thinking with the back due taxes and mortgage coming off the top. I can't say how much would be left over to split between you.

"His last wishes he put in the letter. His funeral service is already planned and paid for as is his burial site and headstone."

Melody and Sammy looked at each other. Andy hadn't said anything about this when they had been in his office earlier in the day. Melody wondered why Andy had offered cremation.

Craig Peterman continued, "He wanted you to keep the place and run the orchard as you can read there in the second paragraph. As you can see by his writing, he is actually commanding you to *live* there, both of you."

Sammy shook her head no and looked unhappy. Melody slumped in her chair.

"Of course, that's unenforceable. It's a letter. It doesn't get filed into probate," Peterman added quickly. "And as you can see, he doesn't really want the property changed in any way."

"You can mow, cut, trim, prune, pick, and generally clean up. But the house stays, the barn stays, the orchard stays. The patch of cattails out back of the barn stays, as do the four cars parked there."

Peterman went on. "In the house you can clean, paint, fix up anyway you want. You can even sell anything in the house, but it has to go into an estate account until we get out of probate."

"This is nuts!" Melody paused before she called him Poodlenuts to his face. "What was our father thinking? He doesn't leave any money to pay the bills. He thinks we are going to want to stay and follow these rules as if we were still children. We'll clean the place up but with the intent of selling it. Or not, I'm not sure. We'll stay for now but my sister and I are grown women with lives of our own and we want to go back to our jobs and lives."

And with that Melody and Samantha got up and marched out of the attorney's office.

Chapter Five

Thursday, October 2, 2014

Melody and Sammy

The sisters stood outside in the rain, each one talking on her own cell phone, trying to iron out staying in Sheridan for the time being and ensuring they would have jobs and apartments whenever it was that they would be returning home.

Then it was off to the grocery store to buy cleaning supplies and basics so that every meal wasn't eaten in a restaurant or fast food place. Coffee was the first thing in the basket, then eggs, bread, butter, milk. Items for making sandwiches. Cookies in case someone dropped by for a cup of coffee and a chat.

Once home they began the work of cleaning the kitchen. Walls and all. The coffee pot worked as hard as the girls, keeping them fueled up and in high gear.

Later, in the afternoon, it began to rain again so Mel decided to take some of the old paper bags and food boxes and make a fire in the fireplace. She sat on the dirty carpet in the front room, slowly adding to the fire as it burned. Sammy came in from the kitchen with an armload of firewood from the side of the barn. She laid it down and turned to Mel. "I found a box of stuff I want to show you." Sammy ran off and soon returned.

In the box were some family pictures and a few odds and ends from school days. A ribbon for running on the track team, a commendation from church for volunteer work, some report cards, but mostly pictures.

The girls looked through the items, laughed at the clothes and hair styles and old boy friends. And then Mel stopped laughing and held up a picture, it was their mother. Sammy took it from Mel.

"Gee, she looks so young. Pretty too. We have her hair and eyes, I think." They were quiet for a minute as they studied the old photo.

"Why do you suppose she looks so sad?" asked Melody. In the photo Sammy and Melody's mother stood next to their father as if she was being forced against her will. The young woman in the photo looked to be in her late teens, early twenties, wearing a dress that was old and worn with an apron pulled tight around her waist. She was thin, too thin. Clearly unhappy, standing in front of the house with their father, Earl. Earl appeared proud and held their mother, Emily, around the shoulders as if she was his prize, his possession.

"She looks like she would run away if she could," Sammy said sadly. "Ya, well, that's what she did," replied Mel. "I wonder why she ever married Dad. She wasn't pregnant with me; I wasn't born until after they had been married about two years or more."

"Maybe she wanted to get away from her parents, you know, just to get out of the house," offered Sammy. "Did she ever finish high school? I mean, really, Mellie, what do we know about Mom? As far as Dad was concerned, she was a forbidden subject once she ran off."

"You know what I don't see in this box?" asked Sammy digging around then dumping the contents of the box on the carpet, "I don't see a single wedding photo of Mom and Dad."

"I never thought of it until you just now mentioned it," said Mel thoughtfully. She stewed on the revelation to herself.

Where was her mother from? They didn't know their maternal grandparents. *How old was Mom when she left us? Why didn't she ever write or send cards at Christmas?* So many questions flooded Mellie's mind. She sat and stared into the fire. Would Pastor Bob know about their mother? Would they find more photos, maybe a box of their mother's things stuck back in a closet somewhere?

"Well, now that we have the front room warmed up, we might as well start dusting," said Sammy as she got up from the floor, heading off to the kitchen to get dust cloths. Soon the girls were back at it. Cleaning away as they waited to hear from Andy Stokes when they might be able to schedule the funeral.

Chapter Six

Friday, October 3, 2014

Samantha Susan Corbbet, age 31

"I don't know when I'm coming home. No, his body hasn't been released. Yes, I want you to hold my job. Can you do that for me? Can I use my sick leave for this? How much time do I have coming? Oh, good. Let me call you tomorrow. Maybe I'll know more then." Mel hung up her phone. "Well, I'm not unemployed yet, Sammy," she said turning to her sister who was making breakfast.

"Good news there. I do need to sit down and at least do some drawings, sketch out some ideas, you know. Maybe I could get inspired if I walk around the place here. Go down to the creek, or around the back of the barn. I brought a few pens. I have plans for a show around Christmas. Stuff always sells around the holidays." Sammy was trying to make this staying at the farm thing work, even though being in the house depressed her to no end. She couldn't tell if it was the fact that the house was old, run down, and dirty or if it was because of the old memories and the never-ending feeling that someone was trying to reach out to her in some way.

Her childhood hadn't been bad. She wasn't abused or neglected. There must have been good times but she couldn't recall them at the moment. There certainly hadn't been anything special or exciting or filled with any strong emotion one way or the other. Nothing more than mediocre. Plain, that was the word she was looking for. Like vanilla without toppings or a date that ends without a kiss. She remembered the year she wore a beige dress to the homecoming dance. That was certainly dull, at least compared to her life now. Oh ya, she'd had friends in school and church, but she didn't stay in touch with them, too boring. The boys she dated? Yes, they had a nice time. Nice time; not a fun time but a nice time. It had been ordinary, all so damned predictable, she mused to herself as she scrambled eggs and buttered toast. But in the back of her mind there was a little tug of a memory that wanted her attention. She pushed it down.

She thought of the girlfriends she had in high school. A few had gotten pregnant before the end of their senior year and had to get married. But that was their plan all along anyway. One married a boy her parents had hired to work on their farm. Most of them still lived right here in Sheridan. Stay-at-home moms who sewed and canned and sang in the church choir or worked part-time at the hardware store. *Yep, that could have been me. I would have been stuck right here on this farm. Wait, I am stuck on this farm,* she realized.

"Here's your God-damned breakfast, Mellie!" Sammy dropped the plate on the table, turned, and stormed out of the kitchen.

"Crap! Sam, you've burnt the stinkin' toast!" Mel exclaimed as she watched Sammy stomp out the backdoor into the yard and head for the barn.

Chapter Seven

Friday, October 3, 2014

Sammy

Sammy marched around the back yard in a drizzling rain. It was just barely the beginning of October and it had rained every day she had been home. It felt good on her hot face and as she moved around from the back yard to the front yard of the house she began to notice where she was and what was out there.

It was clear that Dad hadn't mowed any part of the property in many months. The areas that had once been flower or vegetable gardens hadn't been worked or tended to in a very long time. Sammy went to the back yard again and headed to the barn. Weeds surrounded the old structure as high as her head. The side door to the barn was half opened and hanging on just the bottom hinge.

Sammy pushed her way through and found herself in a dark, foul-smelling space with cobwebs in almost every corner. Light came through the boards and she could hear the rain on the tin roof. She noted that it was still somewhat dry inside so the roof must be holding out okay.

All the animal stalls were empty, old tack from horses long gone hung on the gate posts. The center of the large barn was filled with an old tractor and an even older pickup, their tires flat, their paint replaced by rust. Sammy smiled as she recalled times from her childhood riding on that very same tractor as her Dad drove it out to the orchard pulling a trailer filled with large baskets on their way to pick that autumn's harvest of apples and pears. It was almost that time of year now.

Sammy left the barn and walked over to the orchard. It wasn't as large as she remembered, maybe only ten acres. Some of the trees were dead and had fallen over. Others suffered from massive insect infestations. The weeds had taken over here as well. It made her sad to think about how this orchard had once looked. Back in the day this had been a well-tended farm. Spring smelled so sweet with pink and white blooms on the trees. By autumn the orchard was heavy with fruit ready to harvest. Now there were only a few random apples and pears here and there that appeared ripe.

If this had been twenty years ago, Sammy thought, she and Mellie would be out here right now picking along with neighbors and local people. Locals would u-pick and pay her father. Women laughing and chattering about the applesauce, apple butter, and pies they planned to make or the pears they would put up in jars. Children running this way and that, some climbing the trees to pick the fruit that was out of reach. The men lifting, carrying, and loading the heavy baskets in the trunks of cars or the back of pickups.

And Dad, well, he would be weighing the fruit, taking money and making change. Talking and telling stories the whole time, completely in his element. At one point there for about ten years running Dad had an apple press. He and some of the men from town made apple cider. Now, that stuff was good, sweet and crisp tasting. They tried their hand at making hard cider as well and it was a big hit until a few of the wives and a now long-gone preacher, Pastor Jake, put an end to it. *Pity,* thought Sammy, as she recalled stealing a bottle of hard cider and the flatbed truck with Mellie. Driving crazy on old country roads and listening to '90s hits, like the country-western song *Thunder Rolls*, on the local radio station. Yes, there were some good times.

Sammy found herself smiling, standing in the rain in the middle of a dying orchard. She sighed and looked around.

Then the artist in her took over. She could draw this place in pen and ink. Black, white, and some mossy green tones. Grays and muted blues for the sky.

"That's the ticket," she thought out loud. If she got started right away, she could get maybe five full pieces done before December and have them ready for her holiday show in Seattle. She could work right here and use Dad's old place as inspiration.

Then, out of the corner of her eye, Sammy thought she saw a figure, moving in the shadows, over by the row of abandoned cars. But it was more than just a thing in motion, it was a feeling of hopelessness and dread. The orchard felt darker, heavier. The air thick with the smell of dead leaves. Fog started to move in, covering the ground as it inched toward the barn.

She shivered and started to walk back to the house. She turned around twice to look behind her as it felt like she was being followed. But she saw and heard nothing. It was that jump in heart rate, that dryness and bad taste in her mouth, and an impression of shortness of breath that made her break into a run.

Sammy slammed into the back door of the house and raced into the kitchen.

"Girl, you are as white as a sheet. What happened, Sammy, you see a ghost out there?" Mel said laughing.

"Ya, well, maybe," Sammy said, shaking. She went in the bathroom and got a towel to dry her hair.

Chapter Eight

Friday, October 3, 2014

Melody

Melody had decided that she and Sammy needed a trip into Portland for two reasons. The first one being that after Sammy told Mellie about her idea to turn out some art pieces using Dad's place as inspiration she knew her sister was going to need more art supplies. And secondly, they needed to get out of the house and Sheridan. Go someplace that didn't remind them every second that their Dad was dead and they were stuck in a losing battle regarding the property.

Mel drove as Sammy talked. She had already figured out down to the exact detail two of the pen-and-ink drawings she would do, both being out in the orchard from different points of view. The other three would be the barn, the house, and that row of old cars that they had orders not to move. The dead rose garden also held promise for one or maybe even two drawings.

Mel was impressed with Sammy's ability to create pictures, scenes of the outdoors that spoke to the heart. Some of Sammy's art made Mel think of Van Gogh's work with orchards and trees in their different seasons. There was always so much emotion and movement in Sam's paintings and drawings. One picture could tell a whole story. She could just imagine a series of five or more drawings all coming out of one farm. It would be an entire novel.

Once they had picked up Sammy's art supplies, which took about an hour of fooling around as she changed her mind twice then rethought the whole project, they were off for lunch at one of the trendy downtown cafes.

"You know, I'm thinking that the best way to go about cleaning out Dad's place is to start with his clothes and personal things and at the same time we can look for anything of Mom's. Like, maybe we would find more pictures of her, or a diary, even a jewelry box or a yearbook from her high school days," Mel proposed to Sam.

"Okay, but just so you know once I start in on this series of drawings there isn't going to be me helping out on cleanup so much. I mean, it really takes all I have to keep my focus. I want to include some details about those trees right down to the bark and tiny dead branches. It takes every ounce of attention I have to get those fine lines onto paper. And those cars, I could end up doing a complete study on that rust alone. I hope I bought enough reds..." Sammy's voice trailed off and her eyes stared off into space as if she was looking at the row of derelict cars in her mind. Sammy was already drawing her art pieces in her head and Mel knew not to waste her time trying to talk to her sister when she was in high create mode. It would be words falling on deaf ears.

So Mel got out a piece of paper to make a "to do" list while she ate her lunch of chicken salad and hot tea. She needed light bulbs so she could see what she was doing, garbage bags to throw old clothes in, banker's boxes to put anything important she might find, rubber gloves to wear while she handled the old moldy items, and rags and soap to wipe down the walls and closets.

"Ugh!" Mel said out loud as she thought about the filthy walls and woodwork.

"What?" asked Sammy. "Don't you think that I should use a matte finish on this series?"

Both girls came out of their mental fogs at the same time, looked at each other and laughed. They had each been so involved in their own thoughts that they hadn't really noticed the other or even where they were.

It was good to laugh; it was as if their souls had been washed of cares for that small instance in time. They held hands, each one kissing the other's right hand, a gesture from when they were kids that their mother had taught them.

Chapter Nine

Friday, October 3, 2014

Melody

After stopping at a Fred Meyer to pick up Mel's list of needed items and a few other things like new pillows for the beds, an area rug for the front room, a Crock Pot to make soup for the cold days ahead, and throw blankets for their laps to keep cozy by the fire at night, they loaded up the car and drove back to Sheridan and the old farm.

It was well past 8:00 pm when they returned home, and the house and surrounding area was dark. They had forgotten to leave a light on in the house when they took off after breakfast and the place appeared abandoned as they pulled into the driveway. Actually, it looked haunted. Downright scary. And if Mel didn't know better, she thought she saw something move in Dad's bedroom window.

"Why does it have to get so dark out here?" she asked Sam. "It's early evening and this place looks so gloomy. This is why I live in Southern California. It's like the lights never go out there. The sun is always shining or it's lit up like a Christmas tree after dark."

"Did you lock the door before we left?" asked Sam. She had seen the curtains in her father's room move open a bit and then go back into place as if someone was watching them pull into the driveway.

"No, didn't think of it," replied Mel in a hushed voice. She stared at the window on the first floor of the old farmhouse that had been her father's and mother's room, and then just her father's for so many more years. Was that a figure of a person she saw or just the way the shadows from the trees as they fell upon the side of the house?

"Did you see that?" whispered Sam. She had goose bumps now. Like chicken skin all up and down her arms.

There it was again! A slow dark thing that glided from left to right of the window frame. It stopped mid-window as if to confirm the girls were home then slid off into nothingness.

"Yaaaaaa, but not sure what," came back a shaky Mel. She realized that she and Sam were breathing together, in out, in out, rapidly.

Still raining, still dark out, wind still blowing, tree branches still waving back and forth. Mel turned off the car engine but didn't take her eyes from the window. Shit! What if some nut case had gotten into the house while they were gone, thinking that the place was now abandoned, looking to swipe anything he could get his hands on? Perfect. Maybe an escapee from the State Mental Hospital in Salem less than forty miles away. Some nut who had cut up his family and put them in the freezer then took off for a Mexican vacation and had only been caught because his brother-in-law had stopped by to pick up some ribs for a BBQ and found his sister and the kids instead.

"Fuck!" hissed Sam.

"Shut up" came back Mel.

Slowly they both got out of the car, leaving the headlights on and letting the warning alarm for leaving the keys in the ignition go off, so that whoever was in the house would know the girls were about to enter the home.

The sisters ran from the car at the same time. Mel hit the back door of the house hard with her hand, then opened it slowly, Sam so close behind her that she was breathing in her sister's ear. They moved as if one being from room to room switching on the lights as they went. Back porch, laundry room, kitchen, front room. They stopped to listen: was that hurried footsteps? A tree scratching the side of the house? The house settling? A rat on the run?

"Fuck!" hissed Mel.

"Shut up," came back Sam.

They stood together in front of Dad's bedroom door, which had remained shut the entire time they had been back home. They had had no reason to go in there. They had always known that was Dad's room, his space, and they never went in there as children after Mom left. Never.

Slowly, Mel opened Dad's bedroom door. Sam had her hands-on Mel's shoulders as they both peered in. The shadow flashed to the right, through the door leading to the sewing room, out to the laundry room ending with a bang of the back door. Both girls raced around through the kitchen to the laundry room then the back porch. They found themselves standing in the driveway in front of the car in the rain.

Whatever or whoever it was had dashed out of the house leaving no clue as to which direction they might have gone. Mel and Sam stood there breathless, shaking, eyes open wide, unable to think what to do next.

Chapter Ten

Friday, October 3, 2014

Sergeant Terence Kell

"You two girls need to caaaaaalm waaaaaay down," said the Sergeant from the Yamhill County Sheriff's office in his slow but kind way. He smiled at both Mel and Sam as if they had just told him they had seen a ghost. Well, they had just told him that. His disbelief was impossible for him to hide but he understood the two women, knew their father had just died in an awful accident, and he was there to comfort them and ensure there wasn't any way it could be some stupid teenagers out causing trouble.

When Sergeant Terence Kell got the call about a possible B&E out at the old Corbbet farm, he was having his dinner of a hamburger and fries in his patrol car on Highway 18 at the Dairy Queen. Terry knew Mel and Sam. He had gone through all twelve grades with them. He even remembered the year their mom ran off with an old boyfriend from back in her high school days. What was his name? A real lady's man, his mom had guessed, one night at dinner when his folks were talking about Emily Corbbet leaving Earl Corbbet. Real shame, it was. Leaving behind them two little girls, Earl all heartbroken. Why, Em and her new man were probably holed up in some seedy hotel down at the coast right at that very moment. Em would come to her senses and return home, sooner or later. Most women did after the spark went out of a fling. At least that is what his dad had said that night at dinner as he buttered his corn bread and tried to look wise.

Thing was, Emily Corbbet never did come home. In fact, she was never heard from again by anyone, now that he thought about it. Never once contacted her daughters, at least from what he knew.

What needed to be done right now was settle these two girls down and have a good look around the place. Sergeant Kell went from room to room of the old farmhouse, big flashlight in hand, checking all the closets, looking in the bathroom and under the beds. Followed every inch of the way by Mel and Sam. Every time he stopped short; they'd run into the back of him. Reminded him of Three Stooges movies he saw when he was a kid. Every once in a while, he'd sneeze really hard from all the dust.

Sam and Mel, talking at the same time, both pointing into their dad's bedroom, which hadn't been cleaned or dusted since the 1980s, at least. He pointed this out to the girls. No figure prints, no marks in the dust to show anyone had been there. Did anything look moved or disturbed in anyway? They didn't think so but then they admitted they never went in their Dad's room.

Upstairs, then back downstairs, out the back door. He aimed his flashlight on the dirt-turned-to-mud of the driveway. The only footprints he could make out were from the girls and himself. He walked to the barn and took a quick look inside, moving his flashlight around and listening for any sound of movement. He came out and scanned the orchard from the front edge but didn't go in.

He was unable to go around the back of the barn due to tall weeds, blackberry vines, and cattails. It was then he realized he was looking at four vehicles, all parked in a row facing forward, almost entirely hidden in the overgrowth.

"Hey, do you realize that you have a collector's dream sitting out here going to rust?" Sergeant Kell commented as he walked back to the house.

"I looked at them," offered Sam. "Mostly to see if there was any way to make them part of my next exhibit. There is some very nice rust indeed. But as far as those cars being worth something on their own. I have no idea. Maybe we should look into that."

"Well, ladies, I am going to call it all safe at this time. I can't see where anyone was in the house, no prints left in the dust, which I might add must be half an inch thick in your Dad's room. Nothing in the house moved around, nothing missing that you can tell. Nothing and no one outside but us chickens. Let me help you unload your car and change out some light bulbs up where you can't reach, then I will be on my way." His voice was calm and deep.

"You don't mind if I ask you a rather personal question, do you?"

Both girls shook their heads no.

"Did you ever hear from your Mother? You know, later, after she had been gone awhile."

Both girls shook their heads no. Blank looks on their faces.

"Did you ever think to look her up? You know, in this day and age it might not be too hard to find her. Internet and all. Now might be the time, let her know about your Dad passing. If you know her date of birth and social security number, I could give it a try on my computer at the office. Maiden name might help, some information about her parents or brothers and sisters. Anything, really." Sergeant Kell noted the confusion in Mel and Sam's eyes. He didn't need to be told they didn't know any of this vital information about their mother, he could see it on them. They hadn't even thought to look for their own mother, ever. This lowered his opinion of the two women. Why would they never look for their mother?

"Here's what I'm going to do. I start my shift tomorrow at noon. I'm going to stop by here and have a look around in the daylight. Besides, I want to see those cars up close. Does that make you all feel any better?"

"Yes, Terry, it does. I am so sorry to... no, I'm not sorry, I'm grateful you came out and looked and took some time with us and didn't just write us off as a couple of nuts," said Mel, looking relieved.

Later that night, as Sergeant Kell drove back to the office, rain hitting his windshield, the wipers splashing away, he had time to think about Earl Corbbet, his wife, Emily, and those two women back in that rundown wreck of a house. He had to admit there was a very eerie feeling in that place. It was more than just years of dust and clutter. It was the gloom, an odd sadness that surrounded the entire farm, in the house, by the barn, the orchard, even over by the cars.

Had the girls seen the ghost of their dad in the window? Was that crazy old guy, Earl, going to haunt his kids? Terry half believed in that sort of thing, even after being on the job now for the past ten years. *There could be ghosts, that's for sure,* he thought. *You just can't tell what it is that they want to say to you. That's the problem with them.*

As for the cars out back by the barn he did know why he hadn't really noticed them until now. Of course, they were covered up fairly well and the fact was, he hadn't been out to the orchard since he was a kid in grade school. Any time he needed to go up Rock Creek Road now he was usually in a big hurry on some domestic violence call so he wasn't checking out Earl Corbbet's place from the road. Just more junky cars in someone's yard here in Yamhill County. Well, they had his attention now.

Chapter Eleven

Friday, October 3, 2014

Melody and Sammy

After Sergeant Kell left Sam and Mel moved around the kitchen, putting the groceries away, washing and drying dishes and wiping down the table and counters.

Sam offered to make them some soup and Mel said she was going to take a shower. They would take turns: first Mel showered and put on some clean sweats and fluffy slippers while Sam made up a packaged potato cheese soup. Then Sam showered, donning a pair of pink flannel pajamas with white hearts, while Mel started a fire in the fireplace in the front room.

They moved all the furniture around against the walls and spread out the new area rug they had gotten at Fred Meyer in front of the fireplace. The new pillows and throw blankets were arranged so that once they had their bowls of soup, they could sit down in the little safe space they had created to eat.

Only one lamp was now operational. It had a fresh light bulb with a new white shade and was placed in the corner on an old end table. In this light the front room of the old farmhouse actually looked warm, cozy, and inviting.

The rain outside continued to pour down, the wind blew, and the curtains moved with each gust. *Drafty old place,* thought Mel. She sat on the rug with her bowl of soup, beer, and plate of fresh French bread. *Nice,* she said to herself. When she thought about it, she didn't remember her and Sammy ever doing this before. Never when Dad was around. They had never had a slumber party with girlfriends over. Never a birthday party nor a Christmas party.

Oh ya, they had attended plenty of these sorts of social events as kids at their friends' homes. She remembered how nice it was to be with a family that had a mom. Someone who baked cookies or had sewn you a new summer dress. Or sang while she did the dishes or hung clothes on the line in the yard. A soft voice telling you good night, sweet dreams rather than a loud bark yelling for you to shut up and go to sleep, damn it!

Sam was the first to say something about their fright. "Do you feel it? I don't. It's gone, like, not in the house at this time," she said calmly. She buttered her bread and tore off pieces to dip in her soup. "Damn, that scared the shit out of me, I swear. I bet that took two years off my life."

Mel turned from her daydream to her sister. "Could you tell what it wanted? Could you tell who it was? I sure couldn't"

"No, but I think Terry believes us. He sure looks better than he did in high school." And they both laughed.

Terry had been a freshman the same year as Sam when Mel was in her junior year. He always showed up at the dances alone. All the girls always danced with him when he asked so he didn't feel bad. Besides, Terry was a good dancer; he held you close during the slow dances and wasn't afraid to get crazy during the fast ones.

"Ya, sort of an ugly, skinny guy with glasses and braces," said Sam, "but look at him now. Tall, filled out, great teeth, kind smile. He had his pick of the girls by the time he was a senior but married that short fat... what was her name?"

Both girls thought. "Jan, Janet, Janelle, Jell-O, I don't know." Mel tried to jog her brain into remembering. They both snickered. Jan had been short and fat, alright, but kind and motherly even in high school. She had long blonde hair and a round face that shone bright, as if an angel. A pudgy little cherub angel had come down from heaven and was living amongst humans.

"But I can see it, I see why Terry would marry Jan. Both have kind hearts. Her uncle on the other hand, he was an ass. Always bragging round town about how great he was, how smart he was. Until he had that shooting accident," Mel went on. "Whatever happened to his wife and her daughter? I remember Dad saying it couldn't have happened any better if it had been planned. Good riddance to bad rubbish."

"Is that Jan's Uncle's Ford Crown Vic out back in the car graveyard?" asked Sam. Both girls shivered at the thought.

"We can ask Terry when he comes by tomorrow," replied Mel. They fell quiet again. Mel stirred the fire and put on another log. Sam put the dinner dishes in the sink, then came back and snuggled down on the rug with her pillow and blanket.

The sisters fell asleep there in the front room, both dreaming but of different things. Sammy's dreams found her walking through the orchard at harvest time. The trees full of fruit. *I must get this down on canvas, maybe watercolor is the way to go,* her thoughts floating around like the leaves blowing in the wind. *I just need to catch the light... over there.*

Mel's dreams took her back to high school. Hallways that went on forever, always late for class, losing her pencil, then her pen wouldn't work. The door to the principal's office opens and someone's parents emerge, crying, their boy had been in an accident. The scene changes to the funeral for the boy. Mel sits in the back row of the dimly lit church with four other girls. But they aren't crying, each one's face hard with hate. They nod at her and she nods back as she sits down with them, they lean on each other. She looks up and sees swirls of smoke from candles and incense rising to the intricate ceiling of the church as if carrying away life's force, spirits drifting away.

Then peace; Sam and Mel slept in peace. The fire glowing as the night wore on. A shadow hovered near what had once been a rose garden as if waiting for release.

Chapter Twelve

Saturday, October 4, 2014

Melody and Sammy, Pat Holiday

"Oh God, my back is killing me!"

"My everything is killing me!"

Mel and Sam both tried to get up off the floor.

"What time is it?"

"9:30 for God's sake!"

At that point there was a knock at the front door. The two girls scrambled up, Sammy rushed to the bathroom leaving Mellie to answer the door.

"Hello, oh my, you weren't asleep, were you? At this hour? Well, damn woman, half the day is gone! Don't stand there staring at me, invite me in. Get that coffee pot fired up. You all got anything to eat, cookies, cake, something, anything? Let's get this party started."

Mel couldn't believe her eyes. It was Patricia Holiday, her best friend from high school. The two women flew into each other's arms, laughing and crying at the same time. Pat, she had called her. The idea was that each girl got a name that you couldn't tell on paper if it was a boy or girl. There was Mel, Sam, and Pat. They had planned to go into business together. A bakery or fancy deli. To avoid any problems with gender bias they would use names that didn't tip anyone off who they might be dealing with when applying for a business loan or buying a store front, at least on paper.

"Not only do you sleep all day but you don't keep house for shit, girlfriend!" Pat came in and looked around in amazement. "Just let the good times roll and forget how the place looks. Okay, I can live with that. Well, maybe not. So, you don't have a vacuum?"

"Sammy! Get out here, it's Pat!" Mel yelled to Sam.

"Ya, Sam, get your fuzzy ass out here and give me a hug!" Pat called to Sam.

Sam ran out of the bathroom with the toothbrush still in her mouth, towel in hand, and arms in the air. Pat and Sam embraced, tears of joy all around.

On went the coffee pot and out came the cookies. The girls sat around the kitchen table and settled in for a good gabfest. Mel and Sam explained to Pat what had happened to their Dad and the problems with the property and the strange conditions their father had put in his letter. Pat listened, asking a question as needed here and there.

Then it was Pat's turn. What was happening in her life? So much, but yet so little. Pat had married right out of high school and had three kids ranging in ages from eight to eleven. She was a stay-at-home mom right now but had worked on and off over the years at the local hardware store. Not the bakery they had planned back in those days in cooking class. She sewed and cooked and canned and baked. It was clear she was eating her own cooking; she was at least a size 22. But she was full of life, still funny as hell, and Mel realized how much she had missed Pat.

When Sam went upstairs to get dressed Mel told Pat about her plain life in Glendale, California and her job in the accounting department of the Ford dealership.

"Sounds boring because it is," Mel added. No husband. Dates here and there but not really looking to have to change or share which is what one must do to make any relationship or marriage work. Came close a time or two but chickened out before the deal was sealed.

Sam filled in her story for Pat when Mel went up to change clothes. The art scene in Seattle, the parties, the dates, being broke most of the time. Pat loved hearing Sam talk about her art and the plans to make a series of pictures in pen and ink from the farm for the holiday show. *How clever is that?* Pat thought to herself.

When Mel was dressed, she came back into the kitchen and Sam excused herself so she could go out to the orchard and get started, "because those pictures aren't going to draw themselves."

Pat didn't wait to get started on cleaning. She got right to work scrubbing the stove while she directed Mel to clean out the refrigerator. Then they washed the front of the kitchen cabinets.

Next, they went after the windows, using the cleaning supplies bought the day before. When done there they went to the front room and got going on the woodwork and the walls. Pat took down pictures and paintings that had hung on the walls since Mel could remember as a baby.

The cleaning water in the bucket had to be changed often.

"Say, Pat, how's your mom?" asked Mel.

"Oh, she's okay. She sews a lot, still makes quilts. Enjoys a glass of wine now and then. Likes to go to those New Age conventions. She can do whatever she wants now that Dad is gone," replied Pat as she wiped down the same wall for the third time. "You know, we are going to have to paint the ceiling."

"Did your mom ever say anything about my mom? Did they know each other? Were they friends?" asked Mel.

Pat stopped dead in her tracks. Mel had never asked these sorts of questions before. Everyone knew when Emily Corbbet took off with her old boyfriend. It had been the talk of the town and stayed that way for months after. Earl had no problem spilling his sad story to anyone who would listen. Looking for sympathy, Pat's mom had said. When it was the two girls that should get whatever help there was to offer.

"I have to change this bucket of water again. Let's go in the kitchen," said Pat. "Besides, it's time for a coffee break."

They took off their rubber gloves and washed their hands. Mel poured them both a hot cup of coffee then had to make a fresh pot. Terry was to be there by noon and that would be very soon.

Pat began to tell what she had heard from her mom so many years ago, and which she had never told Mel. Emily wasn't from Sheridan, or at least, hadn't grown up there. Seems she was from somewhere in Montana. Earl had gone off for a summer to work on a ranch there and that autumn had come home with Em as his bride. The talk didn't stop there. Em was pregnant when she arrived in Sheridan, in mid-October, 1980, or so Pat's mom had said. Poor Emily, only eighteen years old and four or five months pregnant. Young, scared, and lonely.

Mel almost dropped her coffee cup. That meant that her Mom *was* pregnant with her. Her mind raced to connect the dots. Her birthday was February 7th, 1981. Not only was 1980 two years after she thought her parents were married, it also meant her mother got pregnant around May, which is spring.

When did Dad go out to Montana? Her mind raced trying to do the math. Was Mom pregnant *before* she met Dad?

Mel laid out her revelation to Pat. Pat nodded, yes, her Mom, Joy, had put two and two together as well. Pat hung her head, "I'm sorry. Maybe, I shouldn't have told you but we were just kids and I figured you knew and so why talk about it when there were pies to bake and plans to hatch for the future?"

Mel got up, crossed the room and hugged her friend. "Maybe I should stop by and visit Joy soon. We want to find Mom, tell her what happened to Dad. Reach out now that we can and should."

"People run off for reasons only they know. They don't always want to be found. I know you want to reach out to your mother. You must have so many questions for her. But maybe you will be disappointed with what you find. I've heard stories where these sorts of family reunions don't live up to some people's hopes and dreams. What they find is worse than not knowing. Just a word of warning," Pat replied. Her voice held kindness and caring.

Mel thought about what Pat was trying to say to her. Would they find her mom an old drunk in some bar at a truck stop who was only happy to see them as it might mean free drinks or a handout? Or would they find her on her deathbed, unable to speak or even remember who her own children were?

Maybe she and Sammy should move slower on this idea of finding their mother.

Chapter Thirteen

Saturday, October 4, 2014

Melody and Sammy

"Well, look who the cat dragged in," Pat said as Sam and the Sergeant entered the kitchen.

"Hey Patty! How's Bud? He still in charge of the big pancake feed next month?" was Terry's reply.

"Oh, ya, he is and he won't have it any other way," answered Pat.

"Sam and I have just been all over God's creation out there and didn't see any foot prints or signs of anyone ever being out there except for you two girls and some raccoons," the Sergeant said, pointing in the direction out back of the house. "And I am telling you that there are some apples and pears that are going to need picking pretty soon. If you girls would get off your butts, put down those coffee cups and get to pickin' we could have some apple sauce for those pancakes. And maybe a pie or two or three for the Sheriff's office. Just sayin'."

"Come look in the front room." Mel motioned to Sam and Terry.

"That's real nice. Smells better," was all Terry said.

"There's light in here! I can see through the windows, front door open and everything. When was the last time that happened?" asked Sam.

"Here, you two, help us roll up this old carpet and take it out to the barn." Pat was barking orders now.

Up came the old carpet and away it went to the barn, the Sergeant making jokes and the girls laughing the whole time. *I wonder when the last time this yard heard laughter?* thought Mel as she struggled under the weight of the old smelly rug.

Sergeant Kell said his goodbyes and asked if he could send his wife out for some apples and pears. Mel and Sam said yes, gladly. *Ya, you send out old Jell-O,* thought Sam.

"What was that all about?" Pat wanted to know when they got back in the house. Mel and Sam filled her in on what had happened the night before. Pat listened and nodded and frowned. "Can the day get any stranger?" asked Pat.

"Sure, it already has," said Mel and she filled her sister in on the new Corbbet family story that had unfolded over coffee not too long before she and Terry had walked in the kitchen.

"Mel is right, Pat. We need to go talk to Joy. Does your mom like visitors?" asked Sam.

"I think she would be happy to see you two and more than happy to share with you what she might know about your mom. I can't say and I don't know if they were friends or not, but hopefully she will be of some help to you both on piecing things together. I bet if we had enough information Terry could help locate your mom." With that said, Pat started in on cleaning the floor in the front room followed by Mel, with Sam finishing up the walls and woodwork.

Once the floor had dried the women placed the new area rug in the middle of the room then moved the sofa, end tables, overstuffed chair, and coffee table into a more functional arrangement. The old pictures and photos were placed in the back sewing room as were the random books that didn't fit the bookshelves on either side of the fireplace. Old magazines and newspapers were moved to the back porch and the mirror over the fireplace was cleaned. The key to wind up the mantel clock was found and the correct time was put on its face. It ticked away happily as Pat said her goodbyes.

"I will call you when Mom is ready to see you. I bet she has some curtains you can have for the front room. And a slipcover for the sofa, although it really should be taken out back and burned. Take that old vacuum to Pete's in town. He can get it running for you." Pat was still barking orders. And in a lower voice she added, "Find some candles, burn those at night. Light them while humming a soft song. Something cheerful. You need light and love to move that... whatever or whoever on out of here. You know what I mean?"

Sam and Mel nodded, and hugged Pat goodbye. "Call us tomorrow, promise," whispered Mel. Pat agreed.

"I am so hungry I could eat a horse. Let's make dinner. I want to fry up those pork chops we bought yesterday. Then I'll show you how much I got done on my first picture. It's going really well; the light was perfect." Sammy was all a-chatter and happy.

Mel stewed on the new information about her mom. It could be that Earl wasn't her dad. Should she have a DNA test done now to see if he was or wasn't? And if Earl wasn't her dad who was? Why would Dad marry Mom if she was pregnant by another man? Did he know he wasn't her father? Did he know who Mel's real father was? Could be Dad had no clue about it at all, about any of this. Did he just marry Mom because he loved her and didn't realize she was pregnant, or didn't care at the time?

And we have four cars in the yard and one of them might belong to Jell-O's Uncle Dickhead who had an odd accident. Plus, there is some being who is lurking about the place. Maybe more than one. Mel thought these things over as she started the fire in the fireplace. Tomorrow she would buy some candles for the mantel.

Chapter Fourteen

Saturday, October 4, 2014

Sergeant Kell

Sergeant Terence (Terry) Kell sat in his patrol car at the Dairy Queen out on Highway 18 and watched the cars and trucks roar past as he ate his dinner. He had a lot to think about and it always helped to watch traffic while he pondered questions his mind wouldn't let go.

The Corbbet farm was two miles outside of Sheridan down Rock Creek Road, almost exactly halfway between Sheridan and Willamina. The night before had been the first time he had been out at that orchard since he was a kid in grade school picking apples with his folks and not just racing past on some law enforcement type of situation.

Sure, he had to drive by from time to time but never had to stop. He'd never dated either of the Corbbet girls in high school and his folks weren't close to Earl like Pastor Bob.

Still, it struck him funny that now he noticed those cars back of the barn in the berry bushes on the Corbbet property. Where before he hadn't given it a second thought, now they pulled his attention. Maybe it was because Sammy and Mellie were seeing things, or a person, or whatever, and he got a chance to tromp around the place a bit. And because of that he started recalling things, incidents, from his childhood.

He had walked in the direction of the four derelict vehicles with the intention of giving them a good looking over when Sammy yelled out a greeting from the area to the side of the barn in front of the orchard. He ended up turning around and going over to visit with her for a bit.

It was clear she was doing some sketching of that area of the farm as she was fully set up out there. She had a chair, an easel with a canvas, a table with pens and pencils, and a mug of coffee. The piece of art was already coming together. He could see what she was looking at and it was going on to the canvas exactly as it appeared in real life.

Terry wondered where Sammy got her talent. He liked her art style. A little spooky but intriguing. She certainly didn't get her gift from her father. Earl couldn't manage to get a coat of paint on his own house.

But before he had gotten distracted and turned away from the cars Terry had realized he recognized three of the vehicles. One had belonged to his wife's uncle, Joe Benton. A Ford Crown Victoria, light blue, uncertain what year the model was, 1992? It was a big boat of a car, had been Joe's pride and joy, and he sported around town in it showing off as much as a person could in a place as small as Sheridan. There was not much more he could remember about Joe, except he had been a heavy drinker, couldn't hold a job, and bragged about all the fights he'd been in, at least that's what his mom had told him. Terry was around seven or eight, he figured out in his head, when old Braggin' Joe fell out of the town Christmas tree while helping to string the lights. It was just before the big tree lighting ceremony Sheridan held every year and this incident should have put a damper on things but it didn't. In fact, there were a couple of people who were quite joyous after they hauled Joe off to the hospital to get checked out.

Then there was Philip Mason's car. 1998 Mazda Miata, charcoal gray. Philip, a senior at Sheridan High, had died at school in a very strange accident when Jeff was a freshman. What a guy that Philip was, huge, manly, loud. On the football team. All the girls were crazy about him. No, that wasn't right. Terry paused and took another bite out of his hamburger. The girls were afraid of Philip. Terry had always thought it was because of Philip's size and loud voice. Just too forward, too aggressive for most of the girls there at school.

Terry, on the other hand, had figured out how to be popular with the girls. He had three older sisters that had taught him all the new dance steps and had kept him up to date on that sort of thing since he was ten years old. Terry attended every school dance and seldom did any of his offers to dance receive a decline. He would just start at one end of the room and ask each girl in turn as a new song was played. And when he had danced with each girl there he would start again back at the beginning. He remembered dancing with Mellie and Sammy.

The smile on his face didn't start until he thought about dancing with his Jan. Yes, she had been plump back then, but he loved the feel of her as he pulled her close during the slow songs. Jan was a junior, in Mellie's class. She wasn't popular but she was sweet and loving. She liked to cook and he liked to eat. Terry knew he would marry Jan from the first time she invited him over for dinner. The age difference was awkward but that didn't matter.

Terry had tried to date several girls from his own freshman class but they seemed jumpy, nervous about being asked out unless it was with a crowd. Like a dance or friends all going to a movie or a group going to the beach.

His mind went back to the puzzle of the four vehicles on the Corbbet farm.

The third vehicle was an old black Chevy pickup, 1973, classic. Had belonged to some guy who worked at the mill. Was that right? Or was it the local bar where the guy had worked. Hmmmm? What had happened to him? Something that had been the talk of the town at the time. What year was that? Had he already left for college?

Now that Terry couldn't remember the owner or what happened to the owner of the black Chevy pickup, he realized he needed to go back to the Corbbet farm and get the VIN off there so he could look up the information on the computer back at the office. In fact, he decided, he was going to do that for all four vehicles because he couldn't place the fourth car in his memory bank either.

There was a fourth car, an old rusted 1980s Chevy Caprice. It appeared to be the first in the row, parked more behind the barn as if to hide it. Blackberry bushes were doing a pretty good job of covering it. No idea whose that was or when that had been parked there.

I must be slipping, Terry thought to himself, when he couldn't correctly place the owners of the pickup and the blackberry car. *Ya, getting senile now that I'm a whole thirty-one years old.* Maybe he would ask around to a few of the old-timers at work. Deputies that had been on the job for the past twenty or thirty years. They might remember the stories behind each of the vehicles. And they might even know the reason these cars ended up in Earl's yard. What was up with that? Why would Earl keep these cars all these years?

Chapter Fifteen

Saturday, April 4, 1998

Sally Evans, age 15

She was so excited to have been asked out on a date by the most popular boy at school that she never asked herself why. Philip Mason, the star football player. Philip Mason, the biggest, handsomest senior at Sheridan High School. Yes, Philip Mason had asked her to go out with him Saturday night. He would meet her in front of the movie theatre at 7:00 pm sharp. She had been caught off guard by the invitation and had forgotten to ask where they were going so she would know what to wear.

Who cared? Nope, not her. Not this little freshman girl. She started getting ready at 2:00 in the afternoon that Saturday. Washing and setting her hair. Running off to the drug store, hair still in curlers, so she could pick out a new lipstick and a fresh pair of pantyhose. She chose a pink dress with white flowers and white sandals, and used her mom's Estée Lauder perfume. She was dressed with makeup on and fully ready to go by 6:00 pm and she arrived at the theatre by 6:20. She didn't care that she would have to wait for forty minutes. If anyone asked, she could say, oh, I'm waiting for my date. Philip Mason, you know.

Just a little before 7:00 Philip Mason rolled up in his new, sleek, gray 1998 Miata. He gunned the engine as he pulled in front of the theatre and motioned for her to get in the car. She jumped in without a second thought. As they pulled away, he handed her a coke in a Dairy Queen cup. "Thought you might like something to drink on our drive to the coast," he said in a smooth, soft voice.

It did occur to her that something wasn't quite right at that very moment, for when she took the paper cup of soda from Philip their fingers touched, just briefly, and the hairs on her arm stood up. But she was young and hadn't yet developed that sixth sense that older girls and women have that tell them all is not well here, get out while you can.

No, she happily took the coke and drank. Within ten minutes they were well on their way to Lincoln City. She felt relaxed to the point that she couldn't feel her hands or feet and she tried to put down the coke. "No, no, don't spill in my new car. Drink up, drink it all."

She couldn't really see the beach house as Philip opened her door and easily lifted her out of the car. She could hear the ocean and smell the sea air but didn't know where she was exactly. It seemed like a beautiful dream, with the sun going down and the wind tinkling the chimes by the front door.

Her vision focused in and out. She was lying on a bed, or maybe it was a sofa. Philip's big face came into view. His lips bright red, his hair covered with a woman's brightly colored scarf. Was that blue eye shadow on his eye lids? Why were his cheeks so pink?

Philip showed the frozen girl a large pocket knife. He opened it up in front of her eyes. She wanted to scream but she couldn't move; she could barely breathe. He carefully pulled her dress up around her waist and looked at her panties and hose. Using the back of the knife he cut off her pantyhose in long strips, going down the length of both legs. Not cutting her skin but leaving behind long red scratches going from waist to toe.

When he pulled back to look at his handiwork she could see he was no longer wearing his jeans and button-up white shirt. Instead he was wearing a woman's white nylon slip, like the kind her mother wore. She could see through it enough to tell he wasn't wearing any underwear and his penis was erect, bulging against the white fabric.

She was frightened, terrified, and if she could have spoken or screamed, she wouldn't have anyway as what stood before her confused her young girl's mind into silence. Her heart pounded; she could hear it in her ears. Her breath short and shallow, mouth open. Her eyes open as wide as possible.

In an instant Philip had pulled his erect penis out from the slip and with a few short jerks of his hand ejaculated all over her face and hair. It went in her eyes and up her nose, but mostly in her mouth. He screamed with laughter as she choked to breathe and could do nothing to wipe away the hot semen.

In her frozen fear, she lost control and urinated where she lay, which thrilled her tormentor all the more. He just stood there and laughed. A cruel, horrifying, pitiless laugh.

She awoke, sitting straight up in bed, soaked in sweat, crying. Sally Evans, now thirty-one years old, still haunted by her ordeal at the hands of Philip Mason, lay back down on her bed and sobbed. She had never told her parents about what had happened that night. And after a time, she found out she wasn't the only one. There were three other girls that she knew of and several others that she suspected.

Philip Mason got away with every single attack. Not one single girl was raped outright. No, he tormented his frightened victims, while dressed like a woman and degrading them to the point that the shame was too great to be told.

That is, until he had his accident.

Chapter Sixteen

Monday, October 6, 2014

Melody

Melody awoke to her sister shaking her. "Wake up, get up, we've got stuff to do!" pestered Sammy.

"The Coroner just called and said he has determined Dad's death was an accident."

"Wow, he must be a Rhodes Scholar. What gave him the clue?" came Mel's retort.

"No time for jokes. I talked to old round Andy at the funeral home. He is expecting us this morning. We still have a few details of the service to plan, people to call, flowers to order. We've got to get some clothes down to him so they can dress Dad and get him ready for the service. Mel, we have to go in Dad's bedroom to get his clothes!" Now Sammy's voice changed from serious to sad with a bit of nervousness thrown in.

"Have we completely given up on the idea of having Dad cremated? What happened with that? Dad doesn't need clothes to get cremated!" protested Melody.

"I already mentioned to Andy that per Dad's last wishes letter Dad paid to get buried so that's the plan. He was like, 'Oh, ya, now I remember.' Goofy old fat guy. Even if we aren't doing an open casket Dad still needs clothes."

"Okay, let's do this thing. But I must have coffee first. Do you think we could not burn the toast today?" Mel asked.

The sisters had slept in their old rooms, in their old beds, that night even though they had gone to all the trouble of cleaning the front room of the farmhouse the day before. They decided that night they didn't want to be caught sleeping in the front room again.

"If I clean another room in this house it is going to be this one." Mel told her sister. "I need to make a safe space somewhere in this house." *And I need a place that doesn't feel like there are eyes watching me,* Mel thought to herself.

Breakfast was put together quickly. Coffee, fried eggs, and toast. It was eaten just as fast. Mel and Sammy got dressed in no time at all. The two young women looked fresh and ready for their short two-mile trip into downtown Sheridan. They were prepared for the task at hand.

They entered their father's bedroom together, moving through the doorway side by side, having to press together a bit to get inside. Slowly they looked around, taking in the sights of a place they never could enter as children.

As with the rest of the house this room appeared to be the color gray, or maybe light brown. Years of dust covered most objects, a lamp shade, a nightstand, the dresser. Who could tell what color the bedspread had been when it was new? The curtains, maybe white at one time, were now a strange gray-green. Clothes and shoes everywhere. On the floor, hanging half in and half out of drawers, piled on top of an old orange overstuffed chair.

There were a few old photos of folks hanging here and there. Some of them were taken on the farm back in its heyday, when the orchard was up and running. One photo had an old flatbed truck loaded with big baskets of apples and a very proud man in bib overalls standing next to it with his arms crossed over his chest.

Sammy carefully opened drawers and pushed clothing around. "I forgot to ask Andy exactly what he needed to be able to dress Dad properly. Socks, yes. Underwear? Really? An undershirt? I don't know. Mellie, check the closet for a suit. I know Dad had a couple. Tie, we need a tie. A tie pin? White shirt, yes. Cufflinks? Shoes? Oh, dear God, I hate this." And she began to cry, wiping her tears on the sleeve of her sweater.

Melody looked through the closet. Mostly casual button-down shirts, a sports jacket, some very odd khaki pants, ugly ties, and old sweaters with moth holes. Off to one side she found a dark blue pin stripe suit. She realized it was the one he had worn to her graduation from Western Oregon University in 2003. The white shirt and tie he had worn was next to it. These would have to do. She lovingly pulled them from the closet and took them to the front room to see them in better light. They seemed fine but she decided they would go to the cleaners first. Then to the funeral home.

She went back into the bedroom to see how Sammy was doing and find a pair of good shoes for Dad to wear. She had this odd feeling, like a parent getting their child ready for a big day, a graduation or prom. It was happiness, mixed with pride and sadness all at once. *Is that possible?* she thought. Well, it was going to be Dad's big day, last day, a service to honor him and for people to remember him in a good way. She found her father's dress shoes and held them up for Sammy to see.

Sammy had an armload of items when she turned to look at her sister and the shoes. "Those look pretty good. How's the suit and shirt?" she asked.

"They need to go to the dry cleaners, so does the tie. Other than that, they'll work fine. What have you got there?" Mel asked.

"Socks, undershirt, underwear, almost like new. Must be Christmas gifts we gave him that he never wore. I even found the tie clasp and cufflinks set we gave him for his birthday when we were kids and thought he was going to marry that gal from the hardware store." Sammy held them out so Melody could look them over.

"And have a look at this!" Sammy walked past Melody into the front room and sat down on the couch. In her other hand she held a child's jewelry box. Melody ran into the front room, put down the shoes, and sat down next to Sammy.

Sammy opened the yellowed white box trimmed in gold. Inside a small ballet dancer popped up and stood still in front of a little mirror attached to the top of the box. Three old photos fell out, each of a girl at different stages of her life, three years old, nine years old, and fourteen years old. Ages and dates on the back of the photos, with the name of their mother, Emily Louise Newberry, written in pencil.

"Emily Louise Newberry, our mother's full name. I never knew her full name, never knew her maiden name. And look, with these dates on the back of the photos we can tell what year she was born. That would be 1962. Sammy! This might be enough information to track her down. Or at least find out more about her, who her family was. Hell, we might have aunts and uncles!" Melody was almost in tears, her voice cracking as she let out her thoughts.

Sammy pushed a finger around inside the bottom of the little box and brought out a broken locket necklace in the shape of a heart. On the back inscribed was the name "Emily"; inside the locket, nothing. The delicate chain was broken but the clasp for putting the necklace on and off was still intact.

There was a pink baby bracelet with the name "Newberry Baby" in tiny white beads. And a woman's high school class ring, a small silver ring with a red oval stone and the name of the school around the stone. Heart-shaped designs on each side enclosed an 8 on one side and a 0 on the other.

"Here is another clue. This class ring is from Hamilton High School, class of '80. Must be from somewhere in Montana!" exclaimed Sammy. "Oh, Mellie, what if our mom went back to Montana when she left Dad? What if she just went home to her folks?"

"What else are we going to find in here?" was all Melody said as she walked right back in to her father's bedroom ready to tear the place apart.

After an hour of pulling out drawers and dumping their contents out on the bed, digging under the bed for old boxes, and rifling through the closet, all the girls had to show for their efforts were some photos of them as kids at Christmas and a few other holidays and a lock box, no key.

One drawer was of some interest as it held what the girls guessed were some of their mother's things, old clothes. Carefully they took out each item and examined it. They asked each other questions. Mostly to voice what was in their minds, not really expecting an answer from the other.

"Okay, a winter nightie with Christmas trees on it. Not very sexy but warm, I'm sure. Who gave *that* to her? Dad?"

"White ankle socks, now yellow. A fashion statement. What do you wear those with?"

"This is a nice scarf, or at least it must have been when it was new. Horses on it. Was Mom into horses?"

"Look, here is her purse! That's odd, wouldn't she have taken her purse with her when she left? Well, I suppose a girl's got to have more than one handbag."

"What's in it? Old lipstick? Twenty-seven-year-old Life Savers?"

"Nope. A wallet, with two dollars and some change and baby pictures of you and me. Library card from the Sheridan City Library for Emily Corbbet. No ID, no driver's license, no social security card."

Mel had to stop and think a minute. Would a woman run off with another man and not pack? Not take her only handbag and wallet? Her last two dollars?

"Well, we've made a big enough mess here. Let's pack up Dad's clothes and head over to the funeral home. We will have to explain to Andy about taking the suit into Mac to the dry cleaners but we will be able to set a date and plan out the rest of the service around that and get the ball rolling on Dad's last party," Sammy said, ready to go.

It didn't take much time at all to iron out the details for Earl Corbbet's funeral service as he had done all that himself. His daughters wanted simple music like "I'll Be Seeing You in All the Old Familiar Places," or "What a Wonderful Life." Pastor Bob would do the eulogy, exact details of what would be said when the girls got together with him later. Coffee and cookies served as people waited to be seated. That would be extra but Melody couldn't understand why. The Archway Cookie factory was in McMinnville, just seven miles away. Didn't Mr. Donuts here have stock in that company by now? Melody was mad at herself for her unkind thoughts.

Pastor Bob showed up at the house just before dinner to go over what Sammy and Mellie wanted said about their father and to fill in vital information such as birth date, parents' names, place of birth, and marriage particulars.

What was Pastor Bob's last name? Melody asked herself. *Snider, Sniper, Snapper, Snickers?* She suppressed a giggle and it came out a snicker which just made matters worse and she had to cover her month and look away. Pastor Bob took it as Melody trying to control her grief.

He was about their father's age, fifty-five to sixty, in there somewhere. Kind face, gentle and caring to his congregation. This was the one man in Sheridan, Oregon that knew it all. All the good, all the bad, and all the unspeakable. If you asked him to keep a secret he would. Sammy knew that for certain.

"I know that you are here to talk about Dad, Pastor Bob, but I was wondering if you could help out Sammy and me regarding our mother," Mel started in after the eulogy seemed finalized. "You know, Dad never talked about her after she ran off with, well, whoever that was she ran off with. Did you know her? What can you tell us about her? Do you think she would come to Dad's service if we tracked her down and invited her?"

The pastor wiped his mouth with a handkerchief he kept in his pocket and cleared his throat. "Well, I came to Sheridan around 1986 and took over the First Methodist Church that year as the pastor. The pastor before me was retiring. Pastor Jake. He planned to move back East after I got all genned in with the congregation. When I first got here, I was pretty busy trying to learn my way around town, find out about the history of the church and what the members needed, that sort of thing. Took me a year or so to get my feet under me and that is when I met your mother at a Fourth of July picnic. She had you two with her, cute little girls in summer dresses. She told me she had made them for you. She loved you both very much, I know that for a fact. Just made it all the stranger she would run off on you and your father a year later. But humans are foolish when it comes to love and matters of the heart."

"Did she attend church? Did she talk about her family? Did they come to visit here?" Both Sammy and Mellie peppered the pastor with questions all at once.

"She attended my church now and then. She wasn't a regular. I think she would have been if she could have gotten a ride every Sunday. Your father, God rest his soul, was not a church-going man and when your mother did talk him into coming to Sunday Services, he would fall asleep. Snore so loud I could hear him all the way up at the pulpit. After service I would stand at the door and shake everyone's hand as they left and have a little visit with each person. One time I asked your father if he had had a nice nap. He got a bit upset and didn't come back for a long time."

"I love it, add that to the eulogy. Could you?" giggled Sammy.

"Sure, no problem. I do need to figure out how to mention your mother being married to your father but not bring attention to the fact of her leaving him. I'll work it out. As far as you girls finding her, well, I doubt you will. If a person doesn't want to be found they won't leave a trail to follow. It was clear, at least to me, that your mother, for as sweet a woman as she was, wasn't in love with your father. She was here, had you girls, and that was her life and she was resigned to it. Your father was an annoyance she put up with. She just didn't have any other choice. He seemed to know and not care. Sorry I can't say more," he ended.

Can't say or won't say, Melody thought to herself. *So, Mom marries Dad because she is pregnant. Moves away from her family to this small town, lonely on this farm and when she gets the first chance she runs off. Would I do the same? Yep, I bet I would. Leave my small girls behind? I don't think so. Not a phone call, birthday or Christmas gift or letter. Never!*

Chapter Seventeen

Saturday, October 11, 2014

Melody

The service for Earl Jackson Corbbet was about sixty minutes long. Fifty-five minutes too long for Sammy. Fifty-nine minutes too long for Melody. Somehow the sisters sat through it, there in the front row by themselves, while what appeared to be the entire town of Sheridan squeezed in behind them.

Some jerk, who would pay for his screw-up later once they figured out who it was, had added the song "Amazing Grace" to the service after they had both made a big deal about not using that song. Not only that but it was the bagpipe version which made Melody's blood boil.

Then there was the part of the service where friends and family got a chance to tell little short personal stories about Earl Corbbet. That had felt like it went on forever.

"I hate this. I want out of here," Sammy sobbed on Mellie's shoulder. Mel put her arms around her sister and they cried together. Yes, their father was gone and it was sad, but mostly because they hated the music and despised listening to people babble away for what seemed like an eternity.

Afterwards there were all the hellos and goodbyes and would you like another cup of coffee to go with that cake at the farm. The house was packed with people and Melody was happy they had spent so much time on cleaning the kitchen and bathroom and painting the front room, if only an off white. People spilled out onto the never-used front porch to smoke and talk, while others stayed in the kitchen to help with dishes and putting out more food.

Melody wandered through the house overhearing bits and pieces of conversation.

"Too bad about not being able to have an open casket, I mean, Earl hit by that pickup and all. Just a shame. True, he wasn't looking so good there near the end anyway."

"Pity the girls never got married. I mean, Earl never got a chance to walk them down the aisle or dance with them at their wedding. Isn't one of them gay?"

"I understand Earl left the girls the farm, lock, stock, and barrel. I just hope they don't start growing marijuana out here."

"Both girls born and raised out here. Run off to the big city to make their fame and fortune. Did you see their dresses? I bet they wear designer clothes and shoes. There isn't a man in Yamhill County that could support and keep them happy. They won't find husbands here. That's for sure."

"Lovely girls. Sort of skinny, not much meat on those bones though. You won't get much farm work out of them and I bet they both get sick this winter."

Melody wandered around, smiling, pouring coffee. She felt so sleepy, so worn out. Her eyelids getting heavier by the minute. Maybe she should head up to her room and lie down for a minute or two. For just a little while.

Melody shuffled up next to her sister. "Hey, Sammy. I have an idea on how to clear this place out and be done with all this social stuff. You and I go around and sell apples. One buck a pound, bring your own basket or crate, cash only, climb the tree yourself or bring a teenager. No deliveries," Melody whispered to Sammy. Sammy almost spit out her iced tea. "I love it, let's roll."

The girls headed off to opposite ends of the house and started in at each grouping of people to lay out their sales pitch. They went slowly at first but soon gathered steam. Within an hour they were standing at the front door together, saying goodbye, kissing goodbye, shaking hands goodbye and waving goodbye.

The last one out the door was Pastor Bob. "You know, your Father would have been proud of you both today. I need to remember that trick the next time I think guests are staying too long." The three of them had a good laugh as the sisters waved goodbye to him.

"Have I told you lately that I love you?" Melody asked Sammy as they walked into the kitchen with their arms around each other. They stopped and looked at the woman washing dishes at the sink. Sammy looked at Melody and shrugged.

"Hey, thanks for helping out with the dishes but I think we have it from here. You must be...?" started Melody.

The woman turned around and smiled. She must have been in her early fifties, carrying an extra thirty pounds, plainly dressed in a dark gray pants suit and flat extra-wide shoes. Her hair was gray as well, pulled back in a French roll, and looked like it had a pink rinse on it. She had a lovely red rhinestone horse brooch pinned to her suit jacket lapel.

"A friend of your mother's. When I heard about your father's accident, I knew I just had to come to the service. But, to be honest, I really wanted to see you both. You know you girls meant so much to your mother. Your father, well, not so much. I don't mean to speak ill of the dead here but not only was he boring, he was a tightwad as well. What your mother had to do to just get enough grocery money out of the guy let alone dress you girls and keep the lights on around here is a wonder."

The woman talked fast but was friendly in the warmest way. Neither girl moved until the woman motioned for them to sit down at the table, which she had cleared of all dirty dishes and half-eaten casseroles and replaced with the last of the fried chicken, mashed potatoes, and a fruit salad.

"Sit down, here. Let's have dinner together and I'll tell you stories about your mother." The woman quickly set the table and the girls, as if under her spell, sat down.

"You knew our mother?" Sammy managed to croak out?

"Oh my, yes, child! She was from Hamilton, Montana, about one-hour south of Missoula. Small town, much like Sheridan. Born and raised there by her parents. The only child of Ned and Willa Newberry. They were sweet, trusting people. Gave Emily anything she asked for and more.

"Emily had always dreamed of going to college after high school. Some place big like Seattle or Berkeley. Anything to get out and meet people, see new places, experience the world. She had hoped to travel as well. You know how young girls dream of going to Paris. Your mother was the same. She loved horses; you know."

The words purred out of the woman as she served up their plates and handed them to each of the girls. She placed a glass of milk by their plates along with napkins and forks. She sat down and urged the girls to eat their dinner before it got cold and they did as she asked.

"You both have grown to be such beautiful women. With careers, no less. Living in cities with friends. Lots of parties, I bet," she said to Sammy and Sammy nodded with a mouth full of chicken.

"It must be wonderful to have your own money, go where you want when you want. No husband to say yes or no, you just get up and go," she said turning to Melody who was putting butter on her potatoes.

"Why yes, it is, now how..." but Sammy got cut off by the woman who went on talking as if she knew Sammy was about to ask more questions.

"This house isn't much to look at is it? I bet it hasn't changed since I last saw it back in the late '80s." The woman laughed. It was a pure, sweet sound, like the tinkling of crystal. "Let's see now, your mother came to Sheridan with your father mid-October 1980. He had been hired by her father to help out on their cattle ranch there in Montana for that spring and summer. He had to get back here by the end of September, first of October for the apple and pear harvest. But they were a bit late and so was the harvest that year."

"So, Mother didn't know Dad very long before they got married?" asked Melody before the strange woman cut her off.

"That's right. Your father came out to Montana first part of June. Maybe late May. He wasn't much to look at. Plain. Didn't have a penny when he arrived. Had driven all the way there in an old pickup truck. Emily's father had hired a whole new crew that year. Lots of work to do, fences to put in or fix, cattle to herd from pasture to pasture. They had to be counted and weighed before shipping. Must have hired ten or more men."

"Did Mom have a boyfriend before she met our Dad? Any one she liked?" asked Melody.

The woman sat and thought a moment. Her eyes went down to her hands resting on the table and the smile fell from her face. Then she let out a sigh, blinked and began to talk again. Only slowly and in a hushed voice now.

"Yes, there was a fellow your mom had a crush on. Not a boy. A full-grown man. Bill Garrett.

"He was the first one of the new crew hired. Must have shown up in April. There was a chill in the air still. Oh, he was a handsome devil. Tall. Dark hair. Green eyes that could look right through you. A charming smile. You could tell he was used to having his way. Emily's father, Ned, loved him from the start. Even had him in the house eating meals at the dinner table with the family. Until it was clear Bill had an unusual interest in Emily, who was only eighteen at the time. She was still in high school, end of her senior year.

"Ned warned Emily to stay away from Bill. Bill was five years older than Emily. But that didn't stop Emily from doing everything she could to get Bill's attention. Tight jeans and low-cut tops. Asking for help to lift this or carry that. Showing off on her horse for him.

"One night first part of June Emily slipped out of the house to meet up with Bill out in the barn. You know, no one knew anything about Bill. No idea about his past or where he had come from or why.

"Emily, she was headstrong, thought she had it all under control. Fool girl thinks romance is a kiss in the moonlight and a man is as thrilled with that as a girl. So, when Bill wants more than a kiss and a hug, she says no. She pushes him away and gives him a slap on the face. Bill decides it's time to show her how this really plays out.

"He starts slapping her around. Slapping her hard. Emily's crying and it's raining out. She calls for help and he hauls off and socks her so hard she came up off the ground and lands flat on her back. Knocks the wind out of her. She can't talk or scream or even breathe. William takes the time to tie her up really good. Turns her over on her stomach, pulls down her jeans and takes her up her... well, where it doesn't normally go. Then rapes her from the front. Two times." The woman's voice trailed off. Tears ran down the faces of the three women at the kitchen table.

Melody put her head down on the table and cried long hard sobs. *The product of a rape.* She was sorry for herself, for her mother and for all that her mother went through. Emily married Earl because she needed to be married to have her child.

Chapter Eighteen

Sunday, October 12, 2014

Melody

Melody rolled over; her pillow wet from crying. She looked at the travel clock on the nightstand; it read 3:00 am. She is in bed, in her room at the farmhouse. How did she get here? Had she been dreaming? The strange woman who never said who she was, the story about her mother's brutal rape, and the realization of why her mother married her father.

Was it true? Was Dad not her father? The man who had always taken care of her and fixed her lunches and sent her off to school and bought her new shoes. Not her father? Her mourning was twice as sharp now. The man she'd lost hadn't even been hers to lose. It was like losing him twice. Could it be true?

But did it matter? This was the man that *had* taken care of her and fixed her lunches and sent her off to school and bought her new shoes. In her heart, Earl was her dad and she was his daughter.

She got out of bed and went downstairs. The kitchen was clean, no dishes or sign of dinner on the table. The front room was clean as well. Melody went to the mantel above the fireplace. She lit the candles she had put there several days before and very quietly sang a song she'd heard many years ago in another dream.

Where is my mother? What happened to her? Did she run off out of shame? Did Dad kill her and hide her body there on the farm? She wouldn't have just run off without us.

In the old, overgrown rose garden a shadow lingered, humming the same lonely tune, agreeing with Melody. *That's right,* nodded the shadow, *she never ever would have left her children.*

Chapter Nineteen

Sunday, October 12, 2014

Sergeant Kell

Terry sat at the kitchen table and looked down at his plate: scrambled eggs and toast. Uneventful. *What sort of Sunday breakfast is this?* he thought. "Can I have more coffee?" he asked his wife, Jan.

"Of course, silly, there is always coffee for you." He loved her now and forever, he thought. She was sweet and caring and they hardly ever fought.

When he started dating her in high school, he had been teased by the other boys in his freshmen class. "Terry's got the balls, dating a junior. Way to go, studly," the boys would call out in the locker room after gym class. "Yep, that's me, the stud of Sheridan High School," he would reply and the whole place would burst out in laugher.

"Hey, Bunny, what did you think of Earl Corbbet's service yesterday? Pretty nice, I thought."

"I thought those girls did a real nice job of putting on something for their dad. It's clear to anyone they loved him, even though they moved away and left him on his own. Oh, you can't blame them for wanting to have their own lives. Just get out of town and put the past behind them, you know, with their mom running off when they were really little and all."

"Earl sure left them a mess out at that farm, you know."

"Oh Lord, don't you know it! I was there in that kitchen helping out with the food and even though it was clear those girls had been cleaning they just hadn't been able to get to the bad places yet. You know, like under the sink. Sweet Jesus! I opened the cupboard door to get some dish soap from under the sink and I just don't have words for the mess and stink under there!" Jan added.

"You know what they have in their yard back over by the orchard? Three old cars and a classic Chevy pickup. While you all were busy putting out the food and getting things going in the house, I took a little walk out there by those cars. I am pretty sure one of those is your Uncle Joe's old Ford. Isn't that odd? Why would that car be out at Earl's farm? And now that I'm thinking about it, what exactly was it that happened to Uncle Joe?" Terry questioned his wife. "All I remember hearing when I was a kid was that he got shot while out doing some target practice. Something odd like that."

"Right you are about it being odd. Gee, how old was I when that happened? Let me think about this for a minute." Jan poured herself a cup of coffee and sat down at the kitchen table with her husband.

Jan had to think for two whole minutes before she started talking. She settled in to her chair with a little wiggle like she did when she was going to tell a story that was going to last a while. Terry loved all her little ways and habits. He smiled at her and he settled in as well to hear the tale.

"It was, oh shoot, well, Uncle Joe died in 1993. That would make me twelve years old. Uncle Joe was Mom's older brother, but he sure didn't act that way. Dad thought Uncle Joe was a complete ass, bragging all the time about how he had this and he had that new car that his wife had bought him and how no one else but him could do something or other.

"About three or four years before he was shot, he married a gal with a daughter from down on the coast. Waldport, I think it was, and they moved to Sheridan. I don't know what they lived on. Uncle Joe never seemed to have a job, at least nothing that lasted very long. Someone once said Uncle Joe's wife, oh what was her name, had gotten a very large divorce settlement from her first husband and that's how they got by. Lilly! That was his wife's name!

"Anyway, she had a daughter, Suzie, who was a couple years older than I was. That would make her fourteen. Nice girl, kept to herself. Poor thing, every time she opened her mouth to say something Uncle Joe made fun of her. He told her how fat she was, how bad her clothes looked on her, how her hair wasn't right. He just couldn't say one good thing about her and he always made it a point to say something cruel to her when other people were around. You know, being a teenager is hard enough for us girls without someone to keep at you about all your insecurities. Well, Uncle Joe would dig at her until he had her in tears. She would start crying and run into the other room and he would just keep at it, even picking at her for crying.

"Lilly hated when he did that, you know, pick on Suzie, and they would fight about it right in front of other people. Start right in there on the spot. They didn't care if they were over at other people's houses or if they were in the grocery store. Mom stopped inviting them over to dinner. She couldn't stand to hear them go at it and she couldn't stand to hear poor Suzie cry.

"All this had been going on for three or four years before the accident. Uncle Joe making poor Suzie's life a misery. Damn, he gave away her dog. One time he hid some of her things and told her he had burned them. She found them later in a closet. It was just some books and cards from her grandparents but it really upset her.

"One day Uncle Joe comes over to the house and asks my Dad if he can borrow a couple small hand guns because he wants to do some target shooting and he wants to show Suzie how guns work. Dad wasn't so keen on the idea but old Uncle Joe, he just wouldn't leave Dad alone and finally Dad gave in and let Uncle Joe borrow two small pistols and some ammo.

"Now, as the story goes, from what I was told and what I could overhear when the adults were talking and thought I wasn't listening, Uncle Joe took the guns and Suzie and goes up out Gopher Valley Road and he finds a good spot, sets up some cans and bottles and shows poor nervous Suzie how great a shot he is. We think he did it to scare the child, just like everything else he did in his bullying fashion.

"Well, he loads up her gun and hands it to her, shows her how to hold it, how to point it, warns her about the recoil and stands her in front of the bottles he had put out on a log. She shoots off a few, and she is missing the bottles completely. Of course, he teased her, called her stupid, ugly, and how she'll never find a husband. She was shaking and crying and she turns to tell Uncle Joe she doesn't want to do this anymore and *pow!* she shoots old Uncle Joe right in the foot. He starts screaming at her, says he's going to beat her when he gets his hands on her. He tries to get her to put the gun down and moves toward her and *blam!* Suzie shoots Uncle Joe just above the knee! I heard she was crying so hard, shaking like a leaf, and he is screaming like a stuck pig. Somehow, he is able to grab her by the shoulder and *kapow!* she shoots Uncle Joe a third time, only this time she gets him in the stomach, right in the guts.

"Dad told us kids there isn't any worse pain in the world than being gut shot. And you don't die right away, you just bleed like crazy inside, because the bullet goes in and bounces around a bit and makes a mess of your innards. Oh, ya, I bet you know about that, don't ya honey? Sorry," Jan apologized to Terry.

"Anyway, big-mouth Uncle Joe is lying on the ground screaming and crying and begging Suzie to put down the gun and go for help. She is shaking and crying, and walks over to him, looks him in the eyes and shoots him square in the forehead. Right between his eyes!"

"God damn it!" exclaimed Terry. "She murdered her stepdad! This is a homicide!"

"Some neighbors had heard the shooting and then heard all the screaming and called the cops. The cops got out there, found Suzie sitting on the ground next to Uncle Joe, gun still in her hand, crying and throwing up. They say the poor girl had peed her pants too. She was just a wreck, couldn't talk for half a day, just cried and screamed. When she finally calmed down, she would just stare into space, not say a word. They got some psychiatrist in to the Sheriff's station in McMinnville and he was able to get the whole story out of her. He later stated she wasn't responsible for her actions because she was so nervous all the time around Uncle Joe." Jan was wrapping up her story.

"What happened to Suzie? What about the trial? Did she get life in prison? Did they try her as an adult?" Terry was worked up at this point.

"It never went to trial; no charges were ever brought up on her for killing Uncle Joe. It was labeled an *accident*. Poor Suzie went into a mental hospital for about six months and as her mother had moved back to Waldport after the funeral, we never saw Suzie again. I heard later, that once Suzie got out of the loony bin, she and her mom moved to some place in Washington. Bellevue or Renton, something like that." Jan completed her story with satisfaction and looked at her husband.

"Damn, Jan, what an amazing story," was all that Terry could manage to say. His brain was starting to smoke, but he didn't have fire yet. "Damn" he said again as he tried to take another drink of coffee from his now empty cup.

"So, why is Uncle Joe's car out there on Earl Corbbet's farm along with the others?" Terry said to himself, but aloud.

"Beats me, hon, but you got to get going here. You are going to be late for work. Want me to pack you a lunch?" Jan asked.

"No, I'll get something while I'm on patrol. But thanks, and damn, what a story," Terry said as he left for work, almost forgetting to kiss his wife goodbye. *An accident? They called that an accident? That shit's murder. Second degree murder? Manslaughter?* He couldn't get it out of his head.

Chapter Twenty

Melody

Melody woke up and looked at the clock. 10:30! *Damn!* She ran downstairs into the kitchen expecting to find her sister cleaning or drawing or getting ready to. On the kitchen table was a note in Sammy's handwriting.

"Dear Mellie, so sorry to have to take off without saying goodbye but got a call from the Gallery up in Seattle and they wanted to see my drawings and talk in person about the holiday show. Packed up what drawings I had and am now headed home. You looked like you were sleeping so nice I didn't want to wake you. I don't think I will be gone for more than a couple days. Keep the home fires burning. Wish me luck. Love you madly, Sammy."

Double damn! Melody wanted to talk to her sister about that woman in the gray suit. Had she been real? Had they both heard the same story about their mom?

Melody decided this wasn't a conversation to be had by phone, besides, she didn't want to talk to her sister if she was driving. What if that woman in the gray suit was just a dream? No need to spill that out while Sammy was driving through Seattle-area traffic.

I'll just go out for breakfast then hop over to see Pat's mom and see what she might remember about Dad and Mom, Melody said to herself as she got ready to leave the house.

First stop of the day was the Fireside Café. Sunday after-church crowd filled the place. The minute Melody walked in she felt like she was a child again. The dining area had been painted a nice light pink since the old day's bright yellow and the curtains were different but the small restaurant smelled the same. Coffee, sausage, cinnamon rolls, and pancakes. She found an empty table for two and sat down. The waitress must have been a local high school student because she was too young to fit into Melody's memory banks.

"Just a cup of coffee and one of those cinnamon rolls, thanks," Melody put in her order. *If I keep eating like this, I am going to get huge,* she thought. *Or worse than that, my stomach problems are going to kick in and then I'll have real troubles on my hands.* Her order arrived in front of her in what felt like seconds. She stuffed a large bite of the roll in her mouth and as she looked up from her plate, holy shit, who walked in the place but *him!*

"Oh, my, Gawd! Melody Corbbet! Is that really you?" came the loud booming voice of Frank Davison. Frank stood six foot four inches, hair on-fire red with a full beard to match. He threw his head back and laughed like a man who had just won a new pickup. He made his way to Melody's table in three steps, grabbed her up in his arms, and gave her a big bear hug. Then kissed her full on the mouth. "You taste wonderful!" he hollered with joy as he put her back in her chair.

Before Melody could invite Frank to sit down, he had already done so and grabbed both her hands. Looking her straight in the eye he added in a calmer voice, "I'm sorry to hear about your Dad. Earl was a great guy, heart of gold, salt of the earth. Sorry for not attending his service, just tied up with work and funerals are not for me. How long you goin' to be in town? You staying for good now? What are you goin' to do with the farm? Your sister here too?" The friendly giant peppered her with questions.

The two old friends talked for an hour, Frank eating his breakfast of ham, eggs, and pancakes, listening to Melody tell him about her Dad's death, the financial mess with the property, and the strange happenings out at the place. She left out the part about the women in the gray suit because she wasn't so certain that really happened.

"You know, I bet you two girls could make a go of that farm. I'd hate to see it sold off to strangers or some investor who turns it into a housing development. Besides, I'd love to have you back here, at home where you belong." Frank's voice was soothing and kind. She hoped he really meant what he said.

He's the same man he was in high school, thought Melody. Outgoing and ready for trouble one moment and sweet as pie the next. How long had they dated? Maybe two years, off and on, before she decided she had to get out of Sheridan or go crazy. When she told Frank her plans he seemed hurt but said he understood. He never begged her to stay, never asked her to marry him, never promised to take care of her, never said he loved her. Maybe if he had, she would have stayed, maybe not.

Everyone in town could tell you the Davison family were self-serving. Known in Yamhill County for owning the biggest lumber mill and for their well-publicized charitable acts. Like the big deal they made at Christmas time handing out bonus checks and turkeys to their employees on Christmas Eve morning. First Frank's dad, Old Ben, would give a speech for ten minutes, nine minutes too long if you asked anyone there. Then the men and woman who worked for the Davison Mill would line up, Ben giving out the checks, $25, $50, or $75, depending on length of employment. Next his wife, Effie, would hand out the turkeys, ten pounds or less.

Lastly Frank, their only child now grown to full manhood and 220 pounds of pure energy, would shake each person's hand before they headed off to the parking lot. No Christmas party, that's it. Frank would laugh and joke, calling each person by name. The men he would slap hard on the back. It was said you could hear Frank laugh all the way to Lincoln City. He had plenty to laugh about too. Heir to the mill and all the family's land holdings which took up half of the county. It just now occurred to Melody that the mill's pole yard bordered on her father's land. No wonder he made the comment about not wanting the farm to go to strangers.

No one dared point out Frank's size and abundant red hair and the fact that his father was only five foot seven inches, 160 pounds soaking wet, and now bald but had once had black hair.

All that known, she wondered to herself if she could have done better if she had stayed in Sheridan. For a few minutes, sitting there talking to her old friend and lover, she felt sorry for herself. Sorry and foolish. *What's so great about living alone in Glendale, California?*

"I want to find my mom. I want to know who she was or is or what happened. Why she left us and never wrote or called or came back to see us," Melody confided to Frank.

"Leave it be, Melody. You are going to just end up digging up hurt and sadness. I had a gal friend back in the day. She found out she was adopted. She thought she needed to find her real mom and hear the reason why she would give her away. This gal traveled all the way to Texas, found her real mom living in some dumpy old trailer park. Come to find out her real mom had been a drug addict for years and had had several kids and gave them all up for adoption. Didn't even remember giving birth to this gal friend of mine. Woman didn't care about anyone but herself. My friend never got over the hurt and disappointment of that one meeting. Don't go down that road, sweetheart. Stay here with the folks who know and love you. Work your daddy's farm the way he intended." His kind eyes looked into Melody's and for just a moment she felt he was right.

"You know, Frank, you are a good man. I love you madly. Always have and always will," Melody said to Frank. He could tell he had made no headway with her and she wasn't about to change her mind.

"I've got to go. Tons to do out at Dad's." Melody got up from the table, kissed Frank goodbye and left. It dawned on her after she had left that she hadn't asked him if he was single and he hadn't asked her either.

Chapter Twenty-one

Sunday, October 12, 2014

Melody

From the café Melody headed straight to Pat's mom's house on Ash Street. She remembered Mrs. Joy Holiday with fondness. Mrs. Holiday had always been good to Melody and Sammy when they came over to play or sew or bake. And Joy never said a word about their mom, ever. Melody was ready to confront Mrs. Holiday on this fact. She wanted answers and she wanted them now.

But no one was home at the Holiday house. At least, if there was someone home, they weren't answering the door. Melody felt frustrated. She tried to call her sister to ask about the woman in the gray suit but it was clear Sammy had turned off her phone as the call went straight to voice message.

Now Melody was both frustrated and pissed off. From there she drove back home. She was tired of crying but cried just the same.

Anger replaced grief. There had to be answers to her questions somewhere in this damned house and she was going to find them if she had to pull the place apart with her bare hands.

Mellie headed for the sewing room as soon as she got in the door. Starting with the first drawer in the highboy she pulled everything out. Clothes, fabric from long-ago dressmaking projects, dress patterns... she stuffed them all into large plastic garbage bags, checking pockets now and then for change or anything that might be of value or use. Once done with the highboy she moved on to an old trunk she and Sammy used to call their "Hope Chest." Nothing found in there of any importance, just old efforts at embroidery on pillow cases and dish towels. Anything she found that might have been her mother's she folded carefully and put aside. Next, she went through the closet. Every sock, shoe, tie, t-shirt. Anything of her father's was going to the dump, damn it!

How could Sammy leave her here like this? Why wasn't Mrs. Holiday home when she needed her? Who was Frank to give her advice on what to do when he didn't have the full picture here? How could her mother just leave her, and never return? And why now, after all these years, did that one thing stand out in her mind and haunt her every waking minute?

She pulled out old bedspreads, blankets, and sheet sets. Those items went into a garbage bag. She pulled the curtains down; dust flew every which way. Those too went into a garbage bag. All the filled bags went on the front porch. Melody found a box and took old childhood art and magazine pictures of heart throbs from back in the day carefully off the walls. There were a few family photos and if the picture contained some one she knew she placed it on the kitchen table. Piles of old patterns, sewing notions, spools of faded ribbon and thread were placed to one side as were prom dresses and half-made quilts. Someone might find those useful.

Melody slowed down and looked around the room. It looked bare but so much better, smelled better too. She went to the kitchen, washed her hands, and put on a pot of coffee. She would take one last look around the sewing room then make herself a sandwich.

Getting on her hands and knees she checked inside the closet again. It was dark in the back. She had to go get the flashlight. There were a few remaining items: old slippers, very old socks, some unidentifiable things, and an old suitcase of undetermined age. She had to go get the broom to retrieve the stuff, which went into the last garbage bag. The suitcase was gently put next to the fireplace in the front room.

Once she had made her sandwich, she went to the front room and started a fire. Maybe the day wasn't a total waste. Maybe there would be more of her Mother's belongings in the old leather case, or at least letters from her family or clues to where she might have run off to. Melody would not allow the thought that her mother might be long dead these many years. And when that stray idea entered her head that her father might have killed her mother out of some sort of jealousy, she cursed herself for being a fool.

As soon as Melody had a few more details about her mother she was going to start in on the internet search for her. Why hadn't she done this before? The question rattled around in her head like a marble in an empty tin can. She felt foolish, went and got her cell phone and tried to call Sammy. The call went to voice mail. Melody texted her sister, "Call me. Need to talk about stuff."

Melody thought about what Frank Davison had said about his friend finding her birth mother only to discover the woman was a wreck of a human being. "Is my mother some old alcoholic living in an old hotel room too embarrassed to call or write?" she wondered to herself out loud.

She put another log on the fire and ate her sandwich slowly. Sweet thoughts of Frank drifted in and out of her mind. She giggled when she thought of looking him up on Facebook to see if he was single. Her heart pounded like it used to when she waited for him to pick her up for a date as she grabbed her phone and started her search.

"Oh, my gawd! He's single!" she whispered. "What's up with that?" Before she could stop herself, she sent him a friend request. Then she hopped off to the kitchen to put her empty plate in the kitchen sink and grab a couple cookies. As she walked out into the front room, she heard the familiar ping from her phone of someone messaging her.

It was not a text from Sammy but a message from Frank. Her friend request accepted and a short, "Hey there, girl!" Melody realized she was smiling. She pushed aside the old suitcase, grabbed one of the throw blankets, and settled in by the fire to message her old friend and lover a return message.

After a few short messages back and forth Frank called. "Hello," said Mellie.

"Now that's better, isn't it?" Frank asked in his calm voice. Mellie loved the sound of his voice. She forgot about the suitcase altogether. Who knows how long they talked?

Chapter Twenty-two

Monday, October 13, 2014

Sergeant Kell

He sat in his patrol car with the engine running in the parking lot of the building that held Yamhill County crime records. The archive structure was plain gray cement of the 1960s-type design. To Sergeant Terence Kell it could have been Fort Knox, for it held the information he needed but had no way to walk in and take it out.

Terry had already been out to the Corbbet farm. He had stopped by early this morning and when he didn't see a light on, he went straight out to the four vehicles off to the side of the orchard and got the VINs he needed. License plate numbers are no good, those can be stolen or exchanged or moved from one vehicle to the next, but the vehicle identification numbers are on the inside and that is how you can tell who actually owned the car or pickup last. With the computer back at the station he was able to access Department of Motor Vehicles records for Oregon, Washington, and Idaho.

On the 1973 Black Chevy Sidestep pickup he got the name Charlie Montgomery. The plates were from Oregon but the registration data showed this vehicle was from Idaho. Sandpoint, Idaho to be exact. He noted that to be quite a long drive from Sheridan, Oregon, so he wouldn't be heading there anytime soon.

Terry had only met Charlie a time or two when he was eighteen years old. It was that summer between high school and college, June of 1999, and Terry was helping out during Sheridan Days at the Chicken BBQ where Charlie was acting as head BBQer.

What Terry knew about Charlie at that time couldn't fill a thimble. Just that Charlie was a new guy in town, worked at the Green Frog as a bartender, and appeared to be charming to the ladies.

But with a few clicks on the keyboard Terry had managed to put together some history on Charlie. Even though Charlie's end had been a brutal unsolved murder in 2003 (a year before Terry joined the Sheriff's department) right here in Sheridan, his old arrests and warrants still showed up online in Idaho criminal records. There were a couple of warrants issued by the Fish & Wildlife department for hunting without a license while trespassing on private property to do so. As one would expect from a lowlife.

There was a list of domestic disturbance calls a mile long for out at some woman's place in Idaho, last name Sanders. Most of those between 1995 and 1999, the last being an actual arrest and some jail time, but true to form, just below that was an outstanding warrant for failure to show for a sentencing hearing. Yep, looked like old Charlie skipped town and headed for somewhere he could hide out and Sheridan turned out to be the place.

Now what Terry wanted was the case file for Montgomery's murder. One way to get that file was to go to his boss back at the Sheriff's office and turn in a formal request to reopen the investigation. To break out a cold case. Terry wasn't so sure he wanted to solve the 2003 homicide of Montgomery as much as he wanted to know how in the world those four vehicles ended up on the Corbbet farm.

Two of the cars were connected to what had been labeled "accidental" deaths. There was Jan's Uncle Joe Benton (who had been accidentally shot by his fourteen-year-old stepdaughter), and his once sky-blue 1992 Crown Victoria Ford. And Philip Mason's charcoal gray 1997 Mazda Miata.

Philip, who had been killed by a stray arrow shot from a group of freshman girls during gym class archery practice. That story he knew from his freshman year, as it had been the talk of the whole high school, whole town for that matter, back in May of 1998.

The 1973 Chevy pickup belonged to the brutally murdered Charlie Montgomery. This vehicle was a classic and if in mint condition today would bring a pretty price. With warrants out for his arrest Sergeant Kell could see why Charlie would have changed out the license plates.

The last car, a dark green 1983 Chevy Caprice, was registered as stolen, last owner Hank Garrett of Yakima, Washington. Name didn't ring any bells with Sergeant Kell. This car appeared to have been out on the farm the longest. The rust was massive, tires flat, mold and weeds growing in and around the car. Blackberries had just about covered it completely. It took a crowbar to get the driver's door opened so he could read the VIN. The license plates were Oregon but the VIN had given the real location of where the car was from.

He needed three case files. Not just the Montgomery file, but the Benton and Mason files as well. Would there be a file for Garrett and the stolen Caprice?

Sergeant Kell turned off the engine to his patrol car, put on his hat, and made sure he didn't have any leftover donut crumbs on his face or uniform. He was going in and he was going to charm the socks off that archives clerk and he was going to get those files, damn it!

Sure enough, as luck would have it, there behind the counter stood a rather thin, middle-aged woman with dyed blonde hair and hot pink lipstick ready to flirt with a young officer and do him a big favor. She even called him "honey" as she handed him the files. In exchange he smiled one of his best

"I'd kiss you if you weren't married" smiles, turned and made fast tracks out of there.

Once back in his patrol car Terry turned straight to the page in the file that showed who the investigator on the murder of Montgomery had been. Long-retired Yamhill County Sheriff's Department, Detective Gus Fuller. Detective Fuller had been with the Sheriff's Department for thirty years, since 1975, before he retired as Sheriff in 2005 at the age of fifty-five. Old Gus had gone into law enforcement after coming back from Vietnam. He had a reputation for being tough as nails but those that really knew him understood that when it came to children, he was the Easter Bunny.

Terry had joined the Yamhill County Sheriff's Department in 2005 after four years of college at Oregon Western University, specializing in criminality and law enforcement. He knew his Oregon Revised Statutes like the back of his hand. He came in young and educated without an ounce of street smarts.

Gus had come in from the battle field as his education, retired the same year Sergeant Kell came on. The two men couldn't have been more different. Even though Gus had retired he still came in and helped out on those hard cases that needed his years of experience and quick thinking.

Sergeant Kell quickly checked the other two files, both Benton and Mason, signed off as accidents by Gus Fuller, who back then had been Detective Gus Fuller.

The young sergeant's heart sank. He had to roll down his cruiser's window to get some fresh air when he felt his stomach start to turn over. "Ah, fuck no!" was all he could think as the smoke in his mind turned to a spark and then a blazing inferno. Old Gus was covering up homicides and had been doing it for years.

Terry knew he could stop by Gus's house anytime for coffee and a nice long talk about anything from the past. Terry pulled the cruiser out of the parking lot and headed for Gus's house. He knew he was in for a long story and welcomed the chance to hear how it was that Gus had let someone, more than one, get away with murder.

Chapter Twenty-three

Monday, October 13, 2014

Sergeant Kell

Sergeant Kell stopped by his home to change out of his uniform into jeans and a sweat shirt; it was his day off after all. Besides, he didn't want Gus to think that the visit was official business or that the Montgomery case had been re-opened. A lie like that would catch up with Terry in a matter of minutes with one call to his superior.

Then he got into his pickup with the case files. He took twenty minutes to review the files so that he would at least be able to ask questions, but not so many as to tip off Gus that Sergeant Kell was snooping around.

When Terry arrived at Gus's house it was 3:00 in the afternoon and he was carrying a six pack of Miller beer. Just in time for happy hour, thought Terry. "Do I know people or do I know people?" he said under his breath to himself.

Gus answered the door on one ring of the bell and Terry held up the beer. Gus gave a big smile and welcomed the young sergeant into his small but cozy ranch style house. Gus's wife came out of the kitchen, saw they already had beer and went back to whatever it was she had been doing.

Terry got right down to business with Gus, no use playing around. He explained he had been called out to the Corbbet farm by Earl's daughters after his death. Poor kids thought they saw someone in the house, they thought it was a ghost. Can you imagine that? Gus drank his beer and nodded, "Ya, could be ghosts," he mumbled. While out there tromping around by the back of the barn Terry saw the four abandoned vehicles and was wondering about them. Mostly the 1973

Chevy pickup, classic, you know, being as he loved those types of pickups. Terry explained how he looked it up and come to find out that pickup had belonged to that loud-mouth bartender Charlie Montgomery.

Gus stopped drinking his beer and looked hard at Terry. Terry looked back plainly, and blinked. No sign of hidden motives, just that "what happened" expectant look.

"You must remember that one, Gus. What a damned mess that must have been to come across. Charlie all cut up, blood all over the place. Of course, I never saw it, in college at the time. I never heard the whole story, only bits and pieces from my gossipy old mother-in-law. If anyone knew what really went on in that old trailer house it would be you," Terry prompted Gus.

Gus got himself another beer and settled in to tell the tale.

"Ya, had to have been end of September, start of October 2003. Still plenty warm out at that time that year. We were never totally certain how long Charlie had been dead before someone from the Green Frog went out to his place to see why he hadn't come to work for two days. By the time we arrived the flies had taken over the entire trailer. Damnedest fuckin' mess you ever saw. Looked like the Viet Cong had tortured the guy.

"Took days to piece together what we think happened. Someone hit Charlie from behind with a baseball bat and knocked him out as he was unlocking the door to his trailer after coming home from working late at the Green Frog. Hit him damned hard but didn't kill him. Nope. Whoever it was drug him into the trailer, pulled off his shirt and pants and cut him open like a can of tuna. Charlie's guts were pulled out of him, laid next to him on the floor, really careful like so as not to let him bleed to death. At some point Charlie wakes up and sees the mess he's in and he tries to get to his phone and call for help. But all the moving around gets him to bleeding bad and he dies, laying there in a swimmin' pool of his own guts and blood and piss. Probably screamin' in pain, if he could catch his breath at all." Gus took a long pull on his beer, wiped his mouth with the back of his hand, and coughed.

"Had to have some fancy-ass detective come in from Multnomah County to look at the scene, took about a ton of pictures. Not a single fingerprint left in all the blood. Place smelled so bad no one wanted to go in there and really investigate the scene. But one thing did stand out. It appeared that whoever had done this to Charlie hated him as much as God hates sin. It looked as if the perp had stood in the corner and watched Charlie thrashing about. Wanted to see Charlie suffer and cry for help. Large bloody boot prints in the corner of the room."

"Who could have done such a thing? Serial killer, maybe?" Terry asked.

"No, didn't match up with anything any of us or other Oregon law enforcement had heard of or seen before. It was a crime of hate, pure hatred. Someone knew Charlie and wanted to see him suffer. We even went up to Sandpoint, Idaho and interviewed his ex-girlfriend. She wouldn't have made much of a witness if she had known anything anyway. He had beaten her so bad over the years they were together she wasn't even able to hold down a job or take care of her kids. She had two boys, one eight and one ten. Both seemed, sort of, well, you know, slow-witted and afraid of strangers. We didn't get anything out of them. She had a teenage daughter, about sixteen years old by the time we got up there to talk to them. Evelynn Sanders was the girl's name. She did hate Charlie, had seen her mom beaten almost to death several times by that bastard. Tiny thing, would have been no more than fifteen years old when Charlie was murdered. She had reason, she had motive, but damn, Terry, it just wasn't possible that she could have gotten into Sheridan unseen, killed Charlie, blood all over her, left town and gotten back up to Sandpoint without one person seeing her or her mom not having known she was gone. Just not possible, I'm tellin' ya!"

"Sure, it's possible! I'm beginning to think teenage girls are capable of just about anything these days," Terry said slowly.

"Now you listen to me, Sergeant Terence Kell! All colleged up, young smart-ass know it all! It's our jobs to see victims get some justice. We arrest assholes, let the courts take it from there. If they are guilty, we let the courts put them away. And we don't go ruining young girls' lives to make a point. Charlie Montgomery got what was coming to him. It's over and done.

"Those cars out at Earl Corbbet's farm are none of your business! The past is the past! Accidents happen! Those that have been wronged have gotten their justice and we uphold that. You understand what I'm saying here? Do you?" Gus was making his point and jabbing his finger at Terry.

Terry didn't need any more explanations out of Gus. The reasons for the vehicles in question being out at Earl Corbbet's were not fully clear to him but it seemed like it might be a cover-up of some very serious crimes committed by, of all things, teenage girls, and Gus felt it had been justice dished out and served up hot to those that deserved it.

On his way home Terry got another call from Melody. She told him she'd found some stuff he might want to take a look at.

Chapter Twenty-four

Tuesday, May 12, 1998

Sheridan High School Principal Cooley

Some days Principal Cooley hated his job and today was one of those days.

"Mason boy's folks are here," announced the school secretary as she poked her head in his office door.

"Okay, send them in."

Principal Cooley stood up from his desk, walked around it and with the greatest of care and sympathy greeted Laura and Scott Mason, Philip Mason's parents, giving gentle hugs to both.

"Please sit down. Can I get you a cup of coffee or a glass of water?"

"No, thank you," was the sad reply from Scott Mason.

"I am certain you are wondering why I asked you both to come see me today. Such a very difficult time for you both. Philip's service was a wonderful tribute to a young man who would have gone on to great things, I'm sure.

"Now, we must get on with details that so often get left behind at times like this. The school, Sheridan High School, and the Board, have a legal duty to ensure that all concerned agree that Philip's death was an accident. Yes, tragic, but an accident, nonetheless.

"The Sheriff's department has done their investigation and has determined that fact. We have also extensively interviewed the four girls. There was no intention to cause harm. The Sheriff's detective isn't even sure which one shot the arrow that went through your son's neck. All four girls did attend the funeral and paid their respects.

"From the information we gathered from the freshman girls' PE class and their teacher we know that the archery segment had begun that Monday. The segment was only going to last through that Friday, May first, the day of the accident. So, the teacher, Miss Hale, was busy checking the girls for form and accuracy, marking grades for each student on an individual basis as the others continued to practice until Miss Hale got to the next student. The four girls in question were the last in line to be checked out so they continued to practice shooting arrows into the targets mounted on hay bales.

"That same day, the senior boys' PE class had started their Spring track segment. Their teacher and coach, Bud Fisher, set them off running around the track to get a good look to see who might be the best candidates for this year's track team.

"Philip was a great football player. He had a wonderful season until he got hurt. That foot injury put him on the sidelines. I know you were so proud of him. He wasn't in shape for track due to that injury and he was lagging behind that group of boys who were running flat out, showing off for the coach.

"As Philip came around the corner at the west end of the track a stray arrow from one of the four girls caught him in the neck and he went down.

"Who knows which one of the kids from the two classes actually made the fatal mistake of pulling the arrow from Philip's neck? So many of them rushed to his aid. The girls got there first but, once again, so many of the kids had his blood on their hands trying to help him. He had been running and his heart on been pounding very hard, so he bled to death before the EMTs even arrived.

"The EMTs we talked to said when they got to the scene they couldn't even get to Philip at first, kids screaming and crying and grabbing at them. Both teachers pulling kids away from Philip, trying to get in there to stop the bleeding. Those four girls were frantically hitting at anyone who came close, trying to protect him, we assume." Cooley's gentle voice trailed off. Laura Mason's shoulders shook as she silently cried. Cooley handed her a box of tissue.

The room was silent except for the sounds of Philip Mason's mother blowing her nose. Principal Cooley moved some papers around on his desk, facing them toward the Mason's sitting across from him.

"So, this leads us to the reason I asked you to come to my office today. The school, the Board, and our attorney need you both to sign this statement of no liability, holding us in no way responsible for the death of your son. It does surrender any rights you might have to file a wrongful death suit against us now or in the future. You understand what I'm stating here, correct?

"I need you both to sign your names, put today's date here on this line, May 12, 1998."

Scott Mason picked up the papers and read them carefully, then looked up at Principal Cooley in disbelief. He had just lost his only son and the school Board wanted to cover their sorry asses before Philip was cold in his grave. *Self-serving bastards, every single one of them,* was the thought that went through his mind.

Principal Cooley's round, kind face looked sadly back at Scott. Both men gave out a huge sigh, then Scott signed and dated the legal documents and handed them to his wife to do the same.

Once Laura finished her task her husband stood up, took her by the arm, helping her out of her chair. They turned and walked out of the office. Cooley watched from his window as the Masons got into their car and drove out of the school parking lot.

Principal Cooley leaned back in his chair and thought about Philip Mason. What did he really know about the young man besides the fact he was the school's football star, popular, good looking? Barely an average student, rude at times. There had been a few reports about bullying younger students over the years. Freshman girls mostly.

The thought that stuck in his mind was the memory of what he found in the trunk of the Mason kid's car the day of the accident. Strange, disrelated items. A wig, women's underclothes, several tubes of used bright-red lipstick. And then there was the small yellow nylon rope, a large folding knife, and duct tape. Looked like a rape kit.

The lunch bell rang and Principal Cooley went out into the hall, greeting students as they hurried to get into line in the cafeteria. Then he headed to his car. Today he would be drinking his lunch.

Chapter Twenty-five

Monday, October 13, 2014

Sergeant Kell

It was late afternoon, early evening, when Terry pulled up in the driveway of the Corbbet farm. The place looked forlorn, almost abandoned, except for a single light from the kitchen.

If ever there was a place for ghosts to hide out, this was the place. Sadness hung in the air like cheap cologne, and a thick fog was forming, moving in from the coast.

He could feel a creeping chill in the air as he got out of his pickup and headed for the back door. *I swear this place has its own climate,* he thought to himself as he knocked hard, then opened the door, letting himself in with a shout of hello to announce it was indeed friend not foe entering the house.

"I'm in the kitchen, Terry," came the shout back from Mellie.

"This had better be good, sister! I'm missing dinner at my house and you know how much I hate to miss a meal," Terry said as he marched into the kitchen.

Terry rounded the corner from the back porch to the kitchen. Laid out on the table were newspaper clippings. Some were in piles, others appeared to be just bits and pieces of what might have been larger stories. He could tell by the yellowing of the paper that some were older than others. They all had fold marks and it was clear that Mellie had tried to smooth them out so they would lay flat. The clippings smelled musty.

"Hey, you've started a clipping service. That should keep you busy while Sammy's in Seattle," Terry said cheerfully.

"How did you know Sammy was in Seattle?" Mellie asked surprised Terry would know such a thing.

"Small town. I work for the Sheriff's department. Besides, she stopped for gas before she drove out of town." Terry seemed pleased with himself.

"So, whatcha workin' on here?"

Mellie explained how she had been doing more cleaning and had come across a briefcase tucked back in a closet in the sewing room yesterday. It held these newspaper clippings. Stories she was certain Terry would find interesting. She had ended up spending the entire day reading the articles, laying them out in date order and piling them up by subject matter.

"If you start here, with the oldest articles," she pointed with her finger to the left side of the table, "and read this way," she pointed to the right side of the table, "you will actually be reading the newspaper stories about deaths of the owners of the three vehicles in Dad's backyard as covered by the Sheridan Sun and the McMinnville News Registrar.

"The first pile is about my Mom and... well, you'll see as you get to reading."

Terry was instantly interested and pulled a chair up to the left-hand side of the table. "I hope you have the coffee pot on, girlie!" He carefully picked up the first pile and began to read.

The first article, dated August 10, 1979, showed the picture of a smiling, bright looking, teenage girl wearing a cowboy hat and a small heart-shaped locket necklace, with a caption, "Senior Court Rodeo Princess, Emily Newberry, from Hamilton High School, will ride her palomino, Archimedes, in the Ravalli County Fair parade on Saturday."

"This is dated August 10, 1979 from the Ravalli Republic newspaper. My God! This must be your mother, Mellie! Look at how sweet and pretty she was," Terry held up the aging article to show Mellie as if she hadn't seen it yet.

"Ravalli County? Hamilton High School? Where is that?" he asked.

"I had time before you got here so I looked it up on my laptop. It's in Montana. The town of Hamilton is small, about one hour's drive south from Missoula," replied Mellie. She didn't mention the strange woman in the gray suit from the day before that had given her these same details.

"Last week Sammy and I found Mom's jewelry box. It contained that same necklace, only the chain was broken. Not all that was broken by the looks of the other articles from Montana," Mellie started in on the story before Terry could read the other articles.

"My mom was raped by one of her Dad's ranch hands near the end of her senior year," Mellie went on sadly. "According to the newspaper articles he was caught and sent to prison. And this article here, look! Seven years later he got out. That was 1987, same year Mom was to have run off with another man. If that's what she really did."

"What makes you think she didn't?" asked Terry. "You think she just disappeared into thin air?" Terry stared at his cup of coffee and thought long and hard, working the pieces of the puzzle around in his mind. Rapists were freaky, evil, and controlling. Rapists weren't about sex as much as they were about control, creating fear. Screams of pain and terror were music to their ears. Ownership and possession. That's why a rapist might come back and rape the same woman over again at a later date.

"Terry, you were at Dad's memorial service and the get-together back here at the house afterwards. Do you remember seeing a middle-aged woman with gray hair, in a gray suit with a red rhinestone horse brooch? Someone not from around here, not someone we all know?" asked Mellie, her voice sounding shaky and uncertain.

"Jesus, Mellie! I saw nothing but middle-aged women with gray hair that day. In a gray suit? Someone I didn't know? No. No one comes to mind. And normally I'm the guy to spot someone new in the crowd. What about her?" Now Terry was intrigued.

Mellie told Terry about the woman who had stayed after everyone had left the house the day of Earl's memorial service. How she had fixed Mellie and Sammy dinner, sat with them at the kitchen table, and told them a frightening story of how their mother had been brutally raped by a ranch hand. Mellie went on to explain she guessed her Mother had gotten pregnant from that rape and that she, Mellie, was the product of that wicked act.

"Dad must have felt sorry for Mom and married her to get her out of that little Montana town, away from the gossip and pity, and brought her home with him here. You know, so she could start a new life. One of the articles in that pile, from October 1, 1980, talks about the trial for the rapist. Mom had to testify. The article states there wasn't a dry eye in the court room when she was done telling what happened to her. I don't know how in the world she had the courage to do that. And all that time she was hiding she was pregnant. She must have been about three months along. Wouldn't have been that hard to cover up with a sweater, I guess." Mellie fell silent.

Terry's mind raced with the information now presented to him and the thoughts of what he could only guess might fill in the holes in the story. He needed time to sort fact from fiction.

And who the hell was this strange woman who shows up with the story of the rape to begin with?

"Hold. Just hold here. This woman who tells you about the rape before you even find the articles about it. Who in the name of Sam Hill is she? When she left didn't you get her name and number? Didn't you ask her how she knew this shocking secret?" Terry pressed Mellie for answers.

Mellie sadly explained how she woke up in her own bed in the middle of the night and wasn't able to tell if the woman had been real or just part of a dream. "But then how would a dream be able to tell a story that later turns out to be true?" she wondered.

According to the articles on the trial Bill Garrett was the rapist. Hot shit! That rusted Chevy Caprice parked in the back yard belonged to a Hank Garrett. If the story Earl told everyone was that Emily and an old boyfriend from her high school days were true, than how did they drive off? What would they have driven away in? Why would she have run off with her rapist? The questions just kept swirling around in the law enforcement officer's mind.

"That is not the end here, Terry! I have a pile of news clippings for each of the other three vehicles out there in Dad's back yard!" said Mellie in a higher than usual voice, pointing to each pile on the table.

"In date order, the next pile of articles from 1993 tells the story of your wife Jan's Uncle Joe Benton's shooting where he gets gunned down by his fourteen-year-old stepdaughter, deemed an accident by local law enforcement. That's his Ford Crown Victoria sitting in the fucking grass out back there." Mellie pointed in the direction of the barn. Terry could tell she was getting worked up by the blush on her cheeks.

"Then we have this pile of articles from 1998. A boy we went to high school with, Philip Mason. You remember him! That's his dark gray Mazda Miata parked next to the Ford, for Christ's sake!" Mellie almost screamed.

"Shit, Terry! You remember, he was shot in the neck with an arrow during a PE class! And that was an accident as well.

"Can you believe it? These cars are parked here and I don't even remember them being towed out to that spot out there by the fucking barn!

"Last, but certainly not least in any way, is the old black Chevy pickup. This pile of articles here tells the gruesome tale of how someone murdered the bartender from the Green Frog in 2003. Doesn't just murder the guy in his broken-down trailer parked on some corner of nowhere but guts the man. At least the Sheriff's department admits it's a murder! Of course, the person who did it isn't ever found." At this point Mellie ran out of steam and sat down hard on her chair.

Sergeant Kell rose from the kitchen table. Looked at the newspaper clippings laid out before him. *Damn it to hell! Damn fucking Earl! Damn fucking Gus! Who the fuck designed this coverup? Who else is in on this coverup?* Sergeant Kell worked to look calm and mildly interested.

"Okay, Mellie. Chill out a minute. Only cool minds will prevail here." Terry wasn't just trying to calm Mellie down but himself as well. He needed time to think, to sort out all the information that Mel had thrown at him.

"I say you are coming home to dinner with me. Jan's waiting. Let's just get out of here for the time being."

Mellie grabbed her jacket and followed Sergeant Kell out of the house. As they drove away in his pickup the fog creeped into the orchard then took over the house and yard.

Chapter Twenty-six

Monday, October 13, 2014

Gus Fuller

The retired Sheriff of Yamhill County sat in his back yard drinking his fifth beer. It was dark out but he had no plans to turn on the porch light. He lit another cigarette and noticed the ashtray on the little outdoor table was full, proof he had been out there for some time.

Nosey-assed Sergeant Kell. Coming over here, asking questions about incidents long ago put to rest. Things Kell had no idea about, like justice and setting matters straight.

Kell knew nothing about how the real world worked. He sure as hell hadn't been to Vietnam and seen the horrors the Sheriff had seen. Grown men, soldiers, standing in line to have sex with frightened little girls. Sold by their own fathers. Women and children running, screaming, set on fire when gas bombs were dropped on villages.

Soon the back yard was filled with the visions of a terrible war that should have never happened. Small grass houses turning yellow and orange with flames reaching to the sky. The sound of screaming and gun fire. Orders shouted to shoot anyone making it outside the village or found in the surrounding jungle no matter their age. The smell of gunpowder mixed with blood and burning flesh and napalm.

"Oh, dear God," he said aloud sobbing into his hands. "No more children being hurt. No more, no more."

Time to call the pastor, he decided to himself, pulling his cell phone out of his sweater pocket. "God damn Earl," he said aloud as he dialed the pastor's number and waited for the ring.

"What's up?" the pastor said instead of hello.

"Come over. Now!" the Sheriff choked out into the phone.

"On my way," was the soft reply, then the line went dead.

Chapter Twenty-seven

Emily Louise Newberry Corbbet

The figure of a young barefoot woman in a gray house dress moved through the old farmhouse on Rock Creek Road. With no one at home she could have the place to herself. Being alone felt good. The quiet felt good. The dark felt good.

She stopped at the kitchen table and looked over the newspaper articles spread out, going through each one, carefully taking her time. The picture of herself as a young girl in a cowboy hat flooded her beingness with fond memories and for a moment she almost felt whole. But that faded away as fast as it came.

Rest is what I need, she thought to herself.

She glided to the living room where the old white jewelry box sat open and her heart locket lay, broken. She recalled her attempted suicide after the rape when she discovered she was pregnant from that act of violence. How Earl found her, held her in his big arms and calmed her, promising to take care of her and the baby. To marry her, take her away from there and bring her to his home where she could forget about what happened. A chance to make a fresh start.

She agreed to marry Earl. It was a relief to her parents; she would be taken care of and could move to another state, out of town and away from there. As if that would erase all that had happened.

The wedding, which was put off until after the trial, had been private, in her parent's front room. No guests, only the minister and her parents. No wedding dress. She had worn a brown skirt and sweater she had bought to wear last fall for her senior year of high school. Earl had worn jeans and a white dress shirt he had bought for the occasion. At least he had taken a bath and gotten his hair cut.

No flowers, no cake, no toasting of the bride and groom.

Once the minister was finished with the wedding vows he shook both their hands and wished them good luck. When the papers were all signed and witnessed she kissed her parents goodbye. Then picked up her small tan leather suitcase and walked out the front door of her childhood home. The place she loved the most.

That evening they stopped for dinner at a small café somewhere in Idaho. Earl made a big deal out of her wanting to order a coke with her hamburger and French fries rather than just drink water, which was free and the coke cost fifty cents. Later in the trip he wouldn't let her order the fries, just the burger, it was cheaper that way.

They stayed in fleabag motels along the highway. Usually next door to some country tavern where the music was loud and went on all night. Earl got rooms with one bed because it was cheaper. She had to sleep with him but he never once tried anything.

Where is happiness? she asked herself. Every day, from then on, she was reminded of her broken locket. Each time she held her baby girl, every time she had to lie in bed with a man she didn't love. Every time she looked in the mirror and saw her face getting thinner, her hair going from blonde to a dull brown. The scar over her right eye which never faded. Neither did the ones on her wrists.

She made few friends in Sheridan, afraid that they would know about the rape. If they did they certainly didn't show it. All Earl's friends knew or cared about was that he had found himself a wife, gotten her pregnant, and brought her home to live at the farmhouse and help out with the orchard. They seemed relieved in some way, as if the whole town had thought he would never marry or be "normal." Oh, yes, there were a few whispers. Stories about how Earl must have gotten her pregnant and when her father found out he forced the marriage. That sort of thing happened often enough in Sheridan so no scandal there.

But every season that passed brought her closer to the time when her rapist would be let out of prison. She knew he had only been sentenced to seven years. What if he got out early? What if he found out she had his baby? Garrett had told her repeatedly during that awful time in the barn that he owned her now. She was his for ever and ever. He had grunted that in her ear each time he climaxed.

Will he come after me? she would ask herself each day as she looked out the window while washing the breakfast dishes.

Yes, he would. And just as she had feared, it was the end of her.

Chapter Twenty-eight

Monday, October 13, 2014

Melody

As Sergeant Kell's pickup moved through the town of Sheridan toward his home, Melody's cell phone rang. It was Sammy.

"Holy shit, sister!! I have been trying to get ahold of you! How could you run out on me like this? What the fuck were you thinking?" Melody screamed into the phone.

"You must chill out! Now listen, I don't have much time to fool around on the phone here. I just wanted to call you and let you know I'm here in Seattle making sure the drawings I've been working on are going to work for my upcoming show. And just so you know, Miss 'losing her mind because she is all alone in that old farmhouse', the powers that be are loving every single stroke. So, I'll be home soon because I have a ton to finish and you can get me back then. Gots to go now. Love you madly!"

And with that Sammy hung up.

"Hey, you, wait a God-damned minute!" Melody yelled into the phone then threw the phone down when she realized her sister had hung up. "Shit! I didn't even get a chance to ask her about the old gray-haired woman who fixed us dinner and told us about Mom to see if she was real or just some wild dream I had!"

"I'm voting on 'wild dream'. Look, here we are. Jan is going to be happy to see you. You know what a great cook she is. I have no idea why I don't weigh three hundred pounds."

Terry chatted away, trying to take Melody's attention off Sammy and the gray-haired woman.

He pulled his car into his driveway and turned off the engine. They got out and went into the house through the garage door, walking through a short hallway into a well-lit kitchen filled with the aromas of fresh-out-of-the-oven home baked biscuits and roast beef.

"Honey! I'm home," called out Terry in a joking way.

"In here!" came the cheerful reply from the living room.

"Look who I brought home for dinner," he announced as he and Melody came into the room.

Jan, who had been sitting on the couch watching the news, smiled at them both. Melody noticed Jan was a shadow of her former self. How much weight had she lost since high school? Thirty pounds? Forty pounds? And her hair? Cut and colored in a simple but appealing fashion. She wore just a touch of eye makeup and some lip gloss, with skinny jeans and a black turtleneck sweater. To state it simply, Jan looked great. Melody realized she must look like something the cat had drug in.

"Melody!" Jan exclaimed and ran to hug her old classmate. Melody was taken back by her old schoolmate's relaxed and confident manner. The offered hug seemed to mean that Jan must have forgotten her shy, timid ways. Growing up changed a person and in Jan's case it was for the better. Melody guessed being married to a confident and loving man didn't hinder Jan developing into her own person, either.

In no time dinner was on the table and the three sat down to eat. It was clear to Melody that in Terry's eyes Jan could do no wrong and the love between them was real and apparent. They didn't gush at each other or call each other pet names.

Their love was shown by respect and kindness and a genuine caring about the other person's feelings.

By all appearances a perfect marriage. Melody thought for a moment how strange it was that Jan and Terry had no children after being married for so long. Ten years was it? Was there a slight tear in the fabric?

Terry steered the conversation away from Melody's troubles at the farmhouse and prompted her to tell Jan all about her life in Glendale, California. Jan was interested in how Melody had gone from college to her job at the car dealership as one of their CPAs. She was even interested in the explanation of exactly how the dealership figured out the price on new and used cars and what the corporation needed to make in order to consider they had turned a profit.

Terry, on the other hand, looked like he would fall asleep. And when the conversation changed to why Melody hadn't found the right man yet, he had to excuse himself from the table and find something on TV to watch. Jan made a joke about "women's business" and men not mixing.

Even though the dishes were cleared from the table, Jan and Melody lingered there over coffee as Melody began telling Jan of the problems at the farmhouse. As if it wasn't bad enough, dealing with the sadness from the death of her father, there were all the old memories, the grief of the loss of her mother so long ago. And with the house being completely filled with disorganized clutter, so badly in need of cleaning and general maintenance, Melody felt her own personal stability shaken.

Cleaning the house was not only unpleasant, it was as if there were intentional emotional land mines left for her under the beds, in every drawer and closet. Some little tidbit reminder of a past that wasn't awful, it just wasn't great at any point. Like going to the same restaurant and ordering the exact same thing over and over again. There was nothing to dread but then there was nothing to look forward to. Life hadn't been black but then it hadn't been cotton-candy pink or sky blue or poppy orange. It had only been beige.

Jan was a good listener. She nodded, made few comments, and let Melody go on without interruption or evaluation.

Melody moved forward with all that had been going on at the house since she had arrived. All the odd little things, like how she and Sammy had come home to find someone in the house but then there had been no sign that anyone had really been there. She told of strange big things like the gray-haired woman who had made her and Sammy dinner and told them the story of her mother's rape. Then finding the newspaper articles about that rape.

At this point of Melody's narrative Jan shot looks at her husband who was sitting in his chair in the front room, pretending to watch TV. Jan and Terry locked eyes several times during the telling of the "intruder in the house" story and during the "rape of Mom" story.

When Melody started to dive into finding newspaper articles about the three deaths (two accidents and one outright murder) and their connection to the cars sitting out in a field at the farm, Jan artfully guided the conversation to a fond memory of her own.

Jan's tale was from back in the day when the Corbbet farm was an actual working orchard. How every autumn her family, and the family of so many others they had grown up with, went out there to pick apples and pears. It seemed the whole town looked forward to this event.

Jan described in detail getting up on a chilly but sunny Saturday morning. Her mother calling out orders for everyone to hurry and eat their breakfast, grab their coats and baskets, and load up into the car.

Once at the Corbbet farm her family was told by Earl where to pick so as not to be in the way of other pickers. Jan laughed as she explained she had been way too chubby to be one of the kids climbing the trees to get at the apples at the top so her Dad would have to get her brother to do it even though he was younger than her.

When all their baskets were full they would take them to Melody or Sammy to get weighed. Melody nodded her head as she too remembered those times. Visions of yellow and orange leaves racked into huge piles dotting the orchard. A bonfire burned close to the weigh-in tables where people could warm up if it got too cold or wet. The smell of damp soil and apples and oftentimes hot cider or hot chocolate if the women's group from church came out to raise a little money for their Christmas charities.

Melody smiled as she looked at the vision in her mind. Jan smiled at her husband and he nodded at her in approval.

"I know that the orchard out at your Dad's place hasn't been cared for in years and who knows what condition those apples are in? But you know what you ought to do? Throw an apple and pear picking party!! You know, I think people would come out and pick. Have a bonfire. Get the Boy Scout troop to help with the weighing and tree-climbing. I bet they would even mow the lawn and trim back the weeds the weekend before so people could actually get to the trees.

"The Women's League from the Methodist church would be thrilled to bring out hot chocolate and donuts to sell. You could put a big ad in The Sheridan Sun. 'Last Harvest' could be the headline.

"You'll have to decide if you want to charge money for your fruit or just let folks come out to pick. I mean, with the orchard not being kept up those apples could have worms or not be as plentiful as in the past.

"What do you think? I'll help you plan it and promote it. Of course, I would be paid in apples and pears."

Melody thought it over. Yes, one last harvest. She liked the idea of packing up her things, loading up her car, and driving back to Glendale once she and Sammy let the town pick at Dad's orchard one last time. A lovely goodbye, only this time for good.

She thought briefly about Frank Davison. Saying goodbye to him again gave her a strange ache in her chest.

Jan pushed the issue, "Well? Come on! It will be a blast. Say yes and we are in motion."

"Yes! I'm not even going to ask Sammy what she thinks about the idea. Let's just do this thing." Melody's reply was made with pretend enthusiasm. Thoughts of Frank and their wonderful long phone call Sunday night made her doubt herself. But Melody wanted out of Sheridan, off that farm and away from the strong emotional feelings. She wanted to go back to her life in Glendale. Her boring, beige, nothing-much-going-on life. To hell with Dad's last-wishes letter wanting her and Sammy to stay and run the farm. Shit, she'd have to spend her entire savings to pay off the past due taxes and other bills. This was the ticket out of here, one last harvest and she'd hit the road for home!

"If you girls are going to do this thing you need to get a move-on and I mean fast. I had a pear off one of those trees a couple days ago and they are pretty much ready to pick now," Terry encouraged his wife and Melody, who both nodded, then began to work out planning and details of Jan's new project.

****

Terry didn't say what was on his mind. He didn't ask about moving those cars out of the way. Instead he sat there pretending to watch TV. Going over in his mind how he could get inside those cars again. Wondering what sorts of evidence might be in them that they had to be placed out at Earl's. He pondered at the reason for putting the cars out at Earl's in the first place. Besides Earl, who was dead, and the retired Sheriff, who wasn't going to be spilling the beans anytime soon, who else might be covering up what was starting to look like a series of murders? All of which appeared to be committed by fourteen- or fifteen-year-old girls. He shivered at the thought of children, little girls, planning and killing someone. Someone that they felt had done them wrong in some way. That they hated so much their revenge would manifest itself in the killing of another human being.

Adults hated that much, a known and acknowledged fact. An adult criminal would kill another person over something as small as a few dollars or a watch. But he couldn't quite force himself to come to terms with a girl, someone he went to school with, killing in cold blood and being clever enough to hide their evil act behind their age and gender.

Smart though, that's for sure. An older man would always feel protective of a young girl. That older man, someone like the Sheriff, would think it wasn't really her fault, she should be protected. Shielded from an unfeeling and harsh judicial system that could and would ship that little girl off to some state hospital for the criminally insane or a juvenile prison that would be a living hell. Mind-numbing drugs, electric shock treatments, rape by doctors, guards, and other inmates. She'd be worse when she got out and more likely to commit the same crime again with less motive.

Sergeant Kell could see the reasoning behind whatever coverup there might be. He didn't want to believe it was a coverup, maybe just lazy police work. Sweep it under the rug because the paperwork on something like this would be too much.

He knew he had a lot of work to do. He needed to read those newspaper articles that dealt with all four cars that Melody had found. Then reread the case files he had pulled. Next, decide who might all be in on the coverup. Pastor Bob? No, can't be. Andy Stokes, the funeral director. Maybe, in small towns where there isn't a coroner the local medical doctor would be the person to sign the death certificate and cause of death. And in towns that didn't even have a doctor, like Sheridan, Oregon, population 6500, the duties would fall to the funeral director.

Kell looked over at the two women at the table. They had gotten paper and pens and were assigning duties and making lists of needed supplies. It was clear Jan had succeeded in taking Melody's mind off the rape of her Mother and the other horrors out at Earl's place. He wished he would have put the two of them together sooner.

"Melody. You're spending the night here with us. You need a good night's sleep anyway. Besides, you two can get up in the morning and go into high harvesting apples and pear picking mode." Kell said it as an order but with enough kindness in his voice that he wouldn't be challenged.

"Come on," said Jan, "let's find you some pajamas to wear. The spare room has a couch that folds out into a nice bed. I bet you'd like to take a hot shower too. You do that and I'll get the bed ready."

Kell smiled as the women took off down the hall to find pajamas and make a bed for Melody. When they were gone he made plans to get back over to Earl's house and have a good look around, check on the cars, and read those newspaper articles. He would do it tonight.

Chapter Twenty-nine

Monday, October 13, 2014

Pastor Robert Snider

Pastor Robert Snider walked through his living room to his front door and paused long enough to let his wife know he was going out to see someone in need and wasn't certain when he would return. She nodded and let him know she would leave a light on for him, knowing that a pastor's work was never done and almost always needed to happen at the most unusual hours. She was long past thinking it was another woman. And so what if it was, she had the TV to herself and could watch whatever she wanted with him out of the house.

The pastor drove slowly over to Gus Fuller's house. He'd known the retired Sheriff for many years. Knew about his time in Vietnam. Helped him through his bouts of drinking. There had been a few years in there when Gus was seeing other women. That was the hardest to deal with. Women who take advantage of someone who wants to help a damsel in distress. Shit, there was one that emptied Gus's bank account and another that ran off with his car once her boyfriend got out of jail.

Gus's wife should get an award. She stood by him the whole time. Well, except those trips to Vegas she went on when Gus's bullshit would hit the fan. Still, she didn't leave him.

What could it be now? The first thing that came to mind was some sort of trouble with the Corbbet girls. *Maybe they want to move those cars in an effort to clean up the farm so they can sell it.* Not really a problem there; all he and Gus would have to do is offer to move the cars somewhere else. He and Gus could even clean out the trunks and burn the few pieces of evidence stored there. Then they could arrange to have the cars crushed at a local junk yard. Now that he thought about it, that was what they should have done years ago.

Why not move the cars?

The answer to that question came to him just as he pulled into Gus's driveway. He sat there for a minute unable to work out a solution. He knew this day would have to come but he really had prayed that it wouldn't.

The pastor walked around to the backyard without knocking on the front door. He knew where Gus would be. No need to bother his wife.

Gus was sitting in the dark, smoking, beer cans scattered at his feet. This was going to be a long night.

"Hey, Gus! What's got your tail in a knot? Can't decide where to go on vacation?" The pastor asked softly but cheerfully.

"Sit," Gus commanded in a husky voice.

The retired Sheriff quietly and slowly explained to the pastor his visit from Sergeant Kell who was now looking into what the abandoned cars and pickup were doing out at Earl Corbbet's farm. Sergeant Kell had gone so far as to pull the case files on the accidents connected to two of the cars and the unsolved murder connected to the pickup. Getting that information out of the file clerk at case archives had been one easy phone call.

"Shit! Did he ask about the car that had belonged to that prick from Montana?" asked the pastor.

"No, but it will only be a matter of time before he figures out something's up there as well," Gus replied. "We are going to have to deal with Kell before he goes any further. We have to put an end to his nosing around."

"What in God's name are you suggesting here?" asked the pastor, alarmed at what he perceived was Gus's plan to "silence" Sergeant Kell. "The man is law enforcement from your own department! He is a young man, well respected and loved in this community, with a wife, both of them from long-time Sheridan families! Have you called Andy yet? Has he been visited by Kell?"

"If he hasn't, he will be, as it's his signature on all those death certs," Gus answered.

"Look, we can still set this right. Just remove the evidence from the trunks of the cars. Burn it somewhere. Move the cars and the pickup to a junkyard where they can be crushed completely. And hope like hell that no one ever decides to plant a garden or dig up where the cars had been parked." The pastor offered his solutions.

"Okay, Bob. Let's go out there and get that evidence. Now!" Gus meant it. He wanted to get going on "fixing" this thing and he wanted it done now and out of the way. He didn't want to give Sergeant Kell any more reasons to keep going forward with his investigation. Had Sergeant Kell gotten approval from the Yamhill County Sheriff to look into these incidents? Gus had no idea. All he knew was that he wanted it all to stop.

"Fine. I'll drive," surrendered the pastor.

"Afraid we are going to break the law?" asked Gus in a snide way.

"No, I just want to get there in one piece," stated the pastor in a flat tone.

The two men stood up and headed for the pastor's silver Ford Taurus.

Chapter Thirty

Monday, October 13, 2014

Sergeant Kell

Once Melody was put snugly into the guest room by Jan and Jan had gotten herself into bed, Terry came into their room, still dressed.

"Aren't you coming to bed, hon?"

Terry climbed into bed, on top of the covers, next to his wife and whispered in her ear with his arms around her.

"No. I'm going out to the Corbbet farm and having a look around. It will be easier without Melody and her sister there. I can take my time; think over what data I have and what holes need to be filled in.

"Sadly, I do have a theory of what happened to Emily Corbbet," Terry said.

"Really? You don't believe she ran off with some old boyfriend then?" asked Jan.

"No, I don't. I don't think you do either. I'm betting she was killed by Earl. Either that or that rapist from Montana. I think her body is buried on that farm," Terry told his wife his theory.

"So, if she was killed by Earl, why? The man had no motive. She cleaned for him, cooked for him, worked that orchard, and had his children. As far as my Mom knew that poor woman never complained a day living out there with that cheapskate. Mom would give her leftover fabric so she could sew dresses for her little girls. Mom told me she even went out there once after Emily had Sammy to take some soup and help out for an afternoon. It was clear Earl was neglectful, not vengeful. Plainly unaware of other people's needs." Jan added her insight into the topic and as Terry listened he added this story to his growing warehouse of information.

"That leaves my other idea on this. Emily's rapist got out of prison, found out somehow that Emily was pregnant and had his child, picked up his brother's car in Washington, switched out the plates, drove to the farm, and killed her with the intent to take his child. He manages to kill Emily but then something happens where he leaves the car behind. He gets killed by Earl, maybe. Earl buries them both and parks the car over the grave. This would explain why Earl's last wish was for the property to stay the same and to leave the cars in place.

"I don't know. I just think I need to go out to that farm and have another good look around. I'll be back later tonight."

"Okay, stay safe. Love you."

"Love you too." With a strong embrace he kissed his wife then left for the Corbbet farm.

.

Chapter Thirty-one

Monday, October 13, 2014

Andy Stokes

Andy Stokes stood in the rain in his driveway, water running off the hood of his raincoat, sadly looking into the car where Gus Fuller and Bob Snider sat with determined postures.

"Get in the car, Andy!" Gus barked at the wet funeral director.

"Take it easy, Gus. Come on Andy, get in the car, we've got to go," said Bob in his soothing minister's voice.

Andy got in the back seat. He smelled beer and guessed it was Gus who had been drinking. Too much time on his hands gave Gus way too much opportunity to think about the past. He felt sorry for his old friend.

The other thing Andy noticed was there were two hand guns on the floor of the car in the backseat. *Great,* thought Andy, *a pissed-off drunk ex-cop, Vietnam vet no less, with guns. If that doesn't say perfect evening, I don't know what does.*

As the car pulled out of the driveway, Bob started filling Andy in on Sergeant Kell's visit to Gus, asking questions about the Chevy pickup parked out at Earl Corbbet's orchard and the deaths connected to each one of the owners of the cars. According to Gus, Sergeant Kell wasn't going for any long explanations about freak accidents or an unsolved murder.

"Who would have thought one of the Kell kids would turn out to be a sharp-thinking Sheriff's deputy with the tenacity of a bull dog?" Bob added.

"So, the plan here is what? Exactly?" turning to Gus, Andy demanded an answer. "Go out to Earl's place, and what? Then shoot anyone who shows up or asks questions? For Christ's sake, Gus! I didn't help cover up these four crimes for you! I did it for those girls, for their families. I don't care about you but I do care about a battered woman in Idaho and her messed up kids. I do care about Melody and Samantha Corbbet. Now that it looks like someone has figured out our secret your solution is to create more problems?" By now Andy was screaming at Gus.

"*Shut the fuck up!*" shouted Gus.

"Do I have to pull this car over?" hollered Bob.

"*Yes!*" shouted both Andy and Gus at the same time.

Bob pulled the silver Ford Taurus into the deserted parking lot of Davison's mill on Rock Creek Road down from the Corbbet orchard. It was still raining and the windshield wipers slapped back and forth as the engine idled quietly.

"This is no time for a prayer, Bob," Andy said, sarcasm in his voice.

"Oh, I don't intend to pray," Bob replied in a serious tone neither Andy nor Gus had heard before.

Bob took a breath to steady himself and then began his sermon.

"Gus, we all know and fully understand that you saw and did things in Vietnam that were so heinous that you've spent the last forty some odd years trying to reconcile that with yourself.

"I know that, in the beginning, at the very start of the coverups, your heart was with the Corbbet girls, they were so young at the time. And as time went along with Suzie, her mother Lilly, and Joe Benton's family. Idea being to protect a young girl from being sent to a psychiatric prison for children where who knows what would have happened to her. Shock treatment? Brain surgery? Really, I can't imagine. But you did. You thought the whole thing through completely. If we call this a murder, her life and the life of her mother and the whole Benton family would be nothing but sorrow. Suzie would have been the victim a hundred times over. First mentally abused and tortured by her stepfather and then abused and tortured by the justice system.

"And those four freshman girls? You know, I know, what they went through at the hands of that evil fuck, Philip Mason. Who knows how many more he would have played his sick game with or when he would have evolved into a killer? Which would have been sooner than later. His parents had no control over him, never did. I counseled that family starting when Philip was five years old after having set some kittens on fire.

"Same thing here. Young girls, victims of a date turned into a horror show. Taking justice into their own hands because they knew, dammit, they knew nothing would ever happen to him in our court system. They would have been dragged through the courts, stories in the newspaper, humiliated over again and again. Then a juvenile prison? More abuse, drugged?

"Lastly, that fifteen-year-old from Idaho who wanted some sort of meaningful conclusion to the years of beatings her mother suffered at the hands of a man who had already gotten away with it time and time again.

"I know you went up there and talked to her mother, heard the stories, met the girl. What was her name? Evelyn Sanders. She told you herself how she had taken her mother's car, dressed like a boy, and drove all the way to Sheridan. Hid in the dark in his trailer parked off the road on someone's property. Waited for him to come home from work, hit him on the back of the head, tied him up, then gutted him while he was still alive. Then sat back and watched him bleed to death.

"These accidents, these murders committed by little girls, young women. In your eyes it was justice served well. As seen through your eyes, which had witnessed the violence of war laid down on Vietnamese girls by soldiers. The rapes, the burnings, the bombings. Their lives and the lives of their families destroyed by those who should have protected and cared for them.

"You covered it all up, Gus, and we helped you. Andy, as the funeral director and only one who could act as coroner at the time, labeled cause of death on both Philip Mason and Joe Benton an accident on their death certificates. The murder of Charlie Montgomery. Gus, you labeled that case as unsolved and hid it away in the cold case files. And I backed you both up by upholding your stories and ensuring all the families understood this was for the best."

Bob stopped and took time to let what he was saying set in with his two friends. They hadn't spoken ever about any of this in one sitting. The whole truth about each incident was too painful to completely confront.

Gus was silent, staring straight ahead. His mouth set in a frown, tears running down his tough weathered cheeks.

Andy sighed a couple of times and was the first to break the silence. "We're all going to prison," he said quietly. "I knew this day would come. How could we ever think that hiding evidence in cars and parking them on Earl's property was the smart thing to do.? I mean really! Earl? I'm surprised he never spilled the beans on us while he was alive. Such a simple fool. We were... we are all simple fools."

Just then Sergeant Kell's pickup passed them on Rock Creek Road on the way to the Corbbet orchard.

Chapter Thirty-two

Monday, October 13, 2014

Sergeant Kell

Terry Kell pulled his pickup into the driveway of Earl Corbbet's property and slowed down looking in his rearview mirror. He had spotted Pastor Bob's silver Ford Taurus in the parking lot of the lumber mill back on Rock Creek Road. Three people, men by the size of them, were in the car. Two in front, one in back. Pastor Bob in the driver's seat.

He sighed as he slowly drove down the driveway, pulling past the house to the right of the barn, in front of the side door. One thing he knew for sure, Pastor Bob was not out here holding a prayer meeting. To his right was the green house. Further up and to the right was the orchard and to the left and straight ahead were the four abandoned vehicles.

Those cars are all the way to the back of the property, Sergeant Kell thought to himself and sighed again. *What on earth was I thinking, coming out here at night, in the dark, in the rain? How am I supposed to see anything back there?*

As the young officer got out of his pickup he grabbed his large flashlight and a crowbar. He checked his sidearm, which he had loaded before he left the house. He pulled the hood up on his black sweatshirt. He thought about how he must look. If anyone saw him out here now they would think he was here to do some B&E, and the truth be known he really was about to break into those vehicles. He just hoped the doors and trunks weren't completely rusted shut.

He stood in the rain and tried to make up his mind: should he go to the end of the driveway and wait for Pastor Bob and his two companions, or should he see how much he could get done in the cars before the men in the Taurus decided they were brave enough to confront him out here in the dark and rain?

Sergeant Kell walked to the back of the house without turning on his flashlight. No sense alerting the men to his exact location. He then walked to the side of the house and looked up the road. His eyes had adjusted to the dark and he could see the car a ways up the road still pulled over in the parking lot, but now with its lights off.

Maybe they plan to walk down here and surprise me. He tried not to chuckle out loud and put the back of his hand to his mouth in an effort to keep any sound from coming out. If he had been correct, the third man in the back of the car was funeral director Andy Stokes, Sheridan's own Pillsbury Dough Boy. No, there would be no walking down here from the mill for Andy.

He waited and listened. When he didn't hear footsteps on gravel or pavement or the labored breathing of overweight older men coming in his direction, he turned and walked back toward the barn and the vehicles parked about twenty yards behind it.

The rain kept coming down, hitting the metal roof on the barn, making a lot of noise. He thought he might not hear them coming if he stayed by the barn so he walked quickly to the orchard and moved along the northern side of the trees to the area by the cars.

He looked up at the sky. No moon, no stars, just dark gray clouds. Now all he could hear was raindrops on leaves and grass. The smell of wet earth and apples left to rot on the ground was a comfort to him.

Then he saw it out of the corner of his eye. A figure, the shadow of a human, rushing from the green house to the barn, without making a sound. *Damn it! How could those old farts make it here without me noticing them? Just not fucking possible!*

It gave him a chill. He shivered. He wiped his nose with the back of his hand. Carefully, slowly, he walked back to the barn and followed the shadow into the darkness.

Chapter Thirty-three

Monday, October 13, 2014

Gus Fuller

"Oh, for fuck's sake!" screamed Gus as Sergeant Kell's pickup drove past them, stopping in front of Earl Corbbet's property then turning into the driveway. "I just can't believe this guy. Does he have super powers or something? Why is he out here tonight of all nights?"

Andy moaned and put his face in his hands. "I am way too old for this sort of shit. Take me home!"

"No, we're in this together. We need to think a minute here. We have time, there's no rush." Pastor Bob worked to calm the other two men.

"Okay, let's say he gets into the cars, digs around in the dark until he's soaked to the bone and cold. Is he going to know what he's looking at? Will he know evidence from garbage or trash? No, he's not. He's going to give up and go home.

"The only people that fully understand anything about these accidents is us and the girls that committed the acts. Do you think he's talked to them? No, there's no way for him to do that. There's no way for him to get that far on this."

"He has the case files from archives, Bob!" came back Gus with disgust.

"Oh shit!" yelled the pastor. Both Andy and Gus sat in shock at one of the rare times the pastor ever cussed. The men sat stunned into silence for a time.

"So, he knows some things. Bits and pieces really. Kell doesn't have the 'why' of things, he just knows something's not right here," the pastor mused out loud.

"Don't be stupid. He knows the accidents were murders, intentional murders. Sure, not the details or why. He knows a murder was given a short, incomplete investigation and dropped. He has some background on that, but who's to say it wasn't just incompetence back before we had some real forensics?

"But does he know the real story behind Emily Corbbet? Does he know how she disappeared and what became of her? How would he? Her own daughters don't know their mother's true story," Pastor Bob said, staring at the Corbbet property through the rain.

"Don't be so sure about that, Bob," said Andy from the back seat. "Those girls have been cleaning out that house of Earl's for a couple of weeks now. The old fool kept everything going back in time since the Stone Age. At least I'm sure he kept everything of Emily's."

"Fine! Earl's dead. Maybe it's time for this story to come out. We can craft this thing any way we want," stated the pastor.

"Do my ears deceive me? Have I just heard a man of God suggest we lie?" Gus finally joined the conversation in a normal tone of voice. "And just who are we telling our little story to? To whom shall we confess our sins? Earl's daughters? Sergeant. Terry Kell? The *district attorney?*"

"Oh, my head is killing me! I have a splitting headache. Take me home," Andy groaned from the back seat.

"You are an old woman!" yelled Gus turning to look at Andy.

"No, asshole! I am an old man! An old, worn out, exhausted, overweight, fed-up old man! I did what I did at the time because I thought it was the right thing to do. I thought there was no way in hell anyone was ever going to look into any of this bullshit in my lifetime. But here I sit in the back seat of this car more scared than I have ever been. I actually see all I have built going to hell before my eyes. I see the happiness of my wife, children, and grandchildren flying out the window. I see myself going to prison along with six little girls, now grown women with their own families. I see suffering and humiliation on the horizon and I don't like it one damned bit!" Andy blurted out as he hit the door with his fist.

"What our fine Sergeant Kell needs is a lesson. He needs some old-fashioned schooling in the ways of the real world," said Pastor Bob thoughtfully.

"We shoot him?" Gus questioned in a shocked voice.

"No, moron!" replied Andy. "That's not what Bob means. Can I go home now?"

"First we get our young Sergeant Kell in the car and we take him for a nice ride. We tell him the story behind the disappearance of Emily Corbbet. Impress upon him the sorrow this would create for his two friends, the Corbbet sisters, and why he would never want this to get out.

"And if he is still on his high horse about this whole thing, we fully explain how the story behind Suzie shooting and killing her stepfather being made public will ruin the lives of his wife and the whole Benton family. We make him part of this. We just bring him into the fold, so to speak," Pastor Bob completed, laying out his plan.

"Then we shoot him!" exclaimed Gus.

"No, fool! We shoot you!" Pastor Bob said looking directly at Gus as he started up the car and pulled out of the parking lot heading for the Corbbet property.

Chapter Thirty-four

Monday, October 13, 2014

Sergeant Kell

Sergeant Kell's heart was pounding as he made his way back to the barn. The hairs on the back of his neck were standing up and his breathing was short and shallow. His mind told him there was nothing here to be afraid of but his heart pounded; his inner self warned him of danger.

He drew his gun and silently moved along the side of the barn toward the door, which was open, hanging on one hinge, squeaking as the wind moved it slightly.

As he came around the door so he could see inside the barn he was alarmed to find the inside of the barn was lit by an unearthly glow, as if someone had lit a lamp or turned on a low-watt light bulb. He heard voices, a man and a woman arguing. The woman's was high, shrill, and frightened in reply to the demanding voice of the male. The pounding of the rain on the tin roof of the barn drowned out the words spoken.

Slowly, trying not to be noticed or heard, Sergeant Kell moved into the barn, inching his way along so as not to knock something over. He could hear the voices but he couldn't see anyone. A command, a plea, a scream of pain, then crying. The male voice laughed in evil glee.

Sergeant Kell moved out to hide behind a support beam so he could see better, so many old tools and ropes hanging from the rafters kept him from viewing a scene that must be happening right before his eyes but which he couldn't see.

Suddenly the big front barn door to his left flew open and a man with a shotgun came running into the lit area ready to shoot, screaming something that the Sergeant couldn't quite understand.

As his eyes focused Sergeant Kell realized he was looking at Earl Corbbet. A young, twenty-something Earl Corbbet, shotgun raised to his shoulder with a look of determination Kell had never thought Earl possessed. Earl fired the gun and a man screamed in pain. Kell moved his gaze to his right and there stood a tall, dark-haired man clutching his stomach with one hand, holding a bloody pair of scissors in the other. At his feet was a young woman with long light-brown hair wearing a bloodied gray house dress.

Sergeant Kell was unable to move. The actors in the scene playing itself out before him were not made of matter but seemed to be part fog and part light. He held his breath as the ghost of Earl Corbbet ran straight to the woman on the floor of the barn and the dark-haired man crumbled to the ground beside them screaming in pain.

After checking the woman on the floor Earl stood over the dark-haired man and shot him in the face. That stopped the screaming. Earl put down his gun and knelt down beside the woman again. The whole front of her dress was red with blood. Earl took her in his arms and appeared to be comforting her, kissing her forehead and saying something in a gentle, loving voice.

Sergeant Kell stepped into the light closer to the man holding what appeared to be a dying woman. Earl looked up at Sergeant Kell and said clearly, "She's dead, Gus." The ghost of Earl began to cry, holding the woman's lifeless body to his chest, saying over and over again, "What are we going to do Gus? What am I going to tell my little girls?"

As the ghosts faded away so did the eerie light in the barn. Sergeant Kell could not remain in there another minute and dashed out the door the ghost of Earl had come in through.

Sergeant Kell ran to the end of the driveway and as he did the silver Ford Taurus pulled up, the back door opened, and two pair of hands grabbed his hoodie and pulled him in.

The door slammed shut and the car drove away heading up Rock Creek Road and away from town.

Chapter Thirty-five

Monday, October 13, 2014

Sergeant Kell

Sergeant Kell realized he was lying in the lap of the local funeral director, Andy Stokes. Pastor Bob Snider was driving the car and Gus Fuller was looking at him like he wanted to beat him up.

"What happened, boy? You look like you seen a ghost!" Gus said with a nasty grin on his face.

"How did you know?" answered Sergeant Kell. The men said nothing for about five miles while Sergeant Kell relayed the story of what he had seen in the barn.

"Lucky thing we came along and saved you, isn't it?" Gus said in a sarcastic way.

"How did you know I was coming out to the Corbbet place?" asked Sergeant Kell.

"Your wife called me," lied Gus. "Ya, she was worried about you, messing around those cars, getting into stuff that is best left be. She's a smart one, that gal of yours."

Sergeant Kell couldn't believe his ears. Jan had called Gus and told him what Kell had planned to do? What the fuck?

"We got to thinking, Terry, that we needed to tell you a little story but it could be Earl Corbbet's already taken care of that," said the pastor.

Sergeant Kell thought about it and then said, "Why not tell me the story anyway. You came all the way out here in the rain and all. Somethings up here and I'm ready to hear what you have to say. Lucky for the three of you I'm not on duty."

"No, lucky for you you're not on duty," Gus said.

"Gus, you need to relax," Andy warned Gus.

Pastor Bob slowed the car, moving over to the left side of the road, and pulled into the front of the old Rock Creek schoolhouse, long abandoned and often used by teenagers for parties and trouble.

"I really can't drive and talk at the same time so we'll just park here a few minutes," the pastor told Sergeant Kell. "Or more. It's sort of a long story.

"I'm sure you've heard many times how Earl Corbbet went off back in 1980 to Hamilton, Montana and came back with a pregnant young wife, Emily. Oh, it was a big deal. First of all, it was a big deal that anyone would marry Earl in the first place, him being kind of odd to begin with and such a cheapskate on top of that. Then there was the fact she was pregnant, which meant to everyone in town it must have been a shotgun wedding. One of those forced things you hear about.

"What we didn't know was that Earl marrying Emily was an act of mercy on his part. She was pregnant from an awful rape that happened right in her father's barn by some ranch hand. Emily went ahead and pressed charges, brave girl. And the bastard was found guilty but only got seven years. Big injustice there.

"So, to protect Emily from this guy, this rapist, from coming back to Hamilton when he got out of prison and killing her like he promised in the courtroom, Earl marries her and brings her home here to his place.

"Do Earl and Emily live happily ever after? No, she's unhappy because Earl is who he is. She never gets over the rape. Jumpy, nightmares, can't eat. Three years later, back home in Montana both her folks pass away, six months apart from each other. The poor girl takes that really hard. The only future she has is her babies: Melody, then two years later she has Samantha. They are the love of her life but she's stuck in that one bad time in the past.

"The rapist gets out of prison right on time. Takes a bus to his brother's place in Washington who somehow knew Emily was pregnant and married to Earl. So, this guy borrows his brother's car, a 1983 Chevy Caprice. Tells his brother he plans on bringing both Emily and the baby back with him being as they are his property to begin with.

"That's where the little blue Caprice you see out back of the Corbbet barn with the Oregon plates came from. Well this guy, he arrives at the Corbbet place when no one is home so he pulls the car to the back of the barn and waits in the barn there to see what happens. I'm sure he hoped Emily would come out to the barn all by herself and sure enough, when she and Earl get home from wherever they had gone, she goes out to the barn looking for something. Who's waiting for her, but Bill Garret?

"Earl's on the back porch doing something when he hears all this screaming coming from the barn and he grabs his shotgun and runs in there to find Emily stabbed in the stomach, bleeding to death, and the rapist standing over her, so he shoots the guy. Twice.

"Earl kills the rapist and Emily dies in his arms begging him not to tell the girls any of this. Not about the rape, the murder, her death, nothing. Earl swears to her and calls Gus here who comes out as part of his job with the Sheriff's department at the time.

"Gus calls out Andy Stokes and they then call out Pastor Jake because he has retired and is taking off for back East as soon as he can. They decide, right or wrong, to bury Emily and the rapist and park the car on top of them so they can't be accidently dug up by animals or kids or something, and make up this crazy story about Emily running off with an old boyfriend from Montana. And nobody really asks any questions because being married to Earl couldn't be great, but it does sit funny with a few because Emily leaving her kids behind doesn't seem like something she'd do.

"The whole thing fades into the wind except once the girls move out of the house Earl starts to see things. Having dreams that Emily is after him. She's angry with Earl, see, even though he kept to her wishes about not telling her daughters what happened. But the damned fool buried her there back of the barn along with her rapist right beside her. He didn't dig two holes, he just dug one and put both their bodies in there together.

"In the meantime, more cars get put out in Earl's field to sort of brush under the rug a couple accidents and stall up a murder investigation. You know, trying to protect the innocent, keep families together, see justice done. Whatever you want to call it.

"I'm thinking Earl was seeing Emily all the time there close to his death. She might have been what he was running from when he ran out into the road in front of that pickup. Hell, could have been the ghost of that freaking rapist. Might even have been the ghost of Philip Mason or Uncle Joe Benton. Either that or he was committing suicide as it was all getting to be too much for him."

Pastor Bob stopped there and waited for Sergeant Kell to answer.

Andy let out a sigh, "We were all in on all four incidents. Gus and I. Pastor Jake was in on the coverup of Emily's murder and Earl killing that Garrett guy. Pastor Bob, he was new to Sheridan at the time, so we didn't call him in on that one. Pastor Jake was taking off for back East somewhere and at the time it seemed like it was all going to work out. But as it turned out there was more to cover up and Pastor Bob was in on the last three."

Sergeant Kell sat there for a short time. The rape story was true and he had been right that the rapist came to find Emily and claim her and his baby. He could even understand the coverup as Earl would have gone to prison leaving the very young Corbbet girls to foster care or an orphanage.

But one thing didn't set right with Sergeant Kell and he was pissed off. "So why would my wife call you, Gus?" Sergeant Kell demanded.

Chapter Thirty-six

Monday, October 14, 2014

Sammy

Sammy sat at the small kitchen table in her one-bedroom Seattle apartment and stared at the cell phone in her hand. It was Monday evening and she knew she needed to call her sister again and let Melody get off her chest her unhappiness with Sammy for having left so suddenly after their Dad's service.

She let out a long sigh and put the phone down. Yes, leaving Melody alone in that old farmhouse was inexcusable but Sammy was angry with Melody after the funeral. "Damn it! Who did Melody think she was? Queen of the World?" Sammy steamed to herself. "How could she just go up to her bed and fall asleep like that, knowing that all those people were coming over to the house, leaving me to deal with the whole crowd on my own?"

Sammy went over in her mind how many times she had to make apologies that day for Melody. "Oh yes, Melody has gone to her room, poor thing, so exhausted. Yes, just so worn out. This whole thing, Dad's death, cleaning the house, dealing with estate issues, just too much for her, I guess."

"Bullshit, lazy-ass sister! Just like when we were kids and there was work to do. 'Oh, I have a headache. I have cramps. I can't shit straight!' Always something."

The more Sammy thought about it the madder she got, until she was just as mad as the moment when the last of the guests and well-wishers had finally gone home the day of the funeral. Once she was able to wipe that pretend grateful smile off her face and close the door to the house she marched straight to her room, packed her clothes, loaded her drawings in her car, and drove off.

"HA! I bet I was home in Seattle less than four hours after leaving that Godforsaken poor excuse of a farm" she said out loud in a proud voice.

And now I'm talking to myself! She kicked at the other chair, hurting her big toe, then she cussed some more.

But her hostility soon turned to sadness and regret as she thought about the old house and orchard where she grew up. The place was so run down she knew there was nothing she or Melody could do to bring it back to a money-making operation, with the trees being uncared for all these years and the weather taking a huge toll on the house, both inside and out. The well needed to be re-dug or city water piped in. That would cost big money. A new roof and siding on the house, more money there. Rewiring the electricity, tearing out old walls to install insulation. Trees pulled out, replanted or another crop of something put in. Flowers? No. Fancy heirloom tomatoes? God, no! Angora goats? Nope!

Then there was the infestation. Sammy laughed as she looked out the kitchen window, then fell quiet returning to her thoughts. Ghosts! The place was lousy with them. If Melody couldn't see it or feel them Sammy certainly could. Them. *That's right, there is more than one running around that place.*

A shiver went down her spine and she pulled her flannel bathrobe closer around her body, folding her arms in front of herself, leaning over the small kitchen table.

How many, exactly? She wasn't sure. Could she name them? Not really. Did they want her attention? Did they want to be heard? Oh yes, they did!

When did she notice them? The minute she walked in the door of the house when she first arrived after her father's accident. She had thought it was her father greeting her but she soon realized the phantom covering the back door had some rather menacing intentions. "Oh, so glad to see you, my dear. Please, do come in. Stay." Sammy looked down at her arms and saw goose bumps.

She thought back to what the man who had hit her father with his pickup had said, that Earl had run out into the road like he was being chased by someone. "I bet he was," she said to no one in the room.

Sammy decided to call her sister in the morning when Melody was more likely to be calmed down and they could have a serious talk. Too bad this had to be done over the phone but Sammy wasn't completely convinced she could return to the farm, ever.

But then Sammy thought about her upcoming art show. The gallery hosting it was gearing up to promote her new spooky themed trees like crazy. *Haunted Orchards* by Samantha Corbbet. Little did they know. So, yes, she was going to have to go back, at least to finish her pen and ink pictures.

Chapter Thirty-seven

Tuesday, October 14, 2014

Melody and Sammy

Melody awoke out of a deep and peaceful sleep to the sound of her cell phone going off. It took her a second or two to remember where she was and why.

"Oh, Sammy! I'm so glad you called!! Jan and I are planning a "Last Harvest" out at Dad's place and… I just need you." At first Melody's voice was happy but trailed off to end in a distracted tone.

"Hey, Mellie. Sounds like you are keeping busy. Do you have time to talk a bit? I know you had more to say after that last call, besides, I should fill you in on my show. Is Jan there with you now? Are you out at Dad's place?" Melody could hear the flatness in her sister's mood. Sammy often did this when she was in the middle of a painting, like she was there listening but not really processing what she was hearing fully.

"Yes and no. I'm here at Jan and Terry's house. I spent the night here. So, yes, Jan is here but in the other room. I… I need your full attention. I have to ask you about someone who attended Dad's service and came over to the house afterwards."

"Sure. Go on. Ask away," Sammy said dully into the phone. *My sister has got all the nerve in the world, acting like she was even there,* she thought to herself.

"Remember the middle-aged silver-haired woman in the gray suit?"

"No," replied Sammy.

"Oh! Come on! She fixed you and I dinner after everyone left, helped us clean up too."

"Really?" Sammy questioned in a sarcastic tone.

"I hate when you play fucked-up games with me. It makes me feel like I don't have a full grasp on reality. Why do you do this?" Melody sounded distressed.

"Well, continue with your story, Mellie. I am listening now. So, this lady fixed us dinner, nice."

"You were sitting right there at the table with us!" Melody's voice had risen an octave. "Whoever this woman was, she knew our mother! She told us about how Mom had come to marry Dad after she got raped by a farmhand on her family ranch in Montana! I swear you have no feelings at all, not in one bone of your body." Melody was yelling into the phone.

Jan opened the bedroom door and peaked in at Melody. "Everything okay in here? You talking to your sister?"

"Ya, all okay here. Just family stuff, you know. I'll be out after this call. Got some things we need to iron out. Details. You know."

"I do know." Jan closed the door. Melody's attention went back to her sister.

"Listen to me, Mellie," Sammy said in a soft voice. "After Dad's service you and I came home and you went straight to your room, closed the door and didn't come out. I checked on you once and you were fast asleep. You flaked out on me. I had to deal with all those people and all their stupid ass boo-hooing over Dad. I had to handle the food, the clean-up, and the general pain of having a crowd in that stinking house for hours. While you lay in bed and cried and slept the whole thing away. Just like you did when we were kids when there was work to do and you didn't want to. So once everyone left the house so did I. I packed and got the fuck out of there."

Melody was stunned into silence for a few seconds. "Wait, you mean there was no lady in the gray suit? Are you telling me she was just a dream?"

"Or whatever. Ya, I'm saying you dreamed her up. It didn't happen. No lady, no dinner, no rape story and *no one to help clean up!*" The last words Sammy screamed into the phone to make her point. She stopped and thought a minute. Maybe her sister was losing her mind, so she asked, "Are you losing your mind, Mellie?"

"Well, being as you didn't see this woman in the gray suit and she is only a dream, maybe I am cracking up here. It just seemed so real, she was so nice. Kind of like a mother would be, comforting a child." Melody paused then went on, "That story about Mom getting raped and Dad marrying her to get her away from it all because she was pregnant, you know, from the rape. It broke my heart. I felt sorry for Mom, and Dad too, even if it meant he wasn't my father."

Melody was starting to sob. Sammy could hear the stress in her voice before she had begun to cry and knew this wasn't one of Melody's made-up stories to get out of a situation she didn't want to deal with.

"Hmmmm, shit. I believe you. You had a bad dream." Sammy did believe her sister but it just presented the fact more clearly that Sammy didn't want to return to Sheridan no matter the reason. That dream was caused by something or someone and not just plain laziness.

"A bad dream with a horrible story that is the truth! I found an old suitcase full of newspaper clippings about Mom when she was in high school, about her getting raped by some guy named Garrett. The guy got caught and she pressed charges. There was a trial and he was convicted, sentenced to seven years, Sammy! I was reading the articles when Terry came over to the house to check on me. I was about to have a nervous breakdown so he brought me here to spend the night," Melody gushed into the phone.

Sammy's brain and mouth lost connection for a moment. "Auuugh," was all that would come out. The only thought that would form itself into words was, "Wait. I... can't think. Let me get back to you." Then she hung up on her sister, again.

Chapter Thirty-eight

Tuesday, October 14, 2014

Sammy

Sammy realized, too late, that hanging up on Mellie like that a second time wasn't just unkind, it was extremely cruel.

Something was up, without a doubt, at Dad's old house. She had thought she was the only one feeling the creepiness of the place but it now appeared Mellie was falling prey as well.

This new revelation about her mother having been raped as a young girl in high school swam around in visions in front of Sammy's face. Where was her mother now? Tightness gathered in her chest; she felt cold.

She pulled her bathrobe tighter around herself as she navigated the small kitchen to the yellow and chrome table by the window. Sitting down she thoughtfully sipped at the steaming cup of Earl Grey tea she had made earlier and looked out on Seattle's Queen Anne neighborhood. From her fourth floor apartment she had a front-row seat to all the comings and goings of the Starbucks across the street and the corner donut shop.

Sammy considered what Mellie had told her about the woman in the gray suit. Rain pattered purposefully on the glass of the kitchen window. Who had this mysterious woman been? Just a dream, some lost spirit pulled forward from the past? Had it been their mother, reaching out from her grave in an effort to set things straight?

The sound of rain pinging on the roof tops and the fragrance of hot tea always gave Sammy a feeling of well-being. Unlike staying in her childhood home since Dad's passing. Had that same feeling been there before when she was a child? It was more than a sensation of unrest in and around the aging ruin of a farmhouse, it was a menacing vibration that made her skin crawl, her breath to come in short gulps followed by a feeling of total grim foreboding.

Yes, she had sensed these things before when she was in high school. Maybe before that as well. Shadows by the barn, fog out in the orchard, the unpleasant smell of ripe decay which she had always thought was just the odor of rotting fruit.

Sammy stared at the amber liquid in the cup she held. She slowly came to recognize, or rather recall, that exact menacing vibration. Something she hadn't felt since the summer before her freshman year. Her breathing came in short gulps, her eyes glazed over, and a memory from many years ago slowly came into focus. A memory she had managed to suppress. First the edges, then the body of the mental image. It moved, unfolded and became solid.

Oh no... not that!!!

Sammy's shoulders shook as she sobbed into the sleeve of her robe.

The rain now beat the window pane as if in anger and hurt.

Chapter Thirty-nine

Tuesday, October 14, 2014

Melody

Melody Corbbet sat in bed staring at her phone. Was it possible that her own sister, her only sister, her only living relative, would or could hang up on her after she had just poured her heart out about what was happening to her? Twice in two days?

She felt broken inside and her chest was hurting as she slowly got dressed. She popped into the bathroom to relieve herself then washed her hands and face, brushed her hair and teeth (glad she had those items in her handbag), put on some lip gloss and a small smile, and headed into the kitchen to see what Jan was up to.

Mel found Jan sitting sideways on the couch in the front room, looking expectantly out the big picture window with a very worried expression on her face.

"Good morning. What's up?" asked Mel who had noticed somehow through her own problems that all was not as it should be with Jan.

"Terry didn't come home last night. I've been trying to call his cell but he doesn't pick up. I haven't called the Sheriff's department yet because he wasn't on the job last night and… oh, I don't know what I should do." Jan wasn't crying but she was keyed up with worry.

Mel sat down next to her on the couch, "What do you mean? Terry left the house last night? What for? I thought he went to bed after we did."

"No, Mellie. He went out to your Dad's place," was Jan solemn reply.

"What the fuck, Jan? Why? That makes no sense. Is that why he brought me here, so he could go out to Dad's and sneak around without me knowing?" Melody was mad and hurt. More than she normally would have been due to the rotten phone conversation she had just had with Sammy.

Jan was taken back by Melody's strong reaction to Terry going out to the farm but she was more hurt by the fact that Melody wasn't getting the real point here. Terry had not returned!

"Mellie! It's been ten hours! He's not back from your farm! It's only three miles away. I think we need to go look for him." Jan pushed the real issue back at Melody.

Melody jumped up off the couch, "Shit, Jan, I'm sorry. Let's go out to Dad's place and see what's up."

Just then the backdoor in the kitchen opened with a bang and loud strong boot stomps could be heard moving at a fast pace across the linoleum floor.

The women were startled. Jan stood up and they both turned in time to see Terry standing in the dining room. He was soaking wet, mud head to toe, and his black hooded sweatshirt was missing. He smelled like he'd been smoking cigarettes.

Jan rushed to her husband but stopped short of hugging him because of the mud, "Thank God, you're home! Oh, where have you been? I've been so worried. I don't think I slept a wink since 3:00 am when I realized you weren't back. What the hell happened out there?"

"You should know," Terry replied dryly. More than that, he actually sounded pissed off.

Jan drew back a step. Her husband had never talked to her like that unless he was about to give her a piece of his mind, with volume.

Terry looked at both Melody and Jan with blazing eyes.

"Here is how this morning is going to go," he said with that edge in his voice that he used when addressing thugs he had just caught robbing a house.

"While I'm taking a long hot shower, you," he pointed at his wife with a filthy finger, his voice getting louder, "are going to call the Sheriff's department and tell them I won't be in to work today as I'm coming down with something. When I come back out here, I want my breakfast on that table." He now pointed at the table. "Then I'm going to bed!!"

"You two," he continued, waving his muddy hand in the direction of both Jan and Melody, making them jump. He then gestured in the direction of the Corbbet farm and went on, "are going to go over to that farm and get rid of those newspaper articles!" At this point he was hollering.

Terry calmed down just a bit, or rather, he talked with less volume. "Go over there, clean up. If anyone comes by and asks any questions you are going to tell them about that last harvest thing you are planning, then get them off the property fast.

"There's a burn pile that has been started out near the back of the barn. Keep it going. Pile on any downed tree branches, old newspapers, anything that will burn. I'll be out there later this afternoon."

His eyes narrowed as he looked closely at Jan. In a harsh whisper he added. "I will deal with you, sweetheart, later."

"Oh, ya, I almost forgot. Melody, get your damned sister back here!" And with that Terry marched off to the garage to remove his muddy clothes and boots.

Chapter Forty

Tuesday, October 14, 2014

Andy Stokes

Andy Stokes had been dropped off at his home by Pastor Bob before the work out at the Corbbet farm was completed. That must have been about around 2:00 am or later Tuesday morning. Andy had gotten a chill standing out in the rain at the farm.

The men had pulled the abandoned Chevy Caprice out of its decades-old parking place behind the barn using Sergeant Kell's pickup. Then Sergeant Kell and Gus had started digging in the mud, weeds, and grass that had been under the car while Andy and Pastor Bob held flashlights.

Andy had told Pastor Bob he wasn't doing so good and he wanted to go home. With the young Sergeant Kell there, Andy knew he wouldn't be needed to take a turn digging. All he had to do was stand there and hold the big flashlight so the other men could see what they were doing in the dark. Still, that small amount of activity took a lot out of him.

Now safe at home, having had a hot bath and a glass of warm milk, he still wasn't feeling well. His headache was worse than ever.

Andy sat in his den-turned-bedroom in the dark, thinking. His den had become his bedroom years ago when his wife, Barbara, had decided she had had enough of his snoring. "You sound like a moose in rut," she had told him, "I can't take it anymore. You have to move to the den."

The arrangement was fine with him; their sex life was long over by the time they were in their fifties. He could come and go as he pleased, get up early for fishing, go to bed late watching an old movie, stay out with the guys (tonight being a case in point), or just hide when he felt people or Barbara and their two boys were getting on his last nerve.

Neither he nor Barbara, Barbie as he called her, had put two and two together on Andy's declining health even with the weight gain, increase in snoring, and lack of sex drive. They had boys to get ready for college and a funeral home that wasn't going to take care of itself.

At the age of seventy-two, Andy was three hundred and fifty pounds. Five foot eight inches in his stocking feet. Barbie was not a cook; even when the boys were little they lived on take-out and fast food. Christmas Eve dinner had always been at the Chinese restaurant on Bridge Street. Christmas day they ate leftovers along with whatever pastries and sweets neighbors had dropped off as holiday cheer.

He had never been much of a drinker, not like Gus. But then he didn't have the reasons Gus had to self-medicate. Sure, both men had seen death a-plenty but in totally different ways.

While Gus had been putting his soldier buddies' bits and pieces in body bags, Andy was gently laying old women to rest in their beautiful white silk-lined caskets. There was a huge gap in reality there. True, both men had been showing respect for the dead with the intended result being eternal rest in a dignified manner, but the circumstances were at opposite ends of the spectrum.

Could be I need a life style change, Andy thought to himself. He got the bottle of Advil out of his desk drawer and threw a couple into his mouth, swallowing them dry, his milk long gone. Some little man was banging on the inside of his skull with a jackhammer and, *fuck lord,* it was killing him. His chest was heavy as were his arms and legs. Breathing was painful.

He got into bed, turned out the lamp on the nightstand, and lay back on his pillow. He thought about Emily Corbbet. Now there was an example of not putting someone to rest in a dignified manner. How can a soul be at peace when there is no ceremony, no care or outward show of love in the way the body is interned? No affinity for a spirit to carry it into eternity. Tortured in life by Bill Garret and tortured in death by the same evil being. *If that isn't grounds for haunting a place I don't know what is,* he said to himself.

Andy Stokes felt himself slip off into darkness. Soon he was standing out in Earl Corbbet's orchard, wind blowing the rain in his face. Two men were digging in the ground out behind the barn. Andy heard Earl Corbbet crying, saying over and over, "I'm so sorry, I'm so sorry."

Two bodies wrapped in blankets lay on the ground next to the large hole that the two men had been working on. Earl walked over to the smaller of the two bodies, kneeled down, picked it up, and cradled the blanketed corpse in his arms. "Forgive me! I'm a fool! Please forgive me, sweetheart," Earl pleaded weakly.

One of the men who had been digging stopped, got out of the hole, walked over to the larger body and gave it a kick, cussing hatefully. "No!" shouted Andy running toward the man, "Never disrespect the dead!" Gus shrugged and walked back to the other man who had been digging with him. They both sat down on the fender of the oddly painted green car and lit up cigarettes.

Andy walked over to Earl, put his hand on his shoulder and said gently, "Come on, Earl. It's time to go. You've got to let her go now, Earl. Let's go in the house and clean up."

The two men sitting on the bumper of the car finished their smokes and stamped out the butts, then threw the larger body into the hole they had been digging and began throwing objects too hard to identify into the hole, on top of the body.

Andy and Earl walk across the yard toward the house. "This goes no further. My girls are never to know. We take this secret with us to our graves," Earl says weakly. "We have," replies Andy reassuringly.

The scene slowly changes before Andy's eyes and he finds himself standing in his own front yard. The rain has stopped and the sun is just starting to rise. Gray clouds move to the north and as Andy watches them float across the sky, he realizes his headache is gone. In fact, he feels great, light as a feather in both body and soul.

The sky clears, appearing light blue with silver clouds that move off to the south. He feels a pull, a gentle tug, that draws him as if toward a warm embrace. He allows himself to let go and surrenders to oblivion.

Chapter Forty-one

Tuesday, October 14, 2014

Jan Kell

After both Jan and Melody had made the needed phone calls, Jan to Terry's work to explain why he wasn't coming in to work that day because he was coming down with "that bug that's going around" and Melody to her sister plainly stating it was time to return home, they begin putting together breakfast for themselves and the very pissed-off Sergeant Terence Kell.

Jan had only seen her husband truly angry a handful of times but never as furious as he appeared this morning.

As she directed Melody to make coffee, Jan got the sausages on the grill and the hash browns in the frying pan. *What could Terry be thinking I've done?* she worried to herself.

Melody decided not to interfere in someone else's marital problems and complied with Jan's instructions to make coffee, then set the table, ensuring there was butter, jam, salt, pepper, and hot sauce placed in front of Terry's plate.

Sooner than expected Terry came out of the bathroom, scrubbed clean, shaved, hair dried and combed back. He wore a clean light blue t-shirt and plaid flannel pajama bottoms, no slippers. His face was a forced calm, as was his voice.

"No coffee for me. I'll take a large glass of orange juice, a large glass of water, no ice, and whatever you have for a backache that will help me sleep," was all Terry said at first.

Jan rushed to comply, placing the two Advil PMs on the table next to the water rather than handing them to him. Just as quickly she scooped scrambled eggs, sausage, and hash browns onto a plate while Melody got the toast out of the toaster. They placed the food in front of Terry. Terry didn't look at Jan one time while he ate his breakfast.

The women got their plates ready and ate with him at the table but with heads down. Terry addressed Melody with more instructions between bites. She and Jan were to go straight to the farm. Gus Fuller would be waiting for them there tending the burn pile out back of the barn. Gus would explain everything. They were not to go into the barn for any reason, nor were they to allow anyone else into the barn. Pastor Bob would come by at some point to relieve Gus. Once Sammy got there Pastor Bob would fill them in as to what was up.

"Let Gus know I'm sleeping with my phone on in case I'm needed and that I've called in sick today so I will be available." Terry got up from the table and headed for the bedroom.

"Jan, I'll call you when it's time for you to come home," he said with his back to Jan and Melody. "Goodnight, Sergeant Kell," Melody said softly, then she turned to Jan who looked contrite and hurt and added. "Come on. Let's get out to the farm."

Chapter Forty-two

Tuesday, October 14, 2014

Sammy

The second phone call with her sister had gone slightly better but not by much. Melody's voice had sounded hushed and urgent in a secretive way, which intrigued Sammy more than anything.

"I just talked to Terry. Something major is up out at Dad's place. Not sure what exactly but he just returned from there all muddy, like he'd been digging. I think he's found something because he is upset in a major way. I'll know more in about an hour but you do need to come back. Do what you need to do. Handle your gallery owner and promoter of your art show. Promise them anything but come back today. Now! Please, Sammy!"

With that Sammy agreed to return to her dead father's haunted orchard to face her fears of the unbodied people who resided there.

It didn't take much to pack back up. She hadn't unloaded the art supplies, and the half-finished drawings had gone straight back into the car after showing what she had been working on to her friend and promoter, Linda Lowry, the day before.

Sammy had known Linda since art school. She was five years older than Sammy. Tall, slender in a willowy way, and just as graceful. Bright, shiny green eyes and short, curly auburn hair. Skin a flawless alabaster white.

Linda had become an art promoter, or patron as they were once called back in the day, after she decided her style of drawing would never sell and her parents had left her a large inheritance to spend as she pleased. She would find new or struggling artists she liked, hold a show for them, and if their art, paintings, sculptures, wood work, etc. sold she kept them as part of a stable and marketed them to galleries far and wide. In short, the woman was a saint of the arts.

Sammy wasn't certain of Linda's sexual preferences. Hell, she wasn't certain of her own. Why would this come up ever? Their relationship was a business one and both women kept it that way even though it was clear Linda loved her little band of creators with all her heart. Some jealous asshole critic once referred to Linda's preferred artists as her "box of kittens." Oddly, the man lost his job at that magazine and was never heard from again, at least in the art world on the West Coast, or East Coast for that matter, now that Sammy thought about it.

When Sammy had shown Linda the dying orchard drawings she had been working on Linda had gone crazy with excitement. She had loved the dark feeling of them, compared them to some of the trees Van Gogh had done. The sagging trees shaded in green, brown, and black; wilting leaves; and ripe pears turning a pale yellow. Skies, the saddest of silver blue and gray.

Linda had told Sammy which direction she wanted the rest of the series of drawings to take to continue the feeling of despair. She wanted to bring it up out of despair slowly, moving into an aura of graceful decay. The women had sat over coffee, talking for almost two hours, working out each drawing so the subject and its progression would flow like a written story in picture form.

This new plan had meant Sammy needed seven drawings, not five. And to fill the gallery Linda planned to make this a double showing by bringing in another artist, whose art would be in contrast but complement what Sammy was doing.

Before taking off from Seattle Sammy had called Linda to let her know she was heading back to Sheridan to continue her work. Linda wanted to know when Sammy could complete the job because she wanted to start promoting the show and needed an approximate time for the opening. Sammy had turned the table on Linda and wanted her to set the date. Sammy would work toward that deadline. For some artists this caused a block in their ability to produce but for Sammy she found the pressure to be inspiring. It forced her to focus intently and deliberately and fed into her obsessive-compulsive nature.

As the show was to take advantage of wealthy holiday shoppers, it could not become lost in the franticness of the season but would use the season (Autumn) of the work to appeal to her buyers. Linda set an exact date, Monday, November 17th.

This had made Sammy choke.

"Would it be possible to put the show off until January?" she had asked. "I can't do it by November, Linda. Even if I didn't sleep for four weeks it's not possible to keep the detail pronounced enough to ensure the correct feel. Decay doesn't happen overnight, you know," Sammy had stated plainly.

"The only thing I can think to do here is promote the other guy as the main artist and you as 'with a preview of Samantha Corbbet's newest study Haunted Orchard', like a taste of what's to come," Linda had offered up as a solution.

"Okay, sounds good for now. Thank you for all your support and the advance. I love you madly but really need to hit the road. I'll check in next week and send you pictures of what I have done," Sammy had replied in an exhausted manner, already worn out before even having gotten back to work. She didn't bother asking who Linda had in mind as the other artist for the show. Any show Linda put together seldom flopped.

Sammy sped up and merged her Kia Soul smoothly onto Interstate 5 South and settled in for the four plus hour drive back to the small town of Sheridan. She had selected the sound track from the movie *Cold Mountain* as her driving music. It was the correct mood. The movie about a doomed love between two almost strangers set during the Civil War. Just the right amount of sadness and despair. She needed those emotions for her days of drawing ahead. *Yes, it's true, you have to feel it to re-create it on canvas.*

Chapter Forty-three

Tuesday, October 14, 2014

Jan Kell

Jan had a lot to do and even more to think about. She had somehow angered her husband more than she ever thought possible and she was almost in a complete state of anxiety. The trick here was not to show it in front of Melody Corbbet or anyone else for that matter, and to follow through on his instructions so that when, or if, he called her home she would have completed tasks to give up as a peace offerings.

Jan and Melody had left the house shortly after Terry had gone to bed. They had not done the dishes nor cleaned the kitchen in an effort to keep the noise down so it would be easy for him to fall asleep. Same reason they had only grabbed their notes from the night before regarding the "last harvest" party and their handbags and left the house as soon as they could.

Neither one spoke until they were in Jan's car on the way to the Corbbet farm.

"I'm sorry, Mel. I don't think I've ever seen Terry that angry in our ten years of marriage. I'm sure that after a nice long sleep he'll be his old self again. Still, if I were you, I'd plan to sleep at your Dad's place tonight. Besides, Sammy will be back by then and by the sounds of things you two have quite a bit to iron out." Jan started the conversation.

"Well, whatever it is or was that has made your husband so angry we are going to find out in about fifteen minutes. Old Gus is out at Dad's tending a burn pile out back of the barn," Melody replied blankly.

Jan considered what Melody just said and how she said it. To Jan, Melody sounded like and looked like a deer in headlights, stunned, or shocked, or overwhelmed past the point of processing all that was unfolding before her.

Terry's orders might be harder to carry out than she had first realized. If she was going to have to do what was needed and take care of Melody until Sammy got there it was going to be a long unhappy day.

Jan pondered to herself. She knew Terry had the story of her Uncle Joe's demise as she had told him that herself. He had heard from Melody last night while at her Dad's place about Emily Corbbet's history and had pieced together Bill Garrett having come looking for her. Had Gus filled Terry in on the rest of that story? What else had Terry found out about? Did he now know the tale behind each of the four cars?

While it was true Jan knew some bits and pieces about the stories behind the vehicles stored out at Earl's orchard, she didn't know complete details or reasons why. Did Terry know more than she did? Did he think that for some reason she had withheld this information from him or should have for some reason told him these things?

"Oh, dear lord!" she accidently mumbled out loud in the car. Melody stared straight ahead and said nothing.

What would Melody and Samantha do once they knew all there was to know about the secrets their father had kept from them about their mother? Would they demand some sort of redress? Who would they demand this from? Would current local law enforcement now be compelled to go after all those involved in the coverups as well the injured young women who they had worked to protect all these years?

Or would it be her husband, Sergeant Terence Kell? Forced to reveal to his superiors at the Yamhill County Sheriff's department how pillars of the community, past-Sheriff Gus Fuller, Pastor Bob Snider, and then-acting County Coroner Andy Stokes had orchestrated a decades-long string of lies that even the cleverest novelist couldn't have devised?

Would he divorce her for never telling him years earlier all that she knew because he felt betrayed and untrusted? Would he then realize she had never fully trusted him not to damage her family in some fashion?

What about the families whose loved ones were connected to all these different situations? They too would be at fault and could end up being brought up on charges for unreported homicides, obstructing law enforcement during an investigation, covering up for each other out of love. She couldn't imagine all the laws that had been broken here.

It could be her ten-year marriage would end in divorce over these matters. She was glad they didn't have children as they would have made the situation harder if the marriage was over.

These questions swirled around in her mind as she drove down Rock Creek Road, almost missing the driveway to the Corbbet orchard.

Jan slammed on the brakes then turned her car into the driveway and steered it to the right side of the barn, getting as close to the back as she could without getting the car trapped in the mud. It was clear some other car had been out here driving around, creating fresh deep tire ruts she now had to artfully avoid so she wouldn't get stuck.

She and Melody got out of the car.

Gus stepped out from behind the barn and greeted both women in a guarded way. He looked exhausted, old, and just as muddy as Terry had been.

"Hey. Glad you're here. I sure could use a hot cup of coffee while I wait for Pastor Bob to come out relieve me," was all he said to Melody.

"Sure. How about a fried egg sandwich to go with it? Won't take but a sec," Melody offered while looking him over carefully.

"Sounds great. Make one for Pastor Bob just in case. I'll eat it if he doesn't want it," Gus answered, but it sounded more like an order.

Once Melody was in the house Gus turned to Jan and motioned for her to come with him. Jan followed the old retired Sheriff back behind the barn where a burn pile supported a slight flame, smoldering. It was clear it had been started in a hole dug in the soft earth which had been covered by the green Chevy Caprice, which was now pulled back about twenty feet.

Gus grabbed a pitchfork and stirred the paper and tree branches that were slowly burning in the shallow pit.

"Your husband get home okay?" Gus questioned.

"Oh, he got home alright. If he is okay is up for debate. And if he and I will still be married a month from now, well, that's another story completely. He's fucking pissed, Gus! Not at you. He's pissed at me. What in God's name did you say to him? What did you guys do out here last night?" Jan scolded the old man.

"I told him you called me," Gus confessed, looking up at her.

"You stupid old fool! All that happens from here on out is your doing! This is your shit show! I'm pretty certain I'm not going to like prison and neither are my folks. Or Lilly, or

Suzie, or Pastor Bob, or Andy Stokes, or anybody else connected to all this," Jan stormed, waving her hand toward the side of the orchard where the cars were parked and until now long forgotten.

"At least the Corbbet girls wouldn't have to see their Dad go to prison for killing that piece of shit Bill Garrett," was all Gus could think to say. He handed Jan another pitchfork and told her to stir the fire.

"It stopped raining. That's good. Lucky for us there is plenty around here to burn." Gus gestured out at the apple and pear trees that had fallen over in years past, and a few branch piles built up around the yard. "It's old and burns easy."

"So, what did Terry say when he got home?" asked Gus.

"Nothing really. He had me call in sick for him. Took a shower, ate, and went to bed. Told me to come out here, tend this fire, stay out of the barn, keep others out of the barn and off the property." Jan didn't say anything about Terry's instructions to Melody to burn the newspaper articles on the kitchen table.

"I guess I'm partly to blame here. He asked me about what happened to Uncle Joe yesterday at breakfast and I told him the whole story. Well, just what had been in the papers at the time. I didn't tell him about how you, Pastor Bob, and Andy Stokes edited the paperwork to state it was all an accident so that poor little Suzie wouldn't end up in a mental hospital for the criminally insane the rest of her life. I didn't tell him about how you worked out parking Uncle Joe's car out here, truck full of odds and ends that no one need know about, being as Earl Corbbet owed you a big favor for covering up something to do with the death of his wife and his killing that fuck Garrett.

"But I'm pretty sure he's got that story figured out. After what all Melody told him from finding... some family stuff in the house," Jan ended there.

"Thank Pastor Bob when you see him. He filled Sergeant Kell in on the whole Bill Garrett end of things and how we had come out here to help out Earl keep it all... underground, so to speak.

"He's a smart guy, that husband of yours. Showed up at my place yesterday afternoon after going to Yamhill County case archives to pick up the case files on some of these here parked cars. Came in sweet as you please with a six-pack of beer asking me about that pickup and the Charlie Montgomery homicide. Wanted to know why it was only given a slipshod investigation which stalled and ended up in cold cases." Gus motioned toward the pickup as he talked.

"What about Philip Mason's story? Does he have all the details about that?" Jan asked Gus.

"Don't know. But there is someone who does have and could tell him, who he would listen to without putting on his law enforcement badge," offered Gus.

"Who is that?" asked Jan.

"Samantha Corbbet," Gus replied.

Chapter Forty-four

Tuesday, October 14, 2014

Sammy

Samantha knew she needed to stay alert and not daydream while driving on the freeway. But that was the problem she was having on her long drive to Sheridan. How many times had she done this very boring trip before? She couldn't begin to count.

She had always been the one her dad had called to come down and help him with things because Melody lived too far away and had a regular nine-to-five job that she couldn't always get away from.

Sure, just call Samantha, she can drive down in a couple hours. Besides she was just doodling on paper and going to parties. She had nothing important to do.

Stop it, she said to herself. *Don't be bitter about the past.*

She had left her apartment without eating any breakfast so as soon as she saw an easy exit to get off and back on the freeway with a decent place to eat, she took it.

The place she picked was nice, not too busy as it was just before the lunch hour on a Tuesday morning. She ordered her favorite, poached eggs on toast, and hot coffee to keep her awake. The food came quickly and she ate it just as fast. She texted Melody to let her know where she was and when she thought she would arrive out to the farm.

After using the restroom and getting more coffee to go she hopped back in the car heading south again.

She stayed alert, paid good attention to the flow of traffic, stopped once for gas just north of Vancouver, and crossed the Columbia River on the Washington-Oregon bridge. It had taken a little over three hours. It was 12:30 pm.

Samantha rolled into downtown Sheridan an hour and a half later. 2:00 pm. At the last minute she turned left at the one stop light in town and drove over the bridge that crossed the Yamhill River heading south, out of town along SW Ballston Road, to Green Crest Memorial Park. She drove into the entrance then around to the west end of the graveyard close to where she knew Philip Mason was buried.

When she got out of the car she stretched her arms, legs, and back. She looked around to see if anyone was watching her as she thought she might look like she was getting ready to go for a jog and didn't want to bring attention to herself. Then with determination she marched straight to the grave of the one person on this planet that she was certain had gotten what he deserved.

"Here lies Philip Mason. You rat fucker!" She said out loud to his headstone in a deep sly voice, cat-like grin on her face.

Samantha looked around again to ensure she was the only person in the cemetery, that no cars had pulled in since she had arrived. In a flash of motion she pulled down her sweat pants, squatted over the gravesite, and peed hard. A full bladder of coffee which she had held for two and a half hours. The sound was unmistakable and she couldn't help but laugh as she looked up to the sky, relieving herself on the grave of a boy who had revealed to her a true face of evil.

Chapter Forty-five

Tuesday, October 14, 2014

Melody

Melody stepped into the house after having been gone only overnight and noticed it felt the same as it had when she had first arrived from California two weeks ago. The air in the place was stale, musty, and laden with grief and despair. For a second she thought she heard a woman crying.

She walked through the laundry room into the kitchen. It was almost exactly as she had left it, the newspaper clippings in divided piles on the table, a few dirty dishes on the counter waiting to be washed, light over the sink still on. The change here was muddy boot prints all over the floor. They went every which way, like several people had come in and just walked around.

Must have been Terry and Gus coming in to use the bathroom or get a glass of water, she thought to herself. But the news articles were still on the table and Terry had told her to burn them. Why hadn't he done it himself? If he had been in the kitchen he could have grabbed them all and done away with them earlier. "Odd," she said aloud.

Melody got the coffee going then went into the front room, grabbed the old tan leather suitcase, returned to the kitchen, and quickly put all the articles back in it. She then placed the suitcase back into its hiding place in the sewing room.

She went back in the kitchen and started eggs frying and got bread in the toaster. She filled the sink with hot soapy water and dirty dishes while keeping an eye on the cooking food. Then she wiped down the table and the counters thinking how strange it was she wasn't finding muddy fingerprints on used glasses or cupboard doors.

The eggs and toast were done before the coffee was ready so she put the sandwiches together with a thin slice of cheese on each as an added touch. As she was wrapping each of the sandwiches in a paper towel she noticed Pastor Bob's car coming up Rock Creek Road toward the house. It occurred to her that he had gotten there pretty fast, twenty or twenty-five minutes after she and Jan had arrived. Gus must have called Pastor Bob to come pick him up the minute he saw Jan's car out on the road. Pretty easy to see the road from behind the barn.

She was glad she had made two sandwiches. She poured coffee into two cups. Holding them by their handles with one hand and carrying the sandwiches with the other hand, she went out the door to greet her new visitor.

By the time she got out the back door Pastor Bob was already heading straight for Gus, Jan, and the burn pile. She followed him and heard him call out to Gus, "I called the fire department to ensure we didn't need a permit to do burning today. They said it has been pretty wet from the rain this past week so there's no problem, but laughed at the idea we could keep the fire going with all this brush and branches being so waterlogged. It's good to know we won't have any law enforcement out here inspecting what we're doing or asking any questions."

Jan ran up to Melody, took both cups of coffee, and handed them to the two men who thanked the women. Gus reached out and took both sandwiches. "Hey, one of those is for Pastor Bob!" said Melody trying to sound playful and lighten the mood.

"No, that's okay. I'm fine. Had a bite at home this morning before the call came in from Barbara Stokes. I have bad news," Pastor Bob said turning to Gus and the two women. "Andy Stokes died in his sleep this morning."

Gus looked stunned, then worried, but said nothing and continued to eat his fried egg sandwiches.

"Oh God, no!" Jan exclaimed in surprise.

"Does Terry know?" Melody asked wondering to herself if Andy's death might have been one of things that had him so completely enraged this morning.

"I doubt it," replied Pastor Bob. "Barbara called me around 7:00 this morning. I was the first person she called. I went straight over to the Stokes place to help in any way I could."

"Well, what happened?" Jan asked, distressed.

"Barbara had gone in to Andy's room to wake him up and he was cold when she touched his face. She knew right away he was dead. She called me, and when I got there she was pretty shaken up. I checked on Andy. He looked quite peaceful, really, had a little smile on his face.

"I helped Barbara call her sons and tell them the news. Then I called the Sheriff's department and they sent out the county coroner and some deputy, nice young man. I didn't expect Sergeant Kell. He normally doesn't get to work until around noon? Am I right, Jan?" Pastor Bob turned to Jan to confirm his information.

"You're right. But he won't be at work today anyway. He's coming down with something. Flu, cold, I don't know what. He's at home in bed. He did say he was leaving his phone on so Gus could call him if he was needed for some reason," Jan informed the pastor.

Pastor Bob looked at the ground, nodded, then looked back up at Gus, who continued to chew large bites from his breakfast.

"I stayed with Barbara," Pastor Bob went on, "until the coroner and the deputy arrived. It took about an hour for them to get there. Talk about slow. They had to stand around and talk in Andy's bedroom with his body still in the bed. In the meantime, Andy's two boys arrived with their wives and the grandkids. Kind of awful, the kids having to see their granddad get hauled away with a sheet covering his face.

"First glance and opinion by the coroner is Andy died of natural causes. Well, if being overweight is natural. But the man was no spring chicken and had been complaining of a bad headache for a couple days, according to his wife. So maybe it was a stroke. They're going to do an autopsy anyway, just can't see why. The family is fine with it, so whatever. From there they will send his body over to a funeral home in McMinnville to get it ready for his service, but the actual service will be here at his own place being as all his friends are here and this is a local event, so to speak. I'll be doing the service, of course, with both boys saying a word or two. I should have expected this family to be able to put together a funeral for their own in such an organized fashion. They've done this for others for years so it all seems natural to them. Date for the service is up in the air as the body has to be gotten back from the coroner. Well, you know the drill," he said, turning to look at Melody who had tears running down her cheeks.

"Well," said Gus with a sigh, "On that happy note I'd like to go home, please. I'm wet, cold, and have been on my feet I don't know how many hours. Bob, do you think you could come back here and help the girls for a couple hours after you drop me off at home? How long before your sister gets here?" Gus turned to Melody.

"Ah, early afternoon, I think. Around 2:00, give or take an hour. More like give an hour." Melody was trying to answer the question but her brain had closed up shop again.

****

"Okay, let's do this; Jan, you and Melody stay here and keep this fire going. You have to stir it with the pitchforks. Burn anything that's not nailed down. See if you can't get someone out here to help you with a chainsaw that can cut up a few of these dead trees." Gus was in his element giving orders and organizing tasks for his troops.

"There's a few guys in town who have been dying to get into the barn since your Dad died. Don't let them or anyone else in there for any reason. You two girls got that?" Gus shook the finger of his now empty hand at Jan and Melody.

"Gus, we've both been menstruating for years," Jan corrected Gus on his use of the term *girls*.

Gus actually blushed and put his head down then gathered himself back up to assigning duties.

"Melody, I understand from Sergeant Kell you have a pile of newspaper articles that need to be burned. Go in the house right now and bring them out here. I want to see you throw them on the fire," Gus directed Melody.

Melody turned and headed for the house. What was she going to do now? She didn't want to burn any of those articles, mostly because that first pile had been about her mother, and any connection with her mother was better than nothing. The other stuff? Well, that was probably what all this creeping around at night was all about but she didn't feel obliged at all to anyone to help cover up anything. Her dad's part in all this, whatever it had been, was over and ended with his death.

As Melody entered the house through the back door she stopped and looked around. The laundry room was stacked floor to ceiling with old yellowed newspapers. She closed the door so she couldn't be seen by anyone out by the barn. Why not fake these guys out? She just had to be fast, run out there with an arm load and throw them on the fire before Gus or anyone asked to take a look at what she had.

Melody began franticly pulling apart newspapers, tearing around any article with a picture, leaving the headlines off so no one could tell if the article was about the local sewage problems or the bloody murder of a local bartender. She found a brown paper grocery bag and stuffed all the loose newspaper stories in there. Then she grabbed a short pile of still intact papers and put them under one arm.

She flew out the back door at a dead run, loaded down but still able to move quickly. When she came around the corner of the barn she halted in front of the burn pile then threw the paper bag full of random articles on the fire. Next she threw the wad of old newspapers on top of the bag before anyone could stop her to inspect what she had. Slowly the load of old paper started to burn.

Everyone standing around the fire coughed and stepped back. Black smoke went straight up, then the wind changed direction, sending smoke into Gus's, Jan's, and Pastor Bob's faces. Melody grabbed a pitchfork and stirred the mess of papers, spreading it out so it would catch fire faster. She had noticed a gas can next to Gus's feet when they had arrived. She figured he had been using that to re-start the fire whenever it appeared it was going out. She grabbed it and threw out a big splash of gas… *whoooooosh!* The small yard fire was now an inferno.

"What the fuck, sister?" Gus yelled at Melody as he grabbed the gas can out of her hand, all the nice gone out of his voice. His eyes ablaze reflecting the fire before them. Instant combustion had unnerved Gus ever since he'd come back from his time in Viet Nam.

Melody looked at him in a shy hurt way, then put her head down and said, "I thought we wanted to destroy this stuff. Just trying to do my part." She pretended to start to cry. She went over to Pastor Bob and leaned against him in a way that he had to put his arms around her to comfort her.

Jan stepped forward carefully and stirred the fire with the other pitchfork. It sparked and popped until it settled down a bit then she threw on another branch from the small pile Gus had built from debris he had found around the yard.

"Hey, Mel! You know, this fire is great. I mean we can use this to clean up the yard, get things ready for the last harvest. If anyone comes out to find out what's going on, we tell them about the plan to let people come out and pick apples and pears one last time. While we stand here waiting for Pastor Bob to come back from dropping of Gus and for Sammy to arrive, we can make phone calls and get the ball really rolling promoting it," Jan offered as a distraction to the commotion Melody had just created.

"Sounds fine," replied Melody resentfully. "But when am I going to get an explanation for what the hell is going on here? Why can't I go in the barn? Why did I just burn all those articles? Why do we have a burn pile to begin with? And which one of you went in my kitchen with your muddy boots and made a damned mess in there?"

"Just as soon as Sammy gets home, I promise I will explain everything to you both. And you too, Jan," Pastor Bob said comfortingly, kissing Melody gently on the forehead like one would a child.

"None of us," Gus said quietly.

"What?" asked Jan.

"We didn't go in the house. None of us went in the kitchen last night!" Gus stated with concern.

184

Chapter Forty-six

Tuesday, October 14, 2014

Pastor Bob

It took the pastor about an hour to return to the Corbbet farm after dropping off Gus at his house even though it was only six miles round trip. Once home, Gus insisted on loading the back of Pastor Bob's car with folding lawn chairs, a small folding table, a medium-sized red cooler, an ax which looked like it had been sharpened recently, and a saw for cutting tree limbs.

"We need to look the part out there at that orchard. You know, yard clean up. Go home, talk nice to your wife, tell her you need to be outside for a while after dealing with the grief-stricken Stokes family and losing one of your best friends. Get her to bring you out some lunch, or better yet, have her take lunch over to the Stokes family. Change into some yard-working clothes. You and those girls need some boots and gloves. If law enforcement shows up you fucking text me like right now, boy! Do you understand?" Gus issued more orders.

The pastor did what he was told. Went home, told his wife what Gus had wanted him to say. It was everything he could do to keep from crying when he relayed the details about Andy's death and asked her to take lunch to the Stokes family. She was a good pastor's wife and did as she was asked. She could tell he was in earnest and needed her help. He changed into some work clothes. Grabbed extra boots (his wife always had several pairs), work gloves, and a few yard tools.

Then he swung around back the other way through town so he could stop at the liquor store for a bottle of medium-priced whiskey. He was tired and his heart was breaking. The woman behind the counter could see it in his face and she knew why, the town being so small and news traveled so fast.

"Do you need a hug, hon?" the long-time store clerk asked.

"No, but thanks, Pammie. God bless you," he said to her, head down while he paid for his whiskey then turned for the door.

"Well, we all love you very much, Pastor Bob. You hear me? We're all going to get through this together," she called out to him, a crack in her voice, as he left the store.

"*Shit!*" he said to himself as he took his first drink from the paper bag-wrapped bottle seated in the parking lot behind the drug store where the liquor store was located. She had no idea what was happening to him or what he was going through.

Not only had his best friend in the world died in his sleep after having helped him, Gus, and Terry move a completely stuck-in-the-mud Chevy Caprice, but last night he had helped to dig up two long-buried dead people Earl Corbbet had made the mistake of putting into the ground together. Poor Emily Corbbet, now wrapped in a black hoodie, what was left of her anyway, was lying on the floor in the back of the barn out at that haunted farm.

Her rapist, Bill Garrett, whose eternal soul was not only burning in the fiery pits of hell, was also burning, literally, his mortal body in a hole behind that same barn as of right now. Along with a few odds and ends from the trucks and glove compartments of the four vehicles which Gus had towed there to hide said odds and ends. Also known as evidence.

By the time Pastor Bob pulled back into the driveway at the Corbbet farm he was feeling plenty sorry for himself.

Jan and Melody, on the other hand, appeared to be doing pretty well. They had a small side table from the house set out close but not too close to the fire. On it were two cups of something hot, he could see the steam from the cups. There was a plate of pastries. Jan had one in her hand, and in her other hand she had her phone up to her ear saying something about a last harvest out at the Corbbet farm and as soon as they had a date it would go in both the Sheridan Sun and McMinnville Registrar and how fast could the Boy Scout troop be out to mow the lawn and, yes, they needed to bring their own mowers and weed whackers.

Melody was on her phone asking someone how soon they could get out to the orchard with their chainsaw and a couple ladders. No, she added, no tools out here, Dad must have sold them. No, barn is off limits, too dangerous, unsafe, about to fall over, no one's going in there. Period! She ended her call and looked at Pastor Bob.

"Good girl!" Pastor Bob called out to Melody as he pulled his car up as close as he could to the back of the barn and the burn pile, which appeared to be burning nicely, putting off a nice warmth against the chilly Autumn air.

"Looks to me like you two got this thing under control. Come help me unload this car. I've got lawn chairs so we can sit down, boots to keep your feet dry, all the comforts of home. Well, hell, you are home." Pastor Bob chatted away, trying to feel light hearted.

It didn't take long before the three fire tenders had their post mocked up to look like an outdoor camping hot dog and marshmallow roast. Just another day out in the country, doing yard work, burning whatnot, enjoying a sunny day for once.

"Who'd you have on the phone?" the pastor asked Melody.

"Frank Davison. He's going to come out tomorrow afternoon with his chainsaw to see what he can do about cutting up those two dead trees. I told him about the last harvest and he's in. Wants to help out as much as he can," replied Melody.

"No, girlfriend! He wants to see you and… well, I can't go on about what Frank Davison wants to do to you in front of the pastor," Jan added.

The pastor smiled only slightly. Normally he would have laughed at a joke like that but not today. Both women noted this.

"Do you think you can get your wife to round up the women's league to sell donuts and hot cocoa the day of the big picking?" Jan asked politely.

"Sure. After Andy Stokes's funeral, may he rest in peace. Right now she's cooking and delivering lunch to that family. She'll be ministering to them until I get back over there later today," he said with a heavy sigh. He prayed silently for God to forgive his dear friend for his sins and welcome him into heaven. He imagined Andy being carried away in the arms of a silver angel to some white and gold paradise.

Jan stirred the fire as Melody brought out more newspaper from the laundry room. Then they traded tasks: Melody stirred and Jan marched around in the boots that she figured belonged to the pastor's wife, with the nicely sharpened ax chopping away at very overgrown but long since dead rose bushes, then throwing the branches onto the fire. The branch pile made by Gus was now burned up.

Pastor Bob napped in his lawn chair, opening an eye every once in a while, to see what the women were doing if they got too quiet. At one point he looked up to see one of them in a tree, throwing apples or pears down to the other one.

This is how they passed the time until Sammy pulled into the driveway looking cheerful and pink-cheeked.

Chapter Forty-seven

Tuesday, October 14, 2014

Sammy

"Okay! What's so damned-fire important I have to drop everything I'm doing to set up my next show and rush back down here?" Sammy demanded from her sister in front of Jan and the pastor.

"Well, Andy Stokes died in his sleep last night, or rather early this morning, to start with," Melody said defensively looking to the pastor for help.

"Please, Sammy. Have a seat here by the fire. Do you need a restroom break or anything before I get started on some things you and your sister really need to understand?" Pastor Bob started off, taking control of his little congregation.

Sammy instantly thought about what she had just done to Philip Mason's grave, smiled briefly, and shook her head no.

"Good, let's give the fire one more good stir and throw on another load of old newspaper and that big log I was saving." Kindly he directed the actions he felt he needed to have done before he started his sermon, or lesson as it was to be.

Once the fire had been properly tended and was burning nicely and Sammy had helped herself to a Danish, they were ready to start.

"Sit down here all of you. Thank you for hearing me out in advance. What I'm about to tell you will, most likely, upset you both very much. You too, Jan," The pastor began.

In a calm, steady voice Pastor Bob told the story of Emily Corbbet to her daughters. He told them about her life in

Hamilton, Montana. Her brutal rape by Bill Garrett. Her marriage of convenience to Earl Corbbet, moving to Sheridan to have her baby, Melody, a town she thought would be safely away from the reach of Bill Garrett. He explained how unhappy she was to be away from her parents, their ranch, her carefree life. How Earl did love her but had no way of knowing how to show it nor the awareness to even see how unhappy his wife had become.

The pastor continued the story with the birth of Sammy and Emily's struggles to make a home for her children. And how on a chilly evening in October, 1987 the Corbbets returned home from some outing to find a light on in the barn. Being as Emily needed some twine from the big spool out there anyway, she put her children to bed, grabbed a large pair of scissors, and went out to get her cutting.

Earl had heard the screaming coming from the barn from where he had been in the laundry room, had grabbed his shot gun and burst through the big front doors of the barn to find Bill Garrett, scissors in hand, standing over Emily who was lying on the ground bleeding badly. When Garrett rushed at Earl, Earl shot and killed him.

"Earl checked Emily, then ran in the house for some towels and to ensure you girls were safely in your beds. Then he called Gus Fuller, Yamhill County Sheriff's homicide detective at the time. By the time Gus got out to the farm Emily had passed away in Earl's arms making him promise with her last dying breath that you girls would never know any part of this.

"Gus found the car Garrett had driven to the farm parked up by the mill. Garrett had gotten this car, a black 1983 Chevy Caprice, from his younger brother Hank in Yakima, Washington." Pastor Bob motioned toward the car.

"Garrett must have switched out the license plates, Washington to Oregon, and then spray painted it the weird green you see now in an effort to disguise it so he wouldn't get caught going across state lines once he had grabbed Emily and you, Melody. We will never know what he really thought he was going to do after that. Who can tell what an insane person like Garrett thought or if he thought at all? Those types are subject to basic gut reactions to life's situations. Like an animal doing things more out of instinct than anything else.

"At any rate, Gus, Andy Stokes, and Pastor Jake helped Earl cover up the murder so that you wouldn't lose both your mother and father all in the same day. What wasn't fully understood by your father was that you can't bury two people like Emily and Garrett in the same grave. But he did. We don't know if it was to save time, with morning coming and you girls needing to be taken care of, or if he just didn't understand these two spirits would be locked in battle here on this farm as long as they were forced to lie in the same ground. Then the Caprice was towed and parked over the makeshift gravesite.

"I don't think any of us really realized that fully until last night when we picked up Sergeant Terence Kell here at the farm. He had just come running out of the barn after he had seen a vision of what appeared to be Emily's last fifteen minutes in this world of the living. Once we had told him the full story, which I have just told you, he then told us the vision from the barn.

"But Andy Stokes fully understood once he heard what Sergeant Kell had to say. And he impressed upon us the importance, more important than the coverup of the stories behind the other vehicles on this property, that Emily must be freed from her prison next to Bill Garrett.

"What we had to do last night, Gus, Andy, Terry and myself, is move the Caprice back about twenty feet to where you see it sitting now, using Terry's four wheel drive pick-up. Then we had to dig up the bodies of Emily Corbbet and Bill Garrett, mostly bones really, Andy holding the flashlight until he was too worn out and needed to be taken home.

"It was a full night of digging, finding the bodies, putting them off to one side. Wrapping Emily in Terry's black hoodie and laying her carefully in the barn. That's where she is right now."

The women, who had sat silent all this time, stared at Pastor Bob, then the oddly green Caprice, then the barn, and the fire that was burning down and needing more fuel.

"Yes, Bill Garrett is at the bottom of this burn pile. Even though he has been in the ground for twenty-seven years and he is just a pile of so many bones, I am certain there is enough DNA to identify him. Nowadays they can get DNA out of teeth, doesn't seem to matter how long they've been buried.

"Even though Earl and now Andy are gone, the rest of us remain. Those involved in the crimes connected to the other cars are all still alive. True, Melody, there are covered up homicides here but to expose those incidents now would ruin many women, who were young, fourteen-, fifteen-year-old girls at the time, now married with husbands and children. Whole families. Jan's family. Families that have already suffered so much at the hands of Joe Benton, Philip Mason, and Charlie Montgomery.

"Earl allowed us to put the two cars and the pickup out here as he felt he owed Gus some protection for his actions to cover up and in turn protect the girls involved. Jan's Uncle Joe shot by his fourteen-year-old stepdaughter in 1993. Jan was twelve when that happened, you remember. Philip Mason, shot by one of four suspected Sheridan High School freshmen in 1998. One of which could be your sister, Sammy." Pastor Bob turned and gave a small nod to Samantha, who stiffened in her chair.

"And last but not least, Charlie Montgomery, beaten, then gutted while still alive by the daughter of his ex-girlfriend in 2003. Each car had either contained too many bad memories for the families of the owners or contained evidence of some sort that would reveal things their families didn't want known.

"We should have been able to see it happening at the time, what was becoming of this farm and orchard. The bitterness buried in the ground slowly rotting the fruit trees. The evil contained in the cars creating an aura of unrest and despair. I can now stand here and see it all around me. No doubt it is what killed Andy last night in his bed. Could be that one of the warring spirits was what was chasing Earl across the road out front of the house and got him killed by that pickup.

"Well, there you have it." Pastor Bob sat down at the end of his grisly sermon. He let out a huge sigh, then picked up his paper bag-wrapped bottle of whiskey and took a big long drink.

Sammy reached over to the pastor and held out her hand expectantly and nodded at the bottle. Pastor Bob passed it to her and she took two big gulps, coughed, then handed it to Jan. Jan drank short sips until Melody reached out her hand. Jan handed her the bottle and Melody took her turn sipping at it until the pastor motioned for it to be returned to him. And so it went, the bottle traveling from one then the next until the whiskey was gone.

Chapter Forty-eight

Tuesday, October 14, 2014

Sergeant Kell

Sergeant Kell was startled awake by the buzzing of his cell phone, which he had put on vibrate and placed under his pillow before he fell asleep. He blinked his eyes while trying to focus in on its glowing face working to determine what time it was and who was calling him.

It was 4:00 pm and it was Pastor Bob calling.

"Hey, Pastor. What's up?" Kell said, his voice heavy with sleep.

"Well, the whiskey's gone and the girls and I are out here hoping you'd come out and bring us something to eat," came back Pastor Bob's slightly slurry reply.

"Aw, Jesus! Have you guys been drinking?" Sergeant Kell asked in an annoyed tone.

"Nope! Jesus didn't join us this time but we would like it if you did." Pastor Bob snickered at his own joke.

"I'll be out there in about thirty minutes. Stay there, all of you. Don't drive," Terry shouted into the phone.

He jumped out of bed, traded his pajama bottoms for jeans, put on an old sweater his mother-in-law had given him for Christmas, stuffed his feet in a pair of work boots, and put a baseball cap on his head, then headed out the door.

He pulled his pickup up to the small grocery store on Main Street and went inside. He hurriedly gathered together hot dogs, buns, mustard, ketchup, potato chips, bottled water, and the makings for s'mores. The items for the s'mores were more for show than for his desire to eat them.

As he paid for his items the spunky twenty-something clerk recognized him and commented, "Hey, shame about old Andy Stokes isn't it?"

Sergeant Kell stared at the young woman with pink hair. "I've been under the weather and spent the day in bed. What's the story on Andy?"

"Oh, my gawd! The dude died in his sleep last night! Wife found him cold this morning!" She shivered as she told him. "Whole town is just falling apart over it. Like, what are we going to do with dead people now?"

This is not good, Terry thought to himself as he loaded the bags of food in his car. *Or maybe it will work out for the best. Earl's dead, now Andy. That's two less people to hang for this mess.*

Terry suddenly realized he was now part of the mess. His stomach turned as he drove down the street toward the Corbbet farm. His head and back ached as well. Maybe he was coming down with something. Can things get any weirder or screwed up? He was no longer angry with Jan but he still felt resentful and betrayed. She might have been trying to protect him, he wasn't certain.

What he did know was that he would never feel the same way toward her again. He would still love her but not in the totally free way as before. He would now have his guard up. Once trust is lost, it's gone. It's like when you find out your spouse has been cheating on you, you always wonder in the back of your mind if they are going to do it again or if there are other times you don't know about. He was glad they didn't have children.

As for the Corbbet girls, he resented them just because it was their father that started this whole batch of problems. It wasn't their fault, he knew that in the analytical side of his mind. He didn't want to take his turn babysitting them, Emily Corbbet in the barn, or the fire with Bill Garrett's bones smoldering at the bottom of the pit. There were other items in that pit as well. Things that right off the bat hadn't made any sense to him. Like women's underclothes and makeup and a wig in the truck of Philip Mason's Mazda. The child's diary in the glove compartment of Joe Benton's Ford. The clothes and boots in Charlie Montgomery's Chevy pickup.

He needed time to think and he didn't have it; he was pulling into the driveway of the Corbbet farm. He was surprised as he got out of his pickup and gathered up his grocery bags to see that the place looked slightly better. Was it because the girls had continued to pull branches out of their piles in order to keep the fire going? Someone had taken the stones from around the rose garden and had put them around the fire pit, which now had lawn chairs, side tables, and a cooler. Most of the dead rose bushes had been hacked from their sad garden, and other bushes that might still be alive had been pruned back.

There was a small basket of apples and a smaller basket of pears sitting on the back-porch steps. It looked as if people were actually living here.

"Hey hon!" Jan called out in a reserved but friendly manner. She ran up to him and took the grocery bags and let him carry the case of water in plastic bottles. She didn't try to hug or kiss him and he didn't try to hug or kiss her either.

Mel and Sam stood by the fire pit leaning on their pitchforks. They waved their gloved hands but looked solemn.

Pastor Bob slumped in his lawn chair and only looked up when Terry spoke to him. "Heard about Andy when I stopped at the store. It must be the talk of the town. I bet you're needed at the Stokes's place right now. How much have you had? What time was your last drink?" Terry took a sniff at Jan.

"Well, we started with a fifth of whiskey a couple hours ago and now that's gone. So, not that much when you think about it. Ahhh, but we didn't have any mixer so we had to drink it straight, out of the bottle. One must make do in times like these," was Pastor Bob's sad reply.

Terry now remembered how angry he was with both Gus and Pastor Bob but only for a minute. He had to get the pastor sobered up and back over to the Stokes's place before someone noticed he wasn't there and started asking questions.

Terry handed the pastor a bottle of water and told him to drink. The rest went into the cooler. Jan placed the other items from the bags that needed to be kept cold into the cooler then ran off to the house to find some ice and paper plates.

Melody headed back to the house saying something about making more coffee. Sammy stirred the fire, then went off to the house to get another pile of the dwindling newspapers.

Terry called Gus and gave him an update and Gus made an offer to come out and get Pastor Bob. No, they shouldn't all be seen together for a while, Terry told Gus. He would get Pastor Bob sobered up and ready for travel in a little while. He planned to stay out at the farm with the women until dark, so just a couple of hours, and then go home for the night. He reminded Gus he was supposed to be sick in bed so he couldn't stay longer. Bed is where he wanted to be right now. He didn't feel good and thought he might be running a slight fever.

Sammy came out of the house with more newspaper and threw it on the fire in little batches so it would burn faster. In between batches she took the ax and worked away on one of the dead apple trees that had fallen over, dragging what she could over to the fire pit and adding it to the ongoing flames.

"You keep this up and you aren't going to have anything to draw," Terry said in a fake cheery tone.

Sammy gave him back a fake smile.

Terry wandered around the yard looking for anything he could make into roasting sticks with his pocket knife.

"Sammy's got a story to tell you around the camp fire tonight," Pastor Bob said finishing his water and going for another.

"Oh, okay. Jan and I won't be staying too much after dark. You heard me talking to Gus, didn't you? I can't play sick and stand out here where someone might see me," Terry said, unimpressed with the idea of a story from Sammy.

"Don't make it any harder on her than it already is, Sergeant Kell." Pastor Bob sounded serious and sober.

Terry turned around quickly. Pastor Bob was staring straight at him with the intention to be taken seriously.

Melody returned from the house with a large bowl of ice, paper plates, paper towels, and a couple wire hangers. "We can use these to roast those hot dogs. Let's get this fire really going, no more paper, more wood." She looked around at the two men staring at each other. "Jan will bring out the coffee when it's ready. That gal, she's in there peeling apples and pears to make a cobbler. She is a wonder woman, I swear."

"Ya, she sure is," Terry said flatly as he looked from Pastor Bob to Sammy and back again. "Wonder woman." *It's a wonder she had been able to keep all this to herself all these years,* he thought.

Chapter Forty-nine

Tuesday, October 14, 2014

Jan Kell

It wasn't long before Jan came out of the house with two mugs of hot coffee and a throw blanket from the front room. She handed one cup to Pastor Bob and the other to her husband.

"Sit down in the lawn chair and put this blanket in your lap. You really aren't looking so good," Jan told Terry. Much to her surprise he complied.

"The cobbler is in the oven, should be out in about forty-five minutes. Those apples are very soft. They taste okay but they are only good for cooking. Same for the pears. We need to be sure to tell people that when they come out to pick," she said to Melody then added, "I don't think we can charge money for them. Too many worms."

Melody nodded her agreement at Jan and continued to bend the metal hangers into weenie-roasting sticks.

Sammy got the last load of wood on the fire for the night. Gave it a good stir to ensure the paper was well distributed and the tree parts were in the right place to catch fire and burn for a while without too much poking or other attention.

Each member of the group took a wire roaster, put a hot dog on it, then held it over the fire. Melody let everyone know her first one was for Pastor Bob even though he had one going for himself already. She figured he needed an extra hot dog to soak up the whiskey he had in him.

"We've really lucked out with the weather today. Nice sunny day, way overdue. No wind to speak of. It will be a nice clear evening and sunset. Perfect for Sammy to share her story," the pastor commented. "You can do this without me being here, right?" he asked Sammy.

"Yes, I believe that I can, now," Sammy told the pastor. "The story is long overdue. It needs telling, all of it."

The five friends ate their hot dogs and chips without much talking. Jan had to go in the house to get more coffee for Pastor Bob and again to take the cobbler out of the oven.

It was almost 6:00 pm and starting to get dark by the time Pastor Bob got in his car to return home. He still needed to change clothes before he headed over to do what he could to comfort the Stokes family.

Sammy stated that she was glad she had brought her camera with her from home. With all the cleanup that had happened that afternoon and with more to come she was about to lose her subject and she'd end up with nothing to draw. She hoped the next couple of days were cloudy and rainy.

Melody had been pretty quiet most of the afternoon but spoke up now. "Before Sammy tells us what happened between her and Philip Mason, I want to let you know what I think we should do with our mother's remains."

Everyone turned to look at Melody.

"At first I thought the perfect thing to do here was have Andy Stokes give her a coffin and proper burial next to Dad. You know, on the sly somehow. Not tell anyone what we were doing. Small little service at the cemetery when no one was around. Then we could visit them both whenever we wanted to. But now with Andy dead I just don't see a way to do it without getting caught. Besides, Mother didn't really love Dad, so why bury her next to him?" Melody started out.

"Then I was thinking we could bury her remains in the rose garden here on the property. Dig up the whole thing and put in a whole new garden with new rose bushes. That seemed very nice but I've changed my mind completely on that idea as well. What I now know about Mother, after all these years, is she missed her parents a lot and Montana and the life she left behind or could have had there. She longed to return some day but never got the chance.

"I want to somehow get what's left of Mother, her bones, I guess, cremated. You know, properly, not out here in the yard. And take her ashes back to her parent's ranch in Hamilton. I know someone else must own the place after all these years so we can't just march around on their property. But maybe leave some ashes there, leave some at her parent's gravesites and maybe a little at the high school and rodeo grounds.

"We can't come out and say who we really are to the local townspeople. But still, I think we could bring our mother some long-deserved peace. Free her soul, so to speak," Melody concluded as she looked at her sister.

"What do you think?" she asked Sammy.

"I like it. We would have to do some sneaking around, but hey, that seems to be the name of the game around here these days. Yes, Melody, I do like your idea," Sammy said to her sister, her tone congratulatory for Melody having had a good plan, pretty well thought-out.

Chapter Fifty

Tuesday, October 14, 2014

Sammy

Jan, Terry, Melody, and Sammy sat in their lawn chairs around the burn pile out back of the barn as it got dark, the sunset turning the sky shades of pink, blue, and orange, the clouds streaks of gray. Each held a bowl of warm apple-pear cobbler Jan had made earlier.

The fire had burned down to just coals, perfect for roasting marshmallows if they had wanted to. The plan was to let the coals die out on their own so they could leave it for the night and not have to worry about it catching the barn or the orchard on fire by accident when they went off to bed.

"I'm ready, Sammy," Sergeant Kell said gently, looking at her.

Samantha began to tell her story, one even her sister knew nothing about.

It had been the summer before her freshman year in high school. Sammy had been in downtown Sheridan at the local drugstore trying on some different colognes, pretending she was at the makeup counter at Nordstrom's in Portland. She ended up buying a new box of crayons and headed out down the street for the two-mile walk home.

She had only gotten half a block down the street when who should pull up beside her in his mom's new maroon Honda Accord but everyone's favorite football player, Philip Mason? He motioned for her to get in his car and she did, without thinking.

Sammy had been totally knocked off her feet at the idea that she was now driving down the street with the hottest, most popular guy in all of Yamhill County. So when he suggested that they go back to his parent's house to "hang out" she easily agreed. Philip let Sammy know that his folks had taken off to Portland for the day so they would have the place all to themselves and they could use the pool.

Sammy protested some about not having a swim suit. Philip reassured her that there were extras at his house for cases just like this.

When they got to the Mason estate Philip parked the car in the four-car garage, then the two teenagers walked around to the back gate going through the back yard and pool area. At first, Philip tried to talk Sammy into skinny dipping but she wouldn't even consider it. He took her into the house through the sliding glass doors off the patio into the kitchen. He offered her some vanilla ice cream. Once she had a bowl in front of her he offered her some hazelnut liqueur to go on it. She happily agreed. He just kept pouring on a little bit more and then a little bit more as she ate her ice cream until he had Sammy giggling drunk.

Sammy laughed at everything Philip said as he pulled her by her hand upstairs into his mother's bedroom. He explained this was where they would find her a swim suit. Soon Philip was pulling swim suits out of a drawer. He had four or five suits, a one-piece and a couple two-piece, one really revealing skimpy red bikini, piled next to Sammy on the bed. Each one he held up to himself and looked in the dresser mirror, admiring his reflection. Sammy almost choked to death laughing.

Then Philip got into his mother's makeup. He smeared bright red lipstick on his lips and blue sparkly eye shadow on his eyelids. Sammy stopped laughing but then Philip took off his shirt, got out one of his mother's bras, put it on and danced around the room. Again, Sammy laughed long and hard, coughing to catch her breath.

At one point she was lying on the bed on her back trying to catch her breath when Philip lay down on top of her, pinning her arms up over her head with his strong hands. He kissed her mouth with his red sticky lips and tried to stick his tongue in her mouth.

Sammy pulled one of her hands free then started slapping his face and punching him in the ribs. She yelled like crazy for him to get off of her. Philip seemed to really enjoy this at first but soon tired of Sammy's fighting. He turned her over and pushed her face into a pillow. Sammy couldn't breathe. She panicked and kicked wildly. She was able to reach around behind her and grab a handful of his hair, pulling his head down hard while pulling her head up to gasp for air. This smashed his face into the back of her head as she raised it up off the pillow to take a gulp of air and he let go.

She rolled over to see Philip holding his nose as it bled down the front of his chest and his mother's bra. He got off of her and stepped backwards away from the bed. It was clear he was in pain but still he had an erection.

He went into the bathroom connected to the bedroom and closed the door. Sammy took off like a jet out of the room, down the stairs, and out the front door of the house. She ran the whole three miles back home.

She forgot she had red lipstick all over her mouth, chin, and nose. When she got home she went into the kitchen to get something to drink and cool down but her dad, Earl, was standing there by the stove. "So, you've been trying on lipstick at the drug store again, have you?" was Earl's only question. "Ya, sure Dad," was Sammy's reply.

This was Sammy's first encounter with Philip.

The second happened again by chance, or at least that's what she thought.

Sammy had decided to go to the movies by herself because Melody was spending the night at Patty Holiday's house and all her friends had already seen the movie twice. As Sammy waited in line to see *Men in Black* for maybe the fourth time, who happens to walk up? Philip Mason.

He apologized to Sammy for the way he acted at his parent's house two weeks before and asked if he could make it up to her somehow. Sammy told him no but Philip continued to talk to her, told her he liked her sun dress, and suggested they go to the Dairy Queen for milkshakes. Being the fourteen-year-old fool that she was, she fell for his act and soon they were back in his mother's car, this time heading out of town toward the highway and the Dairy Queen.

Philip bought her a strawberry milkshake and got himself a coke. Then he talked her into driving up Willamina Mill Road to the old cemetery there to watch the sunset. The guy was pouring on the charm. Once again Sammy was flattered that he would pay any attention to her at all.

Maybe he really did like her, she told herself in an effort to calm her fears. He had tried to kiss her last time. Maybe he just wanted to make out and she had somehow pissed him off when she didn't want to. Guys like Philip always got what they wanted so he probably wasn't used to someone young like Sammy not knowing what she was supposed to do when a big football star shows a girl some attention. Sammy rationalized his bad behavior away as they drove along.

As soon as they were parked Philip brought out a pipe and some pot. The windows in the car were already rolled up as the air conditioning was on so he was able to fill the car with pot smoke in no time. He offered Sammy a hit every now and then, sweetly teasing her until she gave in. She noticed an odd bitter taste at first but forgot about it as she became high. She hadn't noticed Philip had long since stopped smoking with her. At one point she knew Philip was talking to her but she couldn't understand the words he was saying.

Philip got out of the car and came around to her side, opened the door and helped her out, then walked her through the old pioneer graveyard. It was just starting to get dark so she could still see the writing on the tombstones where it hadn't worn away yet. Philip was talking in her ear, said something about murders of young women back in the day. He reminded her of the story about the Donner party, families getting trapped in the snow and eating their dead.

Sammy was afraid and clung to Philip until she realized he had his hands up her dress and down her underwear. She stomped hard on his left foot then punched him in the gut. When he bent over to grab at his middle, she brought up her knee and caught him with a kick under the chin. She turned and ran but then stopped when she ran into a tombstone. It was dark, she couldn't see, she was stoned and scared and didn't know the way back to the road. She was breathing hard and she tried to get herself under control so she could think. She turned and ran right into Philip who yelled "Boo!" as he threw his arms up in the air. She screamed, turned and ran the other way. She could hear Philip running with a limp behind her; he was laughing. Soon he was running closely beside her, an evil grin curled upon his lips. She tripped and fell with a thud. She got up and ran some more, Philip playing his horrible game of chase in the pitch-black graveyard. She had no idea how long this went on but it felt like hours.

The last thing she remembered was hitting her flip-flopped toe on a low-lying headstone, plopping down, holding her foot and crying. Philip knelt beside her, pushed her down in the grass with one hand and with the other he lifted her dress up around her waist. Sammy really couldn't see Philip very good but she could hear him grunting then she felt splashes of something warm and sticky hitting her stomach.

Philip must have drove her home because when she came up out of her stupor she found herself sitting on her front porch steps in the dark with no one around. She went into the house through the back door in to the kitchen and once again there was her Dad, "How was the movie?" he asked. She replied, "Men in black scare me." She went up to her room and closed the door.

Sammy figured she had nightmares about the graveyard incident for a month. She didn't bother going into town alone the rest of the summer or early fall. It was clear she was Philip Mason's prey now and he seemed to be getting better at finding ways to scare her.

One day around mid-August when Dad and Melody had gone into town to do some grocery shopping Sammy found herself home alone. She was outside doing some weeding and pruning in the rose garden when Philip Mason pulled into the driveway, once again in his mother's car.

Oh! God! No! Was all she could think at that moment.

Chapter Fifty-one

Tuesday, October 14, 2014

Sammy

"For Christ's sake, Sammy! I had no idea any of this happened to you. You were being stalked and tortured by that big jerk and you didn't even tell me," Melody yelled at her sister.

"How many girls do you think he did this to? Were you the first? Why didn't you report it?" Sergeant Kell asked in a reassuring voice he saved for doing interviews with victims of domestic violence.

Sammy chose to answer Sergeant Kell. "Oh, there were more girls, for sure. At least four more that I am certain of, maybe more. Knowing what I know now, I think I was his first and he was experimenting on me to find the right drug, the right location, and what exactly were the elements he needed to get off in his preferred manner."

"The third time….," Sammy started.

"There was a fucking third time?" Melody was totally taken by surprise by Sammy's ordeal.

Terry looked at Jan and flicked his eyes in a way that sent her a message to handle Melody so her sister could finish her story. Jan got the message and moved her lawn chair over next to Melody and put her arm around her and told her to hush in a gentle but firm way.

"Go on Sammy. You're doing great. I'm really getting the picture. Keep going," Sergeant Kell prompted Sammy.

Sammy began again, "When Philip pulled up in his mom's car here at the farm I was standing in the rose garden with a large pair of clippers in my hand. So, I walked over to his car feeling like I had the upper hand in this instance. But he caught me off guard again and I fell for his next trick. Which is the same one he used from there on out with other girls.

"I had walked over to the car and asked him what he wanted. He looked surprised and said some bullshit about coming to check on me. He said that the night we went out to the graveyard I had gotten really sick off that pot and I had spent about an hour throwing up. So once he thought I was done barfing all over the graveyard he brought me home and dropped me off. He said he had been in town off and on over the past three or four weeks looking for me, that he really liked me, wanted me to be his homecoming queen, we could go steady, be the big popular couple at school.

"I was not having any of this talk and told him to just take his crazy self right out off the property. He smiled, wanted to make it up to me, yak yak yak. He got out of the car with two cokes and handed me one. It was hot, I was hot, and the coke was ice cold. I did notice that the top had been twisted off already but by the time I mentioned it to him he was mid-drink from the other bottle. I figured what the hell and drank half the bottle down right where I stood.

"He stood there talking, blah blah blah, all about football practice having started all ready, how he was going to be team captain, blah blah blah, him, him, him. His dad was planning on buying him a new Mazda for graduation or something or other.

"I started to feel a little dizzy and he suggested I put down the clippers and gloves and hop in the car, he'd turn up the air conditioning. So, once again being the damned fool that I was and now drugged on cow tranquilizer (it was his drug of choice from then on) I did what he said.

"He said we should go to the beach and have dinner. He was hungry for fish and chips. I mean, the guy talked a blue streak all the way to Lincoln City. He said we needed to stop at his parent's beach house on Devils Lake for just a quick second and that I could freshen up there before we hit Moe's restaurant.

"On the way to the beach I started to feel frozen stiff. He might not have put enough of that cow stuff in my coke. From talking to the other girls he did this to it appeared he wanted us paralyzed but awake so we could see and feel everything but not be able to move or talk. He must have been tired of me hitting him, screaming and yelling and giving him a bad time.

"Dressing up like a woman was another component to his perversion. Well, at least wearing women's underwear, makeup and donning a wig – he wasn't completely dressed.

"Tying us up was important as well. But Philip didn't have that fully worked out yet at this time either. He did have to carry me into the lake house. He laid me on the floor and tied one of my wrists loosely to the leg of a small wooden end table. Oddly just one hand was tied, but not very good. At first I wasn't sure what was going on. I closed my eyes and gave myself time to relax and think. I could hear him opening dresser drawers, talking to himself, laughing a bit. I worked to move my toes, then ankles, wiggled my fingers. He would stop what he was doing and walk over and check on me. I could hear his bare feet making a slapping sound on the hard wood floor. He seemed cheerful. He even whistled a bit. Once I thought I could move okay I opened my eyes and looked around the room.

"He was right there, leaning over me, face in my face. He not only had a big smile on his face, he had on makeup, the works this time, and a wig of some sort. I did try to talk but couldn't say anything. I had heard somewhere that if you ever find yourself in a situation like this don't show fear. Try to stay calm because it is your fear, your terror, that excites the psycho.

"So, even with my heart pounding in my chest so hard I could hear the blood rushing through in my ears, I just looked at him with calmness.

"He had a large folding pocket knife which he showed me and made some threats about me screaming or fighting and this time he'd kill me. I decided I'd rather be dead, but not before I hurt him again, real bad. You see, the one thing Philip hadn't counted on was I that did have some strength from working on the farm. He would take that into account thereafter with the other girls. Only picking out those that were more passive and weren't involved in any sports or farm work.

"Anyway, I think I got a nice boost from the adrenalin surging through my body from my thoughts of this being my last round up and when he started to unbutton my cutoff jeans, I quickly reached up with both hands and grabbed the leg of the little end table, picking it up off the floor swinging it down at his head as hard as I could.

"I hit him in the shoulder but the blow really knocked him for a loop. I think it surprised him more than hurt him. He fell back on his butt on the floor. I stood up, grabbed the table with both hands again and brought it down hard on his left foot, the foot I had pounced on in the graveyard. I heard a crunch, he screamed and grabbed his foot. I hit him one more time in the head with the little wood end table and it broke to pieces. My wrist came free then. What he had tied my wrist with was only a homemade sort of thing made of old nylons or something like that.

"Then I ran out of the house. I wasn't going very fast but I was traveling much faster than he could with what I hoped was a broken foot and a cracked skull. I got up to the main road and crossed over to where tourists buy donuts, candy, and other shit. I saw some old couple heading toward their car and gave them a long sad story about getting lost and my friends leaving me behind. I asked if they were going in the direction of Sheridan, could I please get a ride, blah blah blah and they went for it. I copped a ride all the way into Sheridan as they were heading back to Salem.

"There wasn't a fourth time, believe me. Philip Mason had learned that what he had planned wasn't going to work on me. I had no idea that he would stay on the hunt until he found other girls that he could control better and didn't have any fight in them.

"I never told Dad or you, Mellie, what happened because I was too ashamed of myself for being such a damned fool. I mean really, three times this guy got me in his car just by talking. A couple months after school started I noticed one of the other freshman girls in my class acting jumpy when it came to boys approaching her. I think it was at the Homecoming dance. Terry, you had asked her to dance and I thought she would fall through the floor. I talked to her much later that night. When I mentioned Philip's name she about fainted.

"I tried to keep my eyes open, warn girls in a guarded way about Mason being a strange pervy guy. I even made a joke once about how I bet he liked to dress up in women's clothes in the girl's locker room when we were getting ready to play volleyball. That was how I found out he'd done it again, well, something again to another girl. Now there were two girls with bad stories, each story being worse than the one before it. It was clear he was getting more skilled at what he was doing and more out of control as he felt confident he wouldn't be caught.

"One day in April Sally Evans came to me saying we needed to talk. With the two other girls we set up a sleepover at one of our houses where we knew nosy parents wouldn't butt into a teenage late-night gab fest and Sally told us her story."

At this point Sammy stopped, got up and stirred the fire. It was going out nicely all on its own and it was no longer putting off a nice glow of heat. She knew she had to wrap this thing up so Terry could get home and back to bed. She stood there leaning on the pitch fork and told the story Sally Evans had told her and the other girls at that sleepover in April of 1998.

Sammy told of how they decided they were going to have to be the ones to put on end to Philip Mason and his reign of terror because he would kill the next girl he was able to drug and drag off to his parent's beach house. They were certain of that.

"We knew we couldn't count on law enforcement to do anything here. Guys like Mason never get what's coming to them until they have a couple murders under their belt. Then it's too late, the damage is done, families lost in grief over the needless death of their lovely daughters. We would never be able to live with ourselves if we let this go on. We didn't know how many others Philip had harmed.

"Sure, we had been drugged, kidnapped, scared so bad we peed ourselves, then jacked off on, but we hadn't been beaten, raped, cut, or maimed. All Mason would have gotten was a slap on the wrist along with a big fat football scholarship to some out-of-state university. Mason's folks would just hire a high-priced attorney from Portland or Seattle and our lives would be ruined in the newspapers as "those stupid young fools who should have known better."

"Well, I sort of messed that up that football scholarship thing for him too. I knew I had hurt his left foot twice. So, once I heard at Homecoming that he had terrorized another girl – no, you don't need her name – I told one of the football players who was madly in love with my sister, Frank Davison, what Mason had done to me. I made Frank swear never to tell a soul and then asked Frank to stomp on Mason's bad foot in the next football game, by accident. You get the idea here. I had Frank Davison break Mason's foot. That did slow up Philip Mason, both on the field and off, for a while.

"It was Sally Evans then that put us into the idea we needed a good plan to murder Philip Mason. And as luck would have it we had archery that Spring at the same time as track tryouts. Took us a couple days of hard practice and good coordination to work out the exact time to put our idea into action but it all fell into place perfectly.

"That fuck Mason came limping around the track and the girls and I zoomed in on him like a hunter on his game. It was me that let the arrow fly that downed the motherfucker. He went to his knees, holding his neck. Then we ran as fast as we could to get to him first, three of us girls blocking the view as Sally got the honor of pulling the arrow from his neck. Then we pulled his hands away from his wound and down over his head. He was in such shock at first, he truly thought we were trying to help him so he didn't struggle at all. The other kids from both the girls and the boys PE classes did the rest, crying, screaming, fighting each other to see what had happened to Mason. It took at least five whole minutes for the teachers to pull the kids back and get to him. By the time the EMTs arrived Mason had bled to death.

"As far as law enforcement went, well, who could tell what? We were all covered from head to toe in Mason's blood. Pastor Bob knew all about Philip Mason and what he was doing to little girls because I told him my story and the story of the other girls. He must have told Gus and Andy. We were safe, us girls, all the girls Mason had harmed and all the girls Mason would have murdered once he was off to college and away from his parents.

"At first I never told anyone because... well, we just killed someone. I killed someone. It was something I couldn't tell, and I would get the other girls in trouble too. We never talked about it. After a while I guess it was something I couldn't even tell myself. I can't believe the whole thing, Philip attacking me and then us killing him, just fell out of my memory, until just the other day when I couldn't ignore it any more.

"So, there you have it, Sergeant Kell. Thank you for listening. I do hope you will reconsider if you have been thinking about going to the District Attorney with all that you have learned about my mother's death, your wife's uncle's accident, and myself and the three other girls taking the Mason matter into our own hands. I really don't know much about Charlie Montgomery and his life. He's dead and his Chevy pickup is out here in the yard, so something must be up there.

"It's cold and I want to go in the house," Sammy concluded.

Chapter Fifty-two

Tuesday, October 14, 2014

Melody

Jan, Terry, and Melody followed Sammy into the house and into the kitchen. Jan and Melody bringing in the bowls, coffee cups, and items for the s'mores no one had bothered with.

"Terry, did you or Gus or the other guys come in here and do this to our clean kitchen floor?" Melody asked, pointing to the floor.

"No. No one came in here all night long. We peed outside by the barn. I waited to wash up until I got home," Terry said still thinking about what Sammy had said.

Mel and Sam looked at each other, then at Terry and Jan.

"Sammy, you want me to build you a nice fire in the front room so you can get warm?" asked Melody in a loving way to her sister.

"No thank you, Mellie. I'm going to take a hot shower and go to bed, unless the Sergeant here as some more questions for me," she answered Melody while looking at Sergeant Kell.

"I can't say that I do. I too need to go to bed. I'm not feeling well and... come on Jan. You can come back tomorrow if they need you to help clean up in here or work on that harvest thing." And with that Sergeant Terence Kell walked out the door, got in his pickup and drove off.

Sammy went out to her car and got her bag which she brought in and opened on the kitchen table, got out her pajamas, then headed to the bathroom to take her shower.

Jan and Melody sat down at the kitchen table and didn't speak for a short time.

"I'll call you in the morning and let you know how Terry is doing. If he's real sick I'll stay home with him. If he can manage around the house on his own I'll come out and help you with this floor or anything else you might need," Jan said to Melody.

"I'm just so sorry, so very sorry, for you and your family, Mellie," Jan added.

The two women hugged. Jan checked her pockets to ensure she had her car keys. She took off the work boots Pastor Bob had brought out and put on her tennis shoes, then left out the back door.

Melody watched Jan drive away down Rock Creek Road toward town from the kitchen window. She could hear the water running in the bathroom. She knocked on the door and asked her sister if she needed anything. Sammy told her no thank you, she was fine, and no, she wasn't going to slash her wrists, so go away.

"Whatever!" Melody replied to her sister's smart-ass comment. "Hey, you want some of this chocolate Terry bought for the s'mores to take to bed with you?" Melody added as a second thought.

"*Yes I do!*" Sammy screamed back.

Melody went up to her room and put on her pajamas, her robe, and her slippers. She shivered; it was cold in the house. She went back downstairs and started a fire in the fireplace. Even though she had been tending a fire all day she was cold. She needed the heat, the warmth, the light, the glow. She lit the candles on the hearth and sang a tune she remembered from her childhood.

She rearranged the big décor pillows on the rug and found one of the extra throw blankets and put it around her shoulders. Then she went in the kitchen, got a glass of milk and the graham crackers that were to go with the s'mores Terry had said were "for show." Whatever that meant.

Before Melody sat down with her snack, she picked up her mother's old jewelry box and brought it with her to her place on the carpet in front of the fireplace. She opened up the box and looked at the items inside, one by one. The pictures, the class ring, the broken necklace she now knew had been broken in the rape, and the baby bracelet.

Sammy walked into the front room drying her hair with a towel.

"First thing in the morning we need to get Mother out of the barn and hide her here in the house until we can set up her cremation," Melody said to Sammy.

"Yes, we do. Where's the chocolate?" was Sammy's reply.

Chapter Fifty-three

Tuesday, October 14, 2014

Sergeant Kell

Terry lay on his back in bed, staring up at the ceiling, thinking. He couldn't sleep. He thought he might be running a low-grade fever, but he also had a chill so he wasn't certain. His arms, legs, and back muscles ached. At first, he thought it was from all the digging he had done the night before but he had worked in his own yard a full day and not hurt like this the next. God damn it! He was getting the flu. He would call in sick for himself in the morning rather than have Jan do it for him.

Jan was in the front room watching TV, he could hear it. He decided not to be angry with her anymore. Terry now knew that his wife had no idea about all that had gone on with Philip Mason and what all he had done to Sammy and the other girls. She might have had a small clue with the gossip that travels around a small-town high school about a star football player but not more than that.

He also figured she wouldn't have known any more than anyone else about Emily and Earl Corbbet. She was a small child at the time when Garrett killed Emily and Earl in turn killed Garrett. No one in town knew what happened, really. Terry was pretty sure the only ones left to know that full story now were Gus and Pastor Bob.

No wait, now he knew as well.

In fact, he knew as much as both Gus and Pastor Bob about all four incidents. The Corbbet's event, Uncle Joe Benton's shooting, the Philip Mason accident, and the Charlie Montgomery cold case. This realization made him feel worse.

He felt bad he had been so mean to Jan. None of this was her fault or her creation. He decided to get out of bed and go see how she was doing being as that story Sammy told earlier that evening was a wild one. And, of course, there was the sudden death of Andy Stokes.

Terry got out of bed and went into the front room. There was Jan in her pajamas with a blanket wrapped around her sitting on the couch looking out the window. She looked very sad. It was obvious she had been crying; there were used tissues on the couch in front of her. Her cell phone was lying there as well.

"Hey hon. I can't sleep. Did you call your mom? How's she doing with Andy Stokes passing away this morning?" Terry addressed his wife kindly.

Jan looked at Terry in a surprised way. "Oh, hey. Should you be out of bed? I don't know what I have here in the house that will help you sleep. Nothing more effective than Advil PM, anyway," Jan replied with a voice that confirmed to him that she had been crying.

She got up from her place on the couch and headed past him into the kitchen to see what cold or flu remedy might be in there she had forgotten about. As she walked close to Terry he reached out and grabbed her arm. She jumped and pulled back, and he let go. They looked into each other's eyes for a few seconds. Jan could see he was no longer angry with her.

Terry could see that he had frightened her. He hadn't meant to. "I'm sorry," he said quietly.

"No, no, it's just your hand is so hot. Come sit down in your chair. Here, take my blanket, I'll get another. I'm going to get the thermometer. I bet you have a fever over a hundred degrees," Jan came back in a kind but guarded way.

Terry turned off the TV. He wanted them to be able to talk without the distraction of all that foolishness. Then he followed her order and sat in his chair with a plop. Jan returned with the thermometer and took his temperature.

"Oh damn, hon! You are at one-oh-one," Jan said feeling his forehead. "You are burning up. I'll get dressed and go to the store and see what they might have to help you feel better."

"No, Jan. Stay here with me," he said holding her little hand gently in his big hands. "What about a hot toddy? Do we have anything to make a hot toddy? We could both use one. Make us both one then come sit with me," he said, looking into her eyes and trying to judge how badly he had ruined their relationship with his fired-up emotions.

"Okay," she said and went into the kitchen. He frowned and lay back in his chair. Everything seemed pretty messed up to him at this minute and the one thing he hoped he could fix was his marriage.

When Jan returned from the kitchen she had two hot steaming mugs that smelled of apples, cinnamon, and rum. She carefully handed one to Terry who took it gladly, thanking her.

Jan went back to her place on the couch only now she sat facing him and waited for him to start the conversation.

"Did you call your mom?" Terry asked a second time.

"Yes. Actually, I was returning her call. And yes, we talked about Andy Stokes and his poor wife, Barbara. She is taking it all pretty hard. At least that's what she heard from one of the gals at the church Women's League. The women are each taking turns cooking lunch and taking it over to the Stokes's place and spending a couple hours this week.

"Mom had wanted to know if I could do one day and I told her I didn't think I should with you coming down with something. I'm glad I didn't make any promises," Jan told Terry.

He sipped at his toddy. It was hot but sweet and the fragrant liquid felt good on his throat.

"You put honey in this? It's wonderful," he told Jan. She nodded.

She looked over at the TV set and saw that it was turned off and started to get up to go over and turn it back on.

"No, leave it off, it hurts my head. Besides, I want to apologize to you for being such a total asshole this morning. No matter how pissed off Gus Fuller makes me there is no reason, ever, for me to take it out on you. You are the one good, kind and loving thing in my life. I... I... I'm just very sorry for hurting you. If you can't forgive me, I truly understand. But please, don't pull away from me," Terry finished and looked at Jan.

She looked back without blinking with the same expression on her face as when he started his apology. It was clear he had not moved her back to his side. Just as Jan had pulled away her arm when he grabbed her, she was now pulling away her emotions, drawing away into herself. He had to do something before she built a hard wall of distrust between them. Once she had that wall up it would be a long time before he could get her back, he knew that for sure.

"Do you trust me?" Terry asked Jan gently.

"No, sir. I don't," Jan answered without hesitation. Terry winced as if she had just slapped him. She hadn't called him hon or Terry, she had called him sir, and that really hurt.

Jan put her cup down in a way that showed she had no intention of drinking its contents. She stood up and said, "You're pretty sick and I don't want to get what you have if I can avoid it. Besides, you'll rest better if I sleep in the guest room tonight. I've had a hard day, I'm going to bed. Good night." And with that she walked out of the room and down the hall.

Terry got up out of his chair, his cup of hot rum still in his hand, and walked around the house turning off all the lights and making sure all the doors were locked. He closed the drapery in the front room then sat back down in his chair taking another sip of what could be the last thing his wife of ten years would ever make him. He felt empty and sick, his heart breaking.

He needed to make up his mind about how or when or even if he should ever tell the Sheriff and the District Attorney about everything he had learned in the past forty-eight hours.

Time ticked by as Sergeant Terence Kell sat in his overstuffed rocking chair in the front room of his house on Parker Street in the little town of Sheridan, Oregon. He thought about his future, his career in law enforcement, his ten-year marriage now falling apart. He thought about the lives of every one of the women and their families that had been protected all these years, some longer than others, from the painful realities of the American judicial system. A system that was harder on the victims than on the actual criminal.

Who are the victims and who are the criminals in this series of homicides? He didn't have the answer to that question. One thing he did know, he wouldn't be a hero for reopening these cases and exposing everyone involved.

Jan would leave him before all was said and done, that's for sure.

When he opened his eyes again light was coming into the house through the kitchen window which faced east. It spilled into the dining room from the kitchen and flooded the front room.

Terry tried to get up out of his chair but his legs were too weak to hold him up. He tried again and stood there shaking. He made his way into the bathroom but became dizzy and had to lean against the wall by the toilet. He threw up unexpectedly and violently. When he had thrown up all that was in his stomach he continued to dry heave for a couple minutes. After he finished, he put his back against the wall and slid down on to the floor where he sat groaning, holding his head.

Jan appeared in the doorway of the bathroom. She took one look at him and said, "I'm calling the doctor right this minute!"

Chapter Fifty-four

Wednesday, October 15, 2014

Melody and Sammy

Sammy slowly opened her eyes, her vision focusing in on the ancient blue-and-white flowered wall paper now turned gray-and-beige. She had hated that wall paper when she was a child and she hated that wall paper now. She made a note to herself to begin pulling it down tonight after it got dark and she could no longer work in the orchard on her drawings.

She checked her cell phone, 7:30 am, not exactly sunrise but still early enough that the sunlight at the east end of the property should fall on the dying apple trees in an advantageous way for her purposes. She got out of bed, dressed quickly, then raced down stairs working hard not to make too much noise and wake up her sister.

As she came around the corner into the kitchen she was surprised to see Melody. She was sitting at the table with a cup of coffee and what appeared to be some of the leftover cobbler from yesterday. She was reading something.

"Thanks for making coffee, Mel. Whatcha readin?" Sammy said in an almost cheerful voice as she crossed the room toward the coffee pot.

"Just checking on the list of things Jan and I put together that needs to get done for our Last Harvest."

"When is this little party supposed to happen?"

"Sometime after Andy Stokes's funeral." Melody took another bite of cobbler.

"Now you now know why I hate it here so much. I really don't care that this place goes to the county for back taxes. Let's just walk away, don't even try to sell it. I just want to leave as soon as possible." Sammy paused for a minute, absent-mindedly sipped at her coffee, and stared into space as if actually seeing herself back in Seattle at an art show. A little smile crossed her lips.

"Whatever," Melody came back as she added a few needed details to the list. "We need to go get Mother."

"Not yet. I need to get my camera and get out to the east end of the orchard while the sun is low enough in the sky to give me the right shadows. At least I hope I can get the lighting where I want it." Sammy looked out the uncurtained kitchen window. Damn, it looked clear out, it might be too sunny. She needed gloom, clouds, the threat of rain. The name of her art show wasn't 'Happy Times at the Orchard', it was 'Haunted Orchard'.

"You better hop on out there, then. Not only do we have to get Mother gathered up as soon as possible, we will be having company for dinner. Frank Davison. He'll be here about 4:30 or so with his chainsaw and some ladders. He might be bringing a friend to help him too," Melody informed her sister.

"Why?" asked Sammy as she headed out the back door toward her car, followed by Melody who was explaining madly the big plan.

"It's clean-up for the last harvest so people can come out and pick apples and pears, you know, like back in the day when this place was an actual going concern. Sort of a last hurrah. We aren't going to charge people to pick because, like Jan said yesterday after making the cobbler, there are too many worms in the fruit. We've got the Boy Scouts coming out on Saturday morning to mow and weed, and they'll help climb trees and pick fruit on the day of the event. The Women's League from Pastor Bob's church will be out here to sell hot chocolate and donuts. As soon as we have a date it's going in the newspapers, both Sheridan and McMinnville. I figure once that's over we can pack up our cars, then you can drive home to Seattle and I can drive home to Glendale," Melody finished, standing, arms folded, facing her sister who had now fished her camera out of the backseat of her Kia Soul and was checking its batteries.

"All sounds fine, Mel, except the orchard in its current rundown and overgrown state is the subject of my next big art show. Linda Lowry wants seven pen-and-ink drawings, not five. I need trees that look forlorn, I need a farm that appears abandoned. You can't just cut up the dead trees for firewood and clean up the yard!" Sammy was getting upset and it showed in the now higher pitch of her voice.

The two women stood in the side yard next to the barn where their cars were parked and stared at each other.

Melody was the one to give in. She knew full well that art was her sister's life, it was her oxygen and nourishment. Melody didn't want to stand in her way; she felt Sammy had been through enough after yesterday. Before with that Mason kid.

"I'll call Frank and tell him we'll do the tree trimming on Saturday. I'm sure he can work around the Boy Scouts. It's Wednesday now. Do you think you can get enough pictures between then and now to work with?"

"I hope so. Right now my problem is lighting. Today looks like it's going to be another lovely day like yesterday." And with that Sammy took off toward the east end of the ten-acre orchard in search of trees in a state of decay and hopelessness.

****

Melody went into the house and texted Frank about the change of date for the planned dead tree-cutting and firewood-gathering project he had so cheerfully agreed to do. She knew he would be fine with the postponement. She would have called him but he was at work at the mill and didn't need to be distracted and end up dropping a load of lumber on someone.

Once she was back in the kitchen Melody got busy on cleaning the muddy boot prints off the old linoleum floor. She had to get down on her hands and knees with a scrub brush and a pail of hot soapy water to really get at them. The mystery boot tracks were in a random pattern which set her mind to working out who had been in the old farmhouse while she and Sammy had both been gone and what was it that they had come in here to do.

There were two different-sized boot prints here. It looked like the larger man followed the smaller man into the kitchen, they walked around in circles a time or two and then just… well, she didn't know what but they didn't walk out of the kitchen. The tracks just ended. The men who had been out here two nights ago digging behind the barn swore they hadn't come in the house and there was no reason for them to lie.

Her phone pinged and she got up to check who was texting her. It was Frank saying he was okay with putting off the yard work until Saturday but was sad they wouldn't be having dinner together tonight. She texted back suggesting they go out for hamburgers at Dairy Queen like when they were in high school, her treat. And would it be okay to bring Sammy along, just like in high school.

Before she could get back down on her hands and knees to continue her scrubbing Frank texted her back, "LOL! You've got a deal. Will be at your place to pick you both up around 6:30. Wear your cheerleaders' outfits!" Melody laughed and sent him the thumbs-up symbol. Neither she nor Sammy had ever been cheerleaders.

Melody went back to her chore and decided to go ahead and mop the whole kitchen floor, it needed it anyway. What it really needed was to be completely re-tiled but there was no way she would put any of her hard-earned savings into this rat hole.

As she worked her mind wandered again, only this time to her sister. What would become of Sammy? Last night while sitting around the burn pile out back of the barn Sammy had explained to her, Sergeant Terence Kell, and his wife Jan how she had been abused, bullied, and tormented by high school football star Philip Mason and had then planned and carried out his murder with the help of three other freshman girls, sixteen years ago.

What in God's name was going to happen now? Would Sergeant Kell, Terry, a boy they had grown up with here in town, go to the Yamhill County Sheriff and tell him about the confession he had just heard? Should she be packing Sammy up in her car with as much cash as they can manage to pull together and send her off to Mexico to hide out the rest of her life? What in the world was she doing scrubbing this stupid floor?

Melody got up from the floor and texted Jan.

"Are you coming out to the farm today?"

The answer came in fast from Jan.

"No, Terry is really very sick. Had to take him into the ER in Mac. Getting some tests now. Will text you back when I know more."

"Prayers coming your way!" was Melody's reply text.

Melody sat down on one of the chairs at the kitchen table, stunned. Odd, stray thoughts floated around in her head like cotton candy working its way around the paper stick to form into a fluffy wad.

Andy Stokes was out here Monday night, then went home and died in his bed. Terry Kell was out here Tuesday night, then goes home only to end up in the hospital the next day. Her sister had just copped to killing one of their classmates while they had sat around a fire that burned on top of the remains of Bill Garrett.

And just as soon as Sammy comes back in the house they are going to go out to the barn to gather up what is left of her Mother so they can re-hide her while she and Sammy work out how best to put their long dead mother to rest, properly.

At this point the song, "Strange Days" by The Doors swirled around in her brain. *Yes, strange days certainly have found us,* Melody thought as she stared into space, tears running down her cheeks.

Chapter Fifty-five

Wednesday, October 15, 2014

Jan Kell

Jan sat in one of the waiting rooms at the small local hospital in McMinnville while the techs x-rayed and ran other tests ordered by the doctor on her husband.

When she had taken Terry's temperature the night before it had been 101, and by the time they got to the emergency room this morning it was up to 103. She was so worried about her husband and all that had gone on in the last twenty-four hours it made her chest hurt.

When they had wheeled Terry away for his x-rays, she had squeezed his hand, kissed his forehead, and whispered in his ear that she loved him. He had looked back at her in relief and whispered he loved her too and was sorry.

Sorry? What did that mean? Sorry he had been an asshole or sorry for what he was about to do, as in spill the beans on the stories behind the four vehicles out at the Corbbet orchard?

Now that she had a few moments to herself she called her mom to alert her to what was happening with Terry. She was so glad she had a mom to turn to at times like this and she felt pity and sadness for Melody and Sammy. Right now, things must be looking rather hopeless for them, not knowing what Terry would do about Sammy explaining how the well-deserved but bloody ending of Philip Mason had come about.

Jan explained to her mom about Terry being so sick she had brought him to the hospital, that the doctor ordered some tests and now she was waiting to hear back. The doctor had said that it looked like pneumonia but they needed the results of the tests to be certain.

She walked outside to the parking lot and sat in the car to explain to her mom the rest of what had happened.

Jan told her mom in a very quiet voice that Terry now knew about Uncle Joe and the coverup. When her mom asked how, Jan explained that Terry had started looking into things and asking a lot of questions after being out at the Corbbet farm a couple times. Gus had tried to set Terry straight but he had just made a bigger mess. Now Jan didn't know what Terry would do. Would he hold fast and not tell or would he feel it was his duty to inform law enforcement?

Jan confided in her mom that it could be that her and Terry's marriage might not make it through this test. If Terry did report what he knew she planned to divorce him for sure.

Fanny Miller, Jan's mom, reassured her daughter that Terry was in good hands now and not to worry, he was young and strong and would make it through this fine. She told her daughter to stay at the hospital by her husband's side, that was her place, and to remember her wedding vows: in sickness and in health.

As far as Terry going to law enforcement with his new-found knowledge, Fanny didn't think he would. She told Jan to stay in touch and she would come up to the hospital later this evening if Jan needed her.

Jan felt better after that phone call. She was sorry Terry's parents had passed away so soon in life but at least now she didn't have to call them to alert them to their son's illness. Terry's sisters had all moved away. Jan decided she would call them once she had the doctor's full report, no hurry in worrying them now.

Chapter Fifty-six

Wednesday, October 15, 2014

Fanny Miller

Fanny Miller got off the phone with her daughter, and turned to her husband of thirty-two years, Jon. Jon, now retired, was relaxing in his favorite overstuffed recliner. He looked up from his *National Geographic* with a question in his eyes.

"What's up with Terry? In the hospital, is he? He get shot by someone robbing a 7-11 or something? I knew something like that would happen to him one day. If I told him once I've told him a thousand times, get out of police work. Too damned dangerous." He gave out his opinion with concern.

"He's real sick. Jan took him to the hospital. We should hear back in a while what the doctor has to say," Fanny replied.

"I think it's time you talked to Gus Fuller about moving Joe's old Ford off the Corbbet property," Fanny informed Jon.

"Why? Them girls out there want to sell the place or something?" Jon wanted to know. "I guess I could call Jesse, have him look up on the internet and find out if it's worth anything. Maybe we could sell it, make a little money," Jon said thoughtfully.

"No, leave our boy out of this. Just call Gus," Fanny stated flatly.

Chapter Fifty-seven

Wednesday, October 15, 2014

Sammy

Sammy came back in the house after about an hour of picture-taking in the orchard, the sun now too high for the type of light she wanted. She found Melody on her hands and knees scrubbing the kitchen floor, crying.

Sammy took off her shoes and stepped on the wet floor in her stocking feet to put her camera down on the kitchen table.

"Why are you crying? What in the fucking world have you got to be crying about? Are you going to prison? No, you aren't. Are you feeling some bit of sadness about losing this farm? No, you aren't." Sammy's voice was full of sarcasm. "Or are you hurt because I never confided in you about what Philip Mason did to me or what I then did to Philip Mason?"

Melody was surprised by her sister's tone of voice. She stopped what she was doing and sat back on her heels looking at Sammy.

"No, none of those things," Melody replied sadly, wiping her cheeks on her forearms because she had on rubber gloves. "You're all I have. I don't want to lose you. I don't know what Terry's going to do."

Sammy walked over to the coffee pot, grabbed a cup, and poured the life-sustaining liquid into it. She took a fork and the pan of cobbler with her cup of coffee back to the table and sat down.

She looked hard at her sister sitting on the wet, almost clean, aging green and beige linoleum. Melody had always been weaker than Sammy. Sweeter and kinder for sure. But when times were tough, when the chips were down, when action had to be taken, Melody couldn't hold up. Sammy had always looked upon her sister as if she was not emotionally prepared to stand up to life's hardships. When they were kids Melody never hit back, never stood up for herself.

Sammy felt cheated. Who did she have to lean on? Who would stand by her now that her beautiful artistic life in the Emerald City was about to turn into shit behind gray walls and cold steel bars?

After all this was over Melody would go back to her bourgeoisie life in Glendale. It was unfair and Sammy knew it but she also knew she had to take the reins here and drive this stagecoach out of hostile country, because no one else could or would.

"I'm sorry, Mel. This whole thing has gotten to me as well. No need to take it out on you." Sammy started off what she hoped would be a re-set to the day. "What's your plans? Is Jan coming over? What about Terry, what's he doing? And Frank, is he sorted out?"

Melody could see that her sister had calmed down but knew Sammy well enough that she could go off again at any time. Keep the peace and move along was the way to go here.

Melody filled her sister in on the news. Terry was really sick in the hospital, Jan would call when his tests were in and they knew what was wrong with him. Frank had been put off on the yard cleanup until Saturday but still wanted to do dinner so it looked like it was Dairy Queen for burgers, the three of them.

Sammy stuffed a huge bite of apple-pear cobbler in her mouth and chewed while she thought over this new information. Terry being so ill, his being in the hospital could be good news, a saving grace, so to speak. He wasn't going to be telling anyone anything that wouldn't be considered any more than fever-induced babble. She liked this piece of news and could feel the tightness in her shoulders relax. Good, more time to think.

As for burgers with Frank Davison, that was a flat "no damned way." He was a nice guy. He had helped her out back when she needed him to stomp on Mason's already hurting left foot but he had his own agenda. She knew when she asked him to hurt Mason, Frank would agree to it. With Mason hurt and out for that season of football Frank would take over as captain of the football team. Frank would be the star football player. The glory and the girls would be his.

"Too bad about Terry. Hope he gets well soon. Hope Jan isn't freaking out." Sammy finally said something back to Melody who still sat on her heels on the floor. "But no on dinner with Frank for me. You go without me. You two can talk over old times and you don't need your little sister with you on your dates anymore."

"Really? I don't want to leave you here alone. What will you do for dinner?" Melody came back.

"Honestly, Mel. I'm surprised at you. Now that you know what I'm capable of how can you, for one fucking moment, think I can't take care of myself?" Sammy replied trying to keep any hint of malice out of her voice. Melody looked startled. Sammy realized too late she had come back too hard on her sister again. Her mind worked hard to find logical solutions for her current state.

"I'll just stay home here tonight and work on my drawings. I need more photos at sunset anyway. You two old love birds can go out and have a nice evening. But don't talk about the farm or anything that has happened here or about me, okay? Can you keep your mouth shut? Please?" Sammy said trying to reassure Melody.

"You have explained to Frank you're not staying, right?" Sammy asked her sister.

"Well, not in so many words. But I should, shouldn't I?" Melody said thoughtfully.

"Why don't you let me finish this floor. You go take a shower. I want you to go into town and drop in on the Stokes family with a cake or something. Find out when the memorial service is going to be held. Get information on who's going to take over for Andy. What's his wife's and boy's plans? Tell everyone about the big cleanup out here. Tons of work, tons of burning. Apples and pears are for shit. Your last harvest idea might not work but then it will give you something to talk about. Then call Dad's attorney, Peterman, and tell him we're going to give up the place to the county for back taxes. Let him know we aren't paying Dad's debts either. What we want to know is, now what happens? How long have we got before we have to move out? You get the idea." Sammy gave her sister exact things for her to do. Not only because Melody needed to get out of the house, but because Sammy needed the information so she could make her plans more concrete.

"We still need to go get Mother out of the barn, Sammy," Melody said as she got herself up off the floor, taking off her rubber gloves and throwing them in the sink.

"Yes, we do. But I think doing it after you get back from town would be best. Any idea of where she is in the barn, exactly? We are going to have to put her in something. A shoebox? How much of her is left after being in the ground twenty-seven years? Bones? Hair?" Sammy again noted she went too far with Melody, who started looking sick during

Sammy's questioning about the condition of their mother's remains.

"Mel, get in the shower," Sammy insisted.

Once Melody was in the shower Sammy went to work to finish the kitchen floor. Two boot prints were left and Sammy had a wild idea. She went to the back porch and came back in with her Dad's gardening boots. She placed them over the boot prints on the floor, they matched perfectly. Shit! It was times like this when she hated being so damned smart. She quickly put the boots in the garbage can outside the backdoor then came back in and scrubbed up the last prints from the floor.

Sammy had the rest of the kitchen floor scrubbed and rinsed by the time Melody got out of the shower. She put the cleaning supplies on the back porch which now was looking fairly good with all the newspapers out of there. Sammy noticed that as they cleaned up the place it felt better. She wasn't getting so much push-back from the "other side."

Melody ran, with a towel wrapped around her, past Sammy up the stairs to her room. "Put on something nice but not too nice. Sheridan nice. You're going visiting a dead friend's family. Please do something with your hair!" Sammy yelled up the stairs like her dad used to when trying to get her and her sister ready for school and out the door. She felt like adding, "The bus will be here any minute!"

When Melody was dressed and ready to go Sammy walked her out to her car and went over with her again what it was that Melody was to do and say in town and the order she was to do it in. Pick up the cake first. Call the attorney last. Before she came home stop at the grocery store and get a few things for Sammy for dinner. Don't forget the wine.

After Melody had left Sammy went in the house, set up her studio in the front room, and got to work on one of the already-started drawings to get herself in the doom and gloom mood. It didn't take long and she was in that place where nothing else existed but the picture in her mind and what she commanded her hand to draw. At one point she had to go outside, gather up a few choice dead leaves and a couple sticks. She put them on the small side table she had moved into place beside her easel in the front room. These she studied closely, holding them up to a bare light bulb so she could see the veins better. She went back out to the burn pile and looked at the blackened wood, took a few bits back in the house and held them up to the bare light bulb as well.

Fire. No not fire, not burned wood. Dead or dying wood. No, dead or dying trees. She got her other two practically-done drawings and placed them around the room. This helped create the sad, hopeless feel she needed but not enough. Too much light was coming in the windows. She had to figure out a way to muffle the brightness in the front room so she put old sheets up on the windows. That worked and she was soon back at her drawing. She referred to the photos she had taken this morning whenever she felt she might be going off track again. She wished it would rain so the orchard would look dark and fog up again.

Sammy checked the clock in the kitchen when she went in there to make a cheese sandwich and get a glass of water. It was now early afternoon. She noted Melody had been gone about three hours. Gone longer than Sammy thought should have been needed to get the information she wanted but then that was Melody. Probably got invited to lunch by someone.

Fire. The idea popped up in Sammy's mind again as she ate her simple lunch. Sun was now pouring into the kitchen making it too warm to be comfortable. She wandered out the back door and stood looking at the barn, sandwich still in hand. She imagined flames shooting out the windows, a wall of smoke rolling out the big double doors, forcing them open on the front of the structure. Sparks and embers exploding out its roof, being blown by the wind toward the tinder-dry orchard, igniting one tree then another, turning the small dead forest of fruit trees into an inferno. The last to go would be the house.

Practicality took over her daydream. Too wet still. This was only the second day of sunshine since she had been home. *How long have I been here now?* she asked herself, *only two and a half weeks?* It had been raining off and on all that time, or at least the skies had been gray with clouds. Now, suddenly, two days of bright sunshine and clear skies.

She went back to her other idea. What good would it do to burn the place to the ground? It might make her feel better but it would serve no other purpose. The neighbors were far enough away that they would be safe but the lumber mill was less than quarter a mile away. Too close. Not good.

Sammy finished her sandwich then walked over to the barn and entered through the smaller side door. It was pitch black inside and after the mid-day sunlight it took a while for her eyes to adjust. She moved carefully forward, watching her feet so as not to step on a nail or sharp tool, or her own mother. She looked for a bundle, something wrapped in a black hoodie. She put her hands out to steady herself, her heart pounding in her temples.

Then she saw it, a small bundle, on the ground in front of the old flatbed truck. She spotted it because at first it looked like someone had randomly dropped their jacket on the ground. But as she got closer she could see it was actually folded in such a way as to wrap something up. The black fleece jacket was zipped up, the hood was folded forward and down, the bottom was folded up under the hood, and the arms were tied around the middle over the hood.

If this was, in fact, her mother there certainly wasn't very much left of her. Random bones picked out of a muddy grave late at night by four men, one holding a flash light in the rain as the others tried to decide what bones were Emily Corbbet and what bones belonged to Bill Garrett. Well, they did have Andy Stokes with them. He'd know big bones from small bones. And Gus Fuller, same there. Both men would certainly have the stomach for sorting one person from another.

Mother might not be all here but what was here was Mother. Sammy gently lifted the bundle. She could feel bones through the fabric of the hoodie and a shiver went down her spine.

"Hey, Mama. It's me, Sammy. I'm going to take you in the house now, okay?" Sammy whispered to her mother.

Cradling the precious bundle in her arms Sammy tiptoed to the door of the barn and looked out to see if anyone was driving up to the house or coming down Rock Creek Road, then she raced from the barn into the house and into her dad's bedroom as fast but as carefully as she could.

She gently laid the hoodie filled with her mother's remains on her dad's bed. She and Melody had cleaned the room before the memorial service for their dad as they were certain some nosy neighbor would go in there even though the door was closed. They had taken down all the old pictures, washed the walls, cleaned windows, and replaced the rotted curtains with new white sheer panels. The dresser and chest of drawers had been cleaned out and wiped down and all the items and clothes either thrown out, boxed up, or taken to the Goodwill. On the bed they had put a new simple blue cotton bedspread, no pillows or sheets as there was no point. The room actually looked good and Sammy was glad for the time and effort she and her sister had put into it as here was a decent place to let her mother stay until the details of her final resting place could be worked out.

"Stay here, Mama. As soon as we work things out we are going to take you home." Sammy breathed the words in a hushed tone.

Sammy backed out of the bedroom and turned around. She jumped and let out a sound like a chipmunk. Melody was standing in the front room staring at her.

"Whatcha doin', Sammy?" Melody asked her sister in a mocking voice. Sammy quickly shut the door to the bedroom. Before Sammy could answer Melody motioned to the kitchen. "We've got company, Sammy! Look who's here!" Melody announced loudly.

Patty Holiday and her mother Joy came stomping into the kitchen from the back porch. "Hey, you guys!" Sammy shouted in pretend enthusiasm. She gave a sideways look at her sister who shrugged as if she had had no other choice but to invite the two women back to the house.

Chapter Fifty-eight

Wednesday, October 15, 2014

Jon Miller

Jon Miller dialed his landline phone to call his old friend Gus Fuller soon after his wife left the house to go out for some groceries. He stood in the kitchen next to the back door where the phone had been attached to the wall for the past forty years. Standing to talk on the phone had, over the years, ensured phone calls would be short, at least for him. When Jan and Jesse had been kids they would stretch the cord so that it went all the way into the back yard so they could sit in lawn chairs and talk as long as they wanted with some privacy.

"Hello, Jon! What do you want?" answered Gus in his normal crappy tone of voice.

"How did you know it was me?" Jon asked.

"Caller ID, Jon. Could you please come into the twenty-first century?" Gus replied, "Now, I'll ask you again. What do you want?"

"I'm going to move Joe's Ford off the Corbbet property. Earl's dead and from what I hear his girls aren't so excited to be back in town. Jan told Fanny they want to go back to their lives as soon as possible. They're talking about letting the county have it for back taxes, which means people out there tromping around and asking questions. No reason in the world to have those cars out there like that," Jon said casually to Gus.

"You're right. Do you have a way to tow that thing? It doesn't run, been sitting out there since 1993. What is that?

Twenty-one years? Have you thought where you're going to put it?" Gus had questions.

"Sucker's a gas hog, don't think it will sell, but who knows? I don't have the time to fool with it. I just want it out of town. My boy, Jesse, he likes cars and has a place in Prineville. Figure he could put it in his pole barn and work on it or just give it to someone," Jon said and added, "Jan and the Corbbet girls are having a last harvest of sorts out at that old orchard. Boy Scouts are scheduled to be out there this Saturday to mow and weed. I'm not waiting around for that. I want to move it now. Tomorrow, latest. Who do you know with a big enough rig we can load that hunk of junk onto and drive out of here to Prineville?"

"Let me think on it for an hour or two and make some calls. This is going to cost money. Do you have any?" Gus came back.

"Ya, a couple hundred bucks is all. Unless you know someone who wants it and will just come and get it for nothing. What about that?" Jon wanted to know.

"That might work," Gus said thoughtfully.

"It should be someone outside the county. What about someone from Southern Oregon or Washington?" Jon suggested.

"I like the way you think, Jon. Stay by your phone, I'll get back to you as soon as I have it worked out." Gus sounded ready to move into action on the project.

"Okay, will do!" Jon said and hung up his phone. He walked back to his front room and his old recliner. Time for his afternoon nap.

Chapter Fifty-nine

Wednesday, October 15, 2014

Jan Kell

The doctor's first guess was half correct. Terry had pneumonia alright, but more than that he had viral pneumonia. With his fever so high the doctor insisted he stay in the hospital until that was under control. Also, this way they could use a mist humidifier on Terry while they started him on antiviral medications.

Once Terry was in his room resting in his hospital bed as comfortably as was possible, Jan excused herself so she could make some phone calls. "Hey, hon. I need to step out to call Mom and the Corbbet girls and let everyone know you are going to be okay. You relax here and wait for me. I shouldn't be but a couple minutes," she reassured her husband, holding his hand and giving him a smile.

Terry looked at her with thankful eyes and nodded his agreement. "Why don't you go get yourself some lunch? Take your time."

"Okay! Anything I can bring you back? Magazines with pretty girls? A six pack of beer?" Jan made jokes in an effort to raise his spirits. "I'll be telling everyone no visitors," she added in a more serious tone.

"Now, you wait right here for me." She turned and walked out of his room deciding not to go to the hospital cafeteria but to drive to Third Street to see what nice café might be open.

Jan settled in a small booth in the back of a bustling, trendy place named Oscar's that smelled like cinnamon French toast and maple syrup. She placed her order with the blue-haired waitress then called her mother to give her the doctor's verdict. Her dad answered the phone. "Oh hi, Dad, can I speak to Mom?"

"No, Jannie. Mom's gone to the store. It's her turn tomorrow to take lunch to the Stokes family. Such a shame about old Andy. Damn, he was a good guy. How is Terry?"

"That's why I was calling, to give Mom the update. The doctor says Terry has viral pneumonia. They want to keep him here at the hospital until they can get his fever down and make sure he responds to the antiviral meds. So, he's not going to die but he is one sick puppy."

"Good news there, Jannie. He's young and strong. No reason in the world he shouldn't come out of this in no time. Anything you need me to do? Do you want us to come up and visit?"

"No thanks, Dad. I doubt he wants anyone to see him like this. I'm going to keep people away for now. Hopefully we will be home by this time tomorrow. Love you, Dad. Give Mom my love. Bye bye."

"Bye, bye, Jannie."

Jan hung up her phone. Next, she would call the Sheriff's department and give them the doctor's report so they could arrange to cover Terry's shift for at least three or four days. Then she would call Melody and fill her in, mostly because she wanted to keep track of her and her sister. As far as Jan knew there was still the remains of their mother out in the barn. That needed to be dealt with as soon as possible. Per what Terry had told her on the way to the hospital what was left of Emily Corbbet was wrapped in his black hoodie. Him giving up his jacket like that was probably why he was flat on his back in a hospital bed right now. He had gotten wet and cold on Monday night, digging in the mud in just a t-shirt. Then he had sat out by the burn pile Tuesday night listening to Sammy tell what happened with the Mason kid, where he got a bad chill.

All that added to the stress of finding out about covered-up murders and now being part of those plots was the perfect environment for falling ill in a major way.

Terry might be five foot eleven inches tall and weigh in at 190 pounds with the strength of a bear, but it was clear he was no match for so much heartache. Their recent fall out included.

Jan decided she would get her husband through his illness and do what she could to keep them together. She would suggest he take some vacation days from the Sheriff's Department. They should go on a road trip down the Oregon Coast. Even when the weather was bad the drive was beautiful. They could stop at their favorite restaurant in Depoe Bay for bowls of clam chowder and watch the whales.

She would do whatever she could to persuade him not to report any of what he knew about the cars out at the Corbbet orchard.

Her phone rang and she answered it without looking to see who it was. Gus Fuller's rough voice came through, waking her up out of her daydream.

"Jan, this is Gus. I can't get ahold of your husband, what's up?

"Well, Gus, he's in the hospital with viral pneumonia."

"I'm sorry to hear about that. I really am. I hope he gets well soon." Gus paused then went on with the business at hand. "Say look, Kell's got some case files in his pickup. He got them from archives on the sly, without permission, is what

I'm saying. Those files need to be returned before anyone notices they're gone or decides to start snooping around.

"Your dad and I are working out moving the vehicles off the Corbbet property. Too many people are coming and going from there and if your husband noticed them after his first visit out there someone else is going to do the same. Shit, they are just a red flashing sign that asks the question, 'why are these cars here?' If you get where I'm coming from.

"Besides, I don't trust those Corbbet girls not to fuck things up. Well, Sammy is okay, she's got smarts but her sister is some sort of poodle brain. You realize there's a body in their barn, right? Do you think those two are capable of taking care of that in a discreet manner?" Gus finished his spiel and waited for Jan to reply.

"First of all, you're lucky I'm sitting in a public place. So, I'm going to hold my tongue, for the most part. But if I was the size of my husband I'd drive over to your house and kick your ass," Jan threatened quietly into her phone.

The blue-haired waitress placed Jan's BLT on sourdough down in front of her, taking off quickly with an alarmed look on her face.

"I can't talk here. Thanks for the info. I'll get back to you when I've taken care of everything. Stay home, Gus. Just stay home and out of the way."

Yes, the cars needed to be moved before any more people went out to the Corbbet place. Each one sent far away and separate from the other. How stupid was that, putting them all on one piece of property? Now that she thought about it why hadn't anyone asked about that classic '73 pickup? That might be worth some money.

The body of Emily needed to be handled, that was already on the list. Now there were case files to take care of as well.

Don't forget influencing her husband to decide not to spill the beans. Jan wondered to herself if that was a felony in and of itself as she ate her sandwich and motioned for the waitress for more iced tea. She smiled to herself when she hit her spoon on her glass and the waitress jumped.

Chapter Sixty

Wednesday, October 15, 2014

Sammy Corbbet

Sammy raced to hug her old friend's mother, Joy Holiday. Not just because she was glad to see her but also to draw attention away from the bedroom door she had so quickly closed. She wasn't sure Joy or Patty had noticed but she knew her sister had.

Sammy took control of the visit right from the start.

"Oh, it's so good to see you! I don't recall you being at Dad's service, were you there?" Sammy asked Joy.

"No, I had paid for a retreat months before the date of Earl's memorial and am too much of a cheapskate to not show up for something that cost me money. But my, you girls look well. Healthy, bright, and shiny. Ah, to be young again. My knees are killing me, I need to sit down." With that Joy landed heavily in one of the kitchen chairs.

Patty had helped Melody bring in the grocery bags and they were now unpacking and putting away the items.

"Where did you find them?" Sammy asked her sister, smiling and trying to appear happy to see her guests.

Melody explained how she had run into the two women while dropping off the cake at the Stokeses'. After their visit with the bereaved family the three of them had decided to go out to lunch.

"How are the Stokeses holding up?" Sammy asked to anyone in the room who might want to answer.

"Well, Barbara is making the most of it." Joy was the first to respond. "You know how she thrives on any sort of attention. Did I just see you take a bottle of wine out of that bag? I do believe I'll have a glass as should the rest of you girls."

Sammy stepped forward, took the bottle of Oregon Blossom Rosé and opened it as fast as any professional. There were no wine glasses in the house but there were some new highball glasses she had bought at a local shop that would work.

"Open that box of chocolates too, while you're at it," Joy said pointing to Melody who had just pulled it from the shopping bag. Melody did as she was told then put the opened box of candy on the kitchen table close to Joy.

"Thank you," said the jolly plump gray-haired woman. "I hope you bought more than one bottle of wine, Miss Mellie."

"Yes, she did, Mom," came back Patty.

"Well, let's all sit down here and Joy can fill me in on all the hot scoop. Get your glasses filled, come on. I can't wait to hear this," Sammy said.

Once the other two women were at the table with their wine Joy was ready to "hold court."

The older woman started off, "Nice clean kitchen floor. You girls are working to bring this place back. I can see it. But what this room needs is a fresh coat of paint. A nice light, I mean really light, green. And some cute curtains for that window over the sink. I bet I've got just the right fabric, something I picked up on sale. Sort of a small patterned green and yellow plaid. Cotton, of course. Curtains always help cheer up a place."

"I'm not so sure we plan to do too much with the place…" Melody started off, then Sammy cut her off and finished her sentence, "until we know for sure we won't lose it to the county for back taxes."

"Oh, that would be a shame. But not a surprise. Earl wasn't a man for details. Well, he wasn't much for basics, either, really. Now that I think of it," Joy explained.

"Joy and Patty are here because it came up while at lunch that I found several half-started, half-finished quilts when I was cleaning out the sewing room a couple days ago. You remember what a big quilter Joy is, always working on some thing or other. I told her she could have them. I hope that's okay with you, Sammy." Melody finally explained why she had brought Joy and Patty home with her. Sammy guessed they had muscled Melody into inviting them because Joy was completely unable to control her snooping into other people's lives.

Sammy decided to use Joy's habit of getting into other people's lives to her advantage and see what details she could get out of the senior citizen.

"That seems fine with me," said Sammy. "Now, Miss Joy, please do tell us about how Barbara Stokes and her boys are doing. What are their plans? Are they going to keep the business open? Who would run it? Or are they just going to close it? Are they going to sell it? Will Barbara stay in the house or move in with one of her boys?"

"Slow down, girl!" Joy said with a mouth full of candy. She emptied her glass and held it out to be re-filled, which her daughter did without a word. "Gee, that's good wine. I hope you put the rest in the freezer to chill," she said to Melody.

"I've known Barbara since she, Andy, and their boys first moved here in 1972. She was a young woman then, maybe twenty-five, the boys were little. She's always loved attention. Barbara enjoyed being the wife of a well-respected local business man. Got her hair done once a week just like clockwork. She said she needed to look her best. It was her way of helping to promote the funeral home. Sort of an odd attitude, I always thought.

"Barbara didn't like to cook. She loved going out for dinner and drinks. Lots of new dresses. Any excuse to buy a new one. Christmas, Easter, even other people's funerals if Andy asked her to help out in the reception area. What was she going on about while we were there?" Joy turned to her daughter. "What she was planning to wear to Andy's service. Can you believe worrying about a thing like that? I bet she has ten black dresses."

"And the business?" Sammy tried to get Joy back on the subject she was interested in.

"Oh, Barbara has no intention of running that business. And neither do her sons. They have lives, families, jobs."

"Is she going to live in that house alone then?" Sammy wanted to know, "Or move in with her sons?"

"Well, I thought about inviting her to go on a cruise. But I'm not sure about Barbara being a good travel companion."

"I can't remember, did they offer onsite cremation services or did they have to send people out for that? Melody and I had thought about that for Dad you know, but we found out Dad had already purchased an end-of-life package which included a gravesite." Sammy worked to keep Joy interested and talking.

Joy had to think a minute. She sipped at her wine. She looked like she was measuring the kitchen window in her mind.

"I believe they do have an oven. That's not what it's called. My God, Miss Sammy. Why do you want to know that?'

"What are they going to do with Andy? Cremate him? When is the service? Open casket? I suppose they can use one they have in stock. I don't know. What's the plan?" Sammy acted befuddled. "Has his body been released? Do they have a cause of death besides being old and having a love for pastry?"

"Yes, he had a cerebral hemorrhage brought on by his high blood pressure, caused by his age and weight. Essentially, he died of natural causes. If one has to leave this world, falling asleep and dying in one's own bed is the way to go. Something the rest of us can only hope for.

"Good thing he and Barbara hadn't slept in the same bed for years. He snored something awful, you know, because of his weight or… I don't know, men snore. They do, just one of those things us women have to bear," Joy concluded with a sigh, then held out her glass for more wine.

"It's getting warm in here, don't you think?"

Sammy got up from the table, "Yes, it is. Melody, open the back door, I'll get the front door. Patty, what do you think about us all moving out to the front porch? It's covered so we'll have plenty of shade and it's such a lovely day. No need to stay cooped up in here. I bet it's seventy-four degrees outside."

As Sammy moved into the front room to open the door Patty and Joy followed her. Joy stopped and looked at the drawings Sammy had been working on as well as the others that she had placed around the room.

"Miss Sammy! What is the matter with you, child? These drawings are downright depressing. Is this what is in your heart? Have I failed your mother? Wherever she might be," Joy said with alarm in her voice after viewing Sammy's artwork.

"I am sorry to say this is what is selling in the big city these days," Sammy replied but really wasn't sorry at all because it truly was what was in her heart. Sammy motioned for her sister to bring the chairs out to the porch as she grabbed the little table she had next to her easel and walked outside.

Joy sat down again once her chair was in place and her glass of wine refilled.

"I feel a blackness. It hovers over this property like an evil fog. The malevolence moves as if on the hunt for sweet and dear creatures it can cause pain," Joy said softly. "I felt it at your back door. Creepy, as if whoever it could be is glad to see you on one hand but on the other wishes to hurt you if he can."

"It is true. This place is haunted," Sammy said flatly. "Sad but very true. It's another reason we aren't staying."

Sammy turned to Melody. "Go get the quilts."

Melody was back in a flash with four partially made quilts. She held each one up showing them to Joy and Patty. Both women handled the fabric, checking for strength, fading, and stitch size trying to determine the merit of completing the long-ago abandoned projects.

The diversion worked to change the mood. Joy and Patty agreed to take over the sewing to complete the quilts. They were instantly filled with new ideas on how they would go about making these old quilts look fresh and new. Joy was certain she had fabrics she could add to these quilts that would brighten them up but not show that new material was added to old.

"I'll wash them in cold water with mild soap, first. Then I'll work on matching the fabric. You know, two of these look like ones your mother had started for your winter beds. Do you want me to finish them for you?" Joy looked at both Sammy and Melody.

"Yes!" Melody jumped forward almost out of her chair. "That would be amazingly kind of you. Patty said you knew our mother and maybe could tell us about her."

Sammy gave Melody a worried look and shook her head no in the slightest way. But Melody went on even after the warning from her sister.

"What would you like to know?" Joy asked still carefully checking out her new project.

Sammy frowned, looked at the ground then with one eye looked in the house. Melody didn't care.

"What was her favorite color?"

"Blue. Not navy blue or royal blue. More like a sky blue. I helped her make a dress for a Mother's Day luncheon put on by one of the churches in town. That was in May, 1987. Come to think of it, it was this same time of year, October, when... well, don't need to go there," Joy stammered, not wanting to talk about Emily leaving her girls.

"What was her favorite flower?"

"Carnations! The big white fluffy ones. I know because Harold and I bought her a corsage to wear to that Mother's Day event. I loaned her a pair of shoes and some earrings as well. Earl was a little uneducated on some points of having and keeping a wife," Joy said as if she was giving them unknown insight into their father.

Melody thought about it a minute. Then jumped up and ran into the house. When she returned she held up a simple sky-blue satin dress. Winkled and stained but still in one piece.

"Oh my God, Mellie! We used to play dress up with that dress! All this time that was Mother's special dress and we never knew it. Dad never said a word to us about it. Where was it?" asked Sammy in amazement.

"I found it while cleaning out the closet in the sewing room and had thrown it in a pile of our old prom dresses. It never occurred to me it had been Mother's special dress," said Melody with reverence.

"She loved that dress. I'm happy you girls have something of your mom's now. You know, when I get home I'm going to look through my old pictures and see if Harold took any photos at that luncheon. Maybe the church has something in their archives or one of the other people who attended might have taken a picture. Let me look around for you. Wouldn't it be wonderful if I could find a picture of your mom in her favorite dress?" Joy was on a roll now. She had enough projects to keep her busy, full time, for at least two weeks. The woman was happy as a lark about it.

Now that her mother was loaded down with busywork Patty took the opportunity to suggest she and Joy take their leave.

"Come on, Mom. The wine is gone and you've eaten half a box of chocolates. I think it's time we were on our way. You've got quilts to work on and pictures to find. I bet you could use a nap," Patty said to her mother as she got up from her chair.

It took all three younger women to get Joy loaded into Patty's van. There was a short stopover in the kitchen as Joy measured the window with a tape measure she kept in her handbag for just these types of situations. This embarrassed Patty a bit but no one else seemed to care.

Joy got into Patty's van then turned to Sammy and in a hushed voice told her, "If you want I can come back here and get rid of that monster you have by the back door. I learned about that sort of thing at that retreat I went to at the time of your Dad's funeral. Think it over and let me know. If we do it you're going to need some things. We can go over all that later."

Once in the van Joy waved and shouted out the van window at Mel and Sammy as Patty turned the van around and headed out the driveway toward the road.

"I'll see you both very soon and I'll have those curtains ready to hang. Love you both!" Joy hollered and waved goodbye like someone on a parade float.

Sammy and Melody waved and blew kisses until the van was off down Rock Creek Road headed for town.

"Did you get what you needed out of her?" Melody asked Sammy.

"I think so. We'll need to look up online more about cremation, how to use that sort of equipment, and how long it takes. Let's hope there is a do-it-yourself page of some sort," Sammy said.

"I doubt it will be as easy as baking a cake," Melody said sadly. "How are we going to get in there and do this? Are we going to break in in the middle of the night? What do we say if we get caught?"

"I'm still working out the details. Oh, hey, almost forgot. Come in the house and say hello to Mother."

Chapter Sixty-one

Melody

Sammy slowly opened the door to their father's bedroom. Melody stood in the doorway and looked in. The room was bright and warm with mid-afternoon sunlight, the sheer white curtains adding a softness to the room. Melody realized she was holding her breath and let out an exhale when she saw the black hoodie with its arms tied over its chest sitting on the bed.

She walked over to the bundle, her arms folded across her chest as well, leaned over slightly, and said in a low sweet voice, "Hello, Mama. Did Sammy tell you? We're going to take you home." Her words stuck in her throat and she couldn't say any more for a few seconds. Then she went on, "Just as soon as we iron out some details. You have Andy Stokes to thank for getting you out of that... mess back of the barn. He passed away a couple days ago, so if you see him thank him and be sure to let him know we are taking care of matters."

Melody turned and walked out of the room and Sammy gently closed the door behind her. Then came the sound of a large truck pulling into the driveway.

"God damn it to hell!" Sammy cursed as she and Melody ran to the back door. "Who the fuck is it now?! I swear this place is getting to be like Grand Central Station. We handle this then we hide Mom."

A middle-aged, or so he looked, thin man with greasy jeans and windblown hair got out of a huge tow truck. He smiled at the two women who had just come into the back yard of the house. His face was tanned and wrinkled from years of working out in the heat of summer and cold of winter.

Melody could see he was missing a good many teeth and wondered how the man managed to eat a meal, then decided he probably drank them, so it didn't matter.

"You two must be the Corbbet sisters," the tow truck driver stated as he pulled a clipboard out of the cab of his truck. "I have here a pick-up order for a green Chevy Caprice."

"Who called in that order?" Melody demanded to know.

The guy starred at the yellow paper on the clipboard. "Gus Fuller. I'm to haul the vehicle to the junk yard in... Marion County. You have an issue with that?"

Both girls shook their heads no then led the driver to the back of the barn where the weirdly painted car sat.

Melody pointed at the car, "There it is. Can you get in here okay with your big rig without messing anything up or getting stuck in the mud?" she asked.

"Ya, sure, I can do this without too much trouble," the guy said, then spit on the ground and wiped his mouth with the back of his hand.

Charming, what a catch. This man could have been my husband, thought Melody. Sammy leaned over and repeated Melody's thoughts almost word for word in her ear. Melody didn't laugh.

"Do you need our help in any way?" asked Melody. She didn't plan to help no matter what but thought she should ask, just to be sociable.

"Nope! You girls can just go back to your knitting or whatever you were doing before I got here," the man stated as he pulled up his pants. "I'm going to be in and out of here in no time. You won't even know I was here."

"I bet you say that to all the girls," Sammy said unable to stop herself. Melody snickered.

The man jumped into the cab of his truck, started up the engine, and began turning around so he could back into the area where the old Chevy had been placed by Sergeant Kell in the early hours of Tuesday morning.

He leaned out his window, smiled a half toothless grin at the two women, and came back with, "No, not everyone is so easy."

Easy was right. It took the tow truck driver only twenty minutes to back his truck in front of the car he wanted, connect it to the winch with steel cables, pull it up on to the bed of the truck, secure it so it wouldn't bounce around, and drive off.

With that Melody and Sammy went back in the house.

"I'm sorry about that," Melody said to Sammy once they were back inside. "Gus called me while I was out running around this morning and told me they were going to move all the cars out of here in the next twenty-four hours. Too many people are going to notice them and start asking questions with all the activity we have planned in the next week or so.

"I meant to tell you sooner but then Patty and Joy invited themselves over after lunch and there was no way to stop them.

"There is more news. Jan called. Terry has viral pneumonia. Doctor wants to keep him for observation, you know, make sure his fever is going down and he is responding to the meds. Jan is fine, she just sounds wore out. She's taken away his cell phone and not allowing any visitors. Jan's working for us, Sammy. Besides taking care of Terry she is going to try to impress upon him that staying quiet is the best thing, the right thing to do."

Melody moved around the house, picking up dishes and glasses. She ran hot water for dishwashing and wiped down the table and counters. Sammy carried the chairs back into the house, found a bag of chips which she opened and began eating as she sat at the kitchen table listening and watching her sister.

"Joy is right. Barbara is really enjoying all the attention she is getting. Now that the coroner has determined Andy's death as natural causes, they have set a date for the service. This Saturday, October 18th. She was going to have it at 1:00 but I talked her into having it at 3:00 because of the Boy Scouts coming out here to mow and weed. And Frank Davison will be here with his chainsaw." Melody talked as she washed dishes.

"Barbara wants to have the service here in Sheridan at their funeral home, because, well, it was Andy's home, so to speak, his work at any rate."

Melody finished the dishes then went into the front room and brought back their Mother's blue dress.

"Whatcha doin'?" Sammy asked, her mouth full of chips.

"I'm going to wash Mother's dress for her. I think if I soak it in cold water with baking soda, I can get that musty smell out. As for the stains, nothing can be done about those. I might stitch it where it's torn, maybe embroider little white flowers over the holes. I don't know if we have time," Melody said thoughtfully.

"I found an old tan leather suitcase in the sewing room. We can put Mother in there, arrange her with her favorite dress. Put some white carnations in there too, if we get to it. It will be a safe place to put her and easy to transport when needed.

"Even if we get someone to take Barbara out for the evening some night, or talk her into going to stay with one of her sons for a week or two, we still have to get into that funeral home, turn on the... what's it called? And get Mother in there, wait for her to cool down. Oh Jesus... what am I saying? I'm talking about burning my mother." Melody leaned on the sink, water running, the blue dress in her hands, and she started crying again for the second time in one day.

Sammy came over to her sister and put her arms around her. "Look, girlie. This is almost over. Do not crack up on me now!" She took the dress from her sister and put it in the sink of cold water. She looked her sister in the eyes with determination.

"Here is the plan. While you are out on your date with Frank tonight, he'll be here in two hours by the way, I will go online and find out about how to work a cremation chamber. At least we'll know how long it will take and if this is even possible for us to do. I'll call Pastor Bob. Maybe he helped Andy use the damn thing a time or two. Hell, we don't even know if that machine still works.

"We get Mother cremated. Won't be much there for ashes. We finish up business here, close up the place and take a road trip to Montana. Mother gets to go home to finally rest in peace. You get to go back to your life in Glendale."

Melody and Sammy moved into the front room. Sammy sat in front of her easel and Melody lay down on the couch.

The front door was still open and a nice breeze was now coming into the overly warmed house.

"Anything else you found out when you were in town? Did you call Dad's attorney?" Sammy asked Melody. Melody tried to focus before she fell asleep.

"I set the date of the last harvest, Saturday, October 25th, from 9:30 am until 4:30 pm. I placed the ads in the Sheridan Sun and the Mac Registrar. Told both papers not to run the ad until the Friday before as we didn't want any "early birds.""

"What about calling the attorney?"

"Didn't get that done. After talking to Gus, I thought I would wait until the cars were gone. Peterman couldn't do anything about it but scold us about upholding Dad's last wishes. I decided to tell him people wanted their cars back so we just let them do it. If he gives me a bad time I'll remind him of all the bills and taxes owing and let him know we have no intentions of paying off any of those debts or staying here to try to make a go of it. The county can have this hell hole."

"You going to take Joy up on her offer to do some sort of exorcism out here?" Melody asked her sister in a dreamy exhausted way.

"Maybe," replied Sammy. "You know who that is, don't you? It's Mason. I didn't recognize him at first, I don't why. We'll see if he's still here after his car is towed away. Any idea of the schedule on those cars leaving?"

"No, but Gus did say he didn't have it totally worked out which car was going where yet. You know, maybe we should move Dad's old flatbed truck out where the other cars used to be so there isn't just suddenly some empty space out there. Someone might notice something's not there just as sure as they are to notice something is there!" Melody sat up from the couch looking alarmed.

"Hell, yes," was Sammy's absent-minded reply. She had started to go back into the world of her art. Pen in hand, she worked on a tree that had split down the middle, its fruit still on its branches, touching weeds and tall grass around it.

"Whatcha goin' to wear on your date with Frank?" Sammy asked as if from the other side of the world.

"I don't know," Melody said laying back on the couch feeling too worn out to care. She thought about it a bit. She didn't want to wear anything that would attract Frank, nothing sexy.

"Are you going to have sex with him?" asked Sammy.

"I don't know," Melody replied. She wanted to make love to Frank but she wanted to go home as well. If they had sex Frank would have hope she would stay in Sheridan and he would work toward that goal. He was a very sweet man and didn't deserve to be toyed with. She got up off the couch and went searching for the half-eaten box of chocolates. When she found it she returned to her place on the couch, lying down after rearranging a pillow for her head.

After a short silence Sammy asked, "Why didn't you marry him?"

"I don't know," Melody came back after picking through the candy looking for one with caramel and nuts. Finding one, she chewed the yummy square slowly thinking over Sammy's question. Sure, Frank had asked her, several times. Well, it hadn't been like he did it in a formal way, on one knee presenting her with a ring asking "Will you marry me?" It had been offhand, more like, pass the popcorn and let's get married before your Dad finds out we've been screwing. Handsome, yes. Clever with a phrase, no.

Both women had been so preoccupied with what they were doing, Sammy filling in the dying split tree drawing, Melody with her box of chocolates and thoughts of Frank and their mutual past. Neither one noticed the tall red-haired man standing in the doorway.

"So, this is how you girls spend your day?" came a deep booming voice.

Sammy and Melody jumped. Sammy dropped her pen. Melody spilled the rest of the chocolates on the floor. Little brown papers flew up in the air then floated back down gently.

"*Asshole!*" they both shouted at him in unison.

Frank stomped into the front room laughing hard.

"Jesus, Frank! I think I peed my pants! Don't sneak up on me like that. Didn't you hear this house is haunted?" Melody scolded Frank. "What's up with being so early?"

"It's 5:30, I work next door at the mill. Remember? No point going home then coming back an hour later. Besides, I worked in the office all day so I didn't even break a sweat. Don't need a shower, I don't think." Frank pulled the neck of his shirt out, lowered his head and sniffed. "I think I'm good to go."

"Come here," Melody ordered Frank. He walked over to her while she got up and stood on the couch. She pulled out the neck of his shirt and sniffed. He smelled like fresh-cut lumber, leather work gloves, hours-old shave cream, and something else. What was that scent? She pulled him closer and sniffed his neck, taking in a longer breath this time. Movie theater candy? Fresh baked vanilla cake? It filled her head and gave her the feeling she was falling.

"Hey, stop! That tickles!" Frank backed away from Melody.

"You people make me want to scream," Sammy said looking at Frank and Melody.

"Get ready to go you two. I'm starving. Service at the Queen is slllllloooowwww," Frank said cheerfully to the women.

"No, you and Mellie go. I have to work. I've got a show next month and I must have art to sell or I starve," Sammy explained.

"It's true, Frank. She has to work. It's why we are putting off the yard work until Saturday. She needs dead trees, a haunted dying orchard, gloom, doom, and fog. In fact, it better rain soon because all this sunshine is messing with her lighting," Melody defended her sister.

"Okay, then. Go change out of your peed pants and let's hit the road," Frank said to Melody, half chasing her out of the room. "I'll wait here, like always, on the couch, starving to death."

Melody ran upstairs. When she got to her room she looked in the mirror. Hell, she was smiling. An actual, real, not pretend, smile. Oh no, don't fall in love with Frank. Not here, not now. Why did he have to be so good in every way? Maybe she had just gotten used to lukewarm feelings for boring city types. "I'm a lukewarm city type now," she said to her reflection in the mirror.

She quickly changed into jeans and a dark blue sweater, then brushed her hair and put on some lip gloss. *No need to worry here,* she thought to herself. *Once Frank realizes you are nothing but a boring city type, he'll politely back away and not push the issue of a relationship. Maybe I could have sex with him just once, for old time's sake. To remember how good it felt to be held in his arms.* She zipped up her little black boots then ran down the stairs.

"Let's do this thing," she yelled at Frank as she came into the front room. He grabbed her by the hand and out the front door they went.

Chapter Sixty-two

Sunday, October 19, 2014

Sammy

Sammy awoke to the sound of vehicles driving past her childhood home on Rock Creek Road. She could tell it was raining by the splashing noise tires make on pavement. It gave her the same safe feeling she got in her little apartment in Seattle. When she rolled over she realized she had spent the night on the couch in the front room.

She wasn't surprised to find herself in this location rather than her bedroom. Saturday had been a very long day. The morning had been the big yard cleanup with the Boy Scouts, Frank Davison directing traffic and cutting firewood. Mid-afternoon had been the funeral of Andy Stokes. Then Sammy had worked late into the wee hours on the fourth drawing in what was to be part of her seven pen-and-inks for her art show, which was coming up fast.

She had lain down on the couch, fully dressed, with the idea of either getting back up a few hours later to continue working or greeting her sister when she came home from another one of her dates with Frank Davison. How many nights out had they had in the last week? Three? *Are they becoming an item?* Sammy asked herself.

If she was still on the couch this morning then it meant Mellie had not come home the night before. This made Sammy snicker as she rolled off the couch, stood up straight, and raised her arms to stretch her back. She had to twist from side to side to get the kinks out so she could walk. "My God, I'm thirty-one years old and feel like I'm 100," she said aloud as her feet shuffled on the carpet on their way to the bathroom.

Once Sammy had used the toilet, washed her hands, and face, and had brushed her shoulder-length dark brown hair, she came into the kitchen to make some coffee. She looked out the now brightly colored curtained window. Yes, it was raining. Dark and gloomy, looked like some fog was moving in from the east. A perfect day at last! She grabbed her camera, pulled on some boots that had been left on the enclosed back porch (now fully cleaned of old newspapers and cardboard boxes and swept, with neatly stacked firewood to one side), and flew out the back door.

She stopped, looked around the newly mowed backyard. The smell of rain, grass, and dirt mingled with a slight scent of roses. Odd, she thought. She hadn't noticed any flowers in the yard yesterday during the cleanup done by the Boy Scouts and Frank.

Sammy walked around the old ruin of a house. On the south side, where there had once been a rose and flower garden, was now bare dirt. The dead rose bushes had been hacked to bits by Jan earlier in the week when they were burning the bones of her mother's rapist. The Boy Scouts had dug up and pulled out the remains of the old bushes by the roots. Now it was just a twenty-eight-foot by twenty-foot patch of neatly dug-up earth. Ready for planting any winter crop she desired, one of the Scouts had explained to her.

She had thanked the tall, skinny, fresh-faced young man for his help. She didn't have the heart to tell him she had no intention of planting anything, or staying for that matter.

Sammy walked over to the now completely weedless barn. The old structure still looked forlorn so she took some pictures from several angles. She went around to the back and looked at the burn pit now full of grass clippings and weeds. Where the four vehicles had sat, overgrown with tangles of blackberry bushes and unidentified vines, was Dad's old flatbed truck. It seemed as if the truck was happy to be out of the barn at last where it could enjoy the outdoors.

During the two days before the cleanup the ownerless ghost cars had been towed away. One by one, each vehicle going off to different places. Jan's brother Jesse had come out and gotten the '73 Chevy pickup. It had been good to see him again after all these years. He had told her he had a place in Central Oregon. In the winter he liked having a project to work on to sell in the spring. He thought the pickup might bring him some cash. He had handed her $1,000 in hundred-dollar bills and told her not to worry about a receipt, that he would handle the paperwork on the deal from his end. Jesse invited Sammy to come out to his place in Prineville, she might find something to paint out there. She had liked the idea and thanked him for the invitation.

Of course, the car that was towed away that had made a notable difference to the feel of the orchard was Philip Mason's Mazda. The two men that showed up to do the job of getting the car dug out of the ground and placed on their truck looked like they came out of a Steven King novel.

Firstly, it had seemed like they just randomly appeared out of nowhere, at 8:30 at night no less.

Secondly, they were quiet. If Sammy hadn't gone to the bathroom and looked out the window, she never would have known they were there. Both men had flashlights, which is how Sammy noticed them and their truck. As luck would have it, it was Friday night. Mellie and Frank were on one of their dates, so Sammy was alone in the house. Well, just her and the evil menacing demon once known as Philip Mason, who guarded the backdoor and welcomed all who entered.

Sammy hadn't known if she was looking at real people or ghosts, at first. She had quickly turned out the light in the bathroom, then ran and got her cell phone, then went back to keep an eye the eerie, creeping figures while she called Gus. No way was she going to call the Sheriff's department or Sergeant Kell who was home from the hospital by then but not fully recovered, at least according to Jan.

Gus apologized to Sammy for not having told her that he was sending out someone to pick up the Mazda. He had Melody's number but he didn't have Sammy's had been his excuse. When she asked him if he had called Mellie to warn her that the guys would be coming late at night, he had admitted he hadn't but then he hadn't known they wouldn't get there until late.

Sammy had been in a fit of anger and hatred and had cussed at Gus, calling him an insensitive prick, as she stood in the dark bathroom and watched the figures load the Mazda onto the back of their tow truck.

She would never forgive her father nor Gus for parking *that* car on *this* property. After all she had been put through by Mason, the rush of emotions in carrying out his demise and the short but painful investigation into his death, Gus and her father then parked the instrument of Mason's heinous deeds in this orchard. She couldn't tell her father what had happened to her so there was no way to get him to move the Mason car.

True, Gus had protected her from ending up in prison, or worse, the state hospital in Salem. Still, each day she had to look at that vehicle had cut her soul, the tiniest bit, in the same place, over and over again until the wound felt like a bleeding gash. Once she graduated from high school she rushed to stay with her sister at her small apartment in California until she could go off to college in Washington. Over time she had forgotten all about Mason, her art the healer of her beingness.

Even though she had cussed at Gus, he had stayed on the phone with her until the Mazda was loaded and the strangers had driven away down Rock Creek Road. Sammy apologized to him then and they hung up.

Sammy stood in the empty space where the vehicles had been. Yes, it looked empty, but did it feel empty? She walked to the back door of the house and stood before it, eyes closed. She could feel the rain and a chill in the air but nothing else.

Satisfied that Mason was now gone she walked down the driveway and crossed Rock Creek Road to the mail box. She took a few shots of it with the old tree next to it, blackberry vines winding around its dark trunk, appearing to be squeezing the life out of it.

That's what this place does to me, she thought as she walked back into the house. *It slowly squeezes the light out of me until I feel empty.*

Back inside Sammy changed into dry clothes in her wallpaperless bedroom. Tearing off the wallpaper had felt good at the time but the now bare aging plywood that had been underneath it made the room feel shaggy, like pictures she had seen of people living in shacks during the depression in the 1930s. She decided she would sleep in the front room from now on, well, until she left here, which she figured out would be a week to the day. The idea of driving away from Sheridan, Oregon lightened her mood.

While she was upstairs, she checked her sister's room just to ensure she had been correct about Mellie not coming home last night. She opened the door and peeked in. No Mellie there.

This bedroom was wallpapered in pink with white and yellow daisies. The furniture was white, trimmed in gold. The bed was unmade, the bedding was Mellie's from her home in

Glendale as was the green glass lamp with the white lampshade on the nightstand.

On the bed was their Mother's blue satin dress. She picked it up to examine it. Melody had washed the garment as best she could and had pressed it carefully to get out set-in wrinkles. There were several tears that had been stitched up with light green thread to look like flower vines and little white flowers embroidered on the vines. Holes had been stitched over in the same manner, flowers with white thread, yellow or pink centers, and green leaves. The frayed raggedy bottom of the dress had been cut off and hemmed with a chain stitch in blue thread. Her sister must have put in many hours, staying up late at night, working on this labor of love.

Tonight would be the night she and Mellie would begin the work of giving their mother a peaceful rest. It was perfect. Rainy, cold, and a Sunday when most people stayed home and got ready for their work week. They would sneak into the West Valley Funeral Home through the back door. Go down into the basement, turn on the cremation unit like Josh Stokes, Andy's younger son, had showed her yesterday after his dad's funeral. It had been easy to get Josh to leave the house and go next door to the funeral home. The house had been crowded with as many townspeople as could fit, talking about Andy, paying tons of attention to Barbara. Lots of people drinking coffee. Everyone eating donuts, cake, and cookies brought in by those who knew Andy.

Josh just wanted out of there and any excuse was a good one. He hadn't even asked Sammy why she wanted to know how to work the machine. He not only explained in detail how to run it, he also showed her around. She had noted there were no security alarm systems and asked Josh why that was. He had laughed and asked her who in the world would want to break in to a place that stored dead bodies. Sammy had just smiled and shook her head trying not to laugh out loud. When they left Sammy made sure the back door was left unlocked by distracting Josh with a little kiss of thanks. He was much older than her, about 47, and long married. So, a kiss from a younger woman splattered his attention like a hand hitting a puddle of water. He forgot the important detail of locking up.

Sammy and Melody would have to wait for the oven to warm up to 1400 degrees but that shouldn't take long, maybe an hour, put Mother in on the conveyor belt, wait another forty-five minutes, then let her cool for an hour. Lastly, they had to put Mother in the grinder, if there were any bones left, then pour her in a box and scram out of there without being seen. It seemed doable. Grisly but doable.

Sammy went in the kitchen and poured herself a cup of coffee, then decided to add some cream, a bit of sugar, and a shot of whiskey. Yes, this was going to be a truly grisly chore. If Andy would have been here, he could have done this for them but he wouldn't be. They'd have to do it themselves. It gave her a shiver thinking about it.

She needed to check on a few things to ensure her plan would go off as she imagined. Sammy would have to make certain Barbara had left today with her oldest son, Andy Jr. She and Mellie had worked hard to talk Barbara into the idea late yesterday afternoon. Andy Jr. and his wife had been happy with the arrangement but Barbara had needed some persuading to get her to want to go. Finally, Mellie had told Barbara how sad and lonely it was after a funeral when everyone goes their own way and no longer pays any attention to a dead person's loved ones. Barbara realized that after yesterday's well-wishers had left her house she would be all alone and no longer the center of attention. The only way to ensure she continued to be in the middle of things was to take off with her son and his family for Albany. At least for a little while, a couple of weeks maybe. Then she could come back and handle loose ends.

Sammy got out the crock pot, turned it on high, and started throwing in whatever she thought would make a good soup. There was leftover roasted chicken from several nights ago, a package of frozen mixed vegetables, a chopped onion, several cups of water, some leftover rosé wine, salt, pepper, dried parsley, garlic powder, and a handful of bouillon cubes.

She checked the clock to see what time it was as well as to judge when to turn the crock pot down to low. 10:00 am. Mellie still wasn't home. Sammy made herself another cup of spiked coffee then went into the front room and made a fire with the last of the old newspapers. She lit the candles on the mantel, then pulled back the sheets she had hung on the windows.

The lighting and feel of the old farmhouse were just right for Sammy to feel inspired and she sat down with a large fresh canvas and began sketching out her new subject, Dad's beat-up old mailbox sticking up from the ground on a rotting timber and the strangled dying tree next to it. From her seat in the front room she had a perfect view of this scene out the front room window facing the road. Soon nothing else existed for the artist but her subject, the way she interpreted this in her mind, and what she was laying down with pen and ink.

A long time had passed before she noted she was looking at Frank Davison's pickup pulling into the driveway. She sighed, put down her pen, took a sip of cold coffee, and waited for the lovers to come in the back door. She hoped they wouldn't be announcing their engagement.

Frank and Mellie didn't disappoint Sammy's expectations. They bounded into the house calling her name with joyous voices and stomping quick steps. They rushed into the front room, their faces pink from the chilly autumn air and their unconcealable re-found love. Mellie held a bouquet of large white carnations, looking like a blushing bride, Frank right behind her with a grocery bag and a doggy bag container from some local restaurant. *God damn it, they look happy,* Sammy said to herself.

"Hey guys! Where ya been? Church?" Sammy joked with her sister.

"Yes, we have! How did you know?" came back Mellie.

"We brought you leftovers from that trendy new place on Third Street in Mac." Frank held them out for Sammy to see. "You should take a break and come eat," he added as he put them on the kitchen table.

Sammy got up from her seat in front of the easel and went into the kitchen to turn down the soup. She opened the box of leftovers: chicken and waffles! She grabbed a syrup- and butter-laden waffle and stuffed it in her mouth. It tasted wonderful. She hadn't realized she was hungry. "Wow!" she managed to say with her mouth full.

"I know, right!?" said Frank, a big smile on his face.

"What's up with the flowers? You get married while at church?" Sammy said between bites of waffle and deep-fried chicken. "I've got a pot of chicken soup on, should be ready in time for an early dinner."

Melody and Frank stared at Sammy with odd expressions on their faces, as if their minds had been read or their futures had just been predicted.

Frank pulled a tape measure out of his pocket and turned to Melody telling her he'd been back in a couple minutes.

Melody laid the flowers down on the counter then sat down at the table with her sister. Sammy knew she was in for a news report.

Sammy listened while Melody filled her in quickly before Frank came back in. Melody and Frank had gone over to his place and he had cooked her dinner after Andy's funeral. She had spent the night there. She and Frank had done a lot of talking about the future. Melody had explained to Frank that she wanted to go back to Glendale after the last harvest. Frank had told her he wanted her to stay here with him. Nothing was settled.

Yes, she and Frank had been having sex. Yes, it was the best she had had in a very long time. Was she falling in love? She didn't think so. How did Frank feel? Melody was uncertain, she hadn't asked him. Sammy could tell this was a conversation they would need to have later and told her sister so. Sammy also reminded Melody that Frank had a tendency to be controlling, not taking no for an answer, and working things out so they would be to his advantage.

When they had gotten up this morning Frank had talked Melody into going to church. She told him flat out she didn't believe in God but he promised her it was just an hour then he had a great place he wanted to take her for breakfast so she gave in. Sammy noted Melody's powers to resist Frank were lessening. Did Melody see this? Sammy wondered.

Melody then told her about running into Jan at church. Terry was home recovering and should be back to work by the time of the last harvest this coming Saturday. Jan felt confident that Terry wouldn't be telling anyone what he knew. He had told Jan that and she believed him. Still Jan thought it best for both Melody and Sammy to get out of town as soon as possible after the last harvest in the event that something happened that was out of anyone's control. Sammy nodded her agreement with Jan's evaluation of their situation.

When Frank entered the kitchen Melody had moved on to telling Sammy about the wonderful place Frank had taken her for breakfast in McMinnville. From there Frank had taken her to a nursery off the highway where they looked for something to plant where the rose garden had once been. That's where he bought her the big bunch of carnations.

Frank jumped in at this point, talking about having just measured the empty piece of earth outside the kitchen window giving his calculations for how many plants would fit in that space and what sort might be put in this time of year.

Sammy stopped eating and looked at Frank then at Melody. "We aren't staying, Frank," she said as gently as she could.

"Didn't Mellie tell you? There are many years of back taxes owed on this place. We don't have the money to pay the debt. This means the property reverts to the County. Dad's attorney knows all this and told us the County will soon take over possession," Sammy explained.

"I don't understand. Why hang curtains in the kitchen? Why do all the work cleaning up the orchard? Why hold a harvest? Why make such a big deal out of it?" Frank asked leaning back against the counter with his arms folded over his chest, his voice firm as if asking one of his employees for an explanation of why something hadn't gotten done on time.

"It's a last harvest, Frank. It's our farewell to the farm and Sheridan. We had to make the property safe for people to come out and pick." Melody joined in trying to get Frank to understand. "Sammy and I are packing up and leaving here the day after the last harvest. She's going home to Seattle and I'm going home to Glendale."

Frank put his hands in his jeans pockets. He staring at the floor and said nothing for a whole minute. Sammy could feel him thinking over what had been said to him. You could almost hear the gears in his mind working.

"I understand what you're both saying. I do get you can't stay here." Frank pointed to the floor of the kitchen making his point.

He let out a deep sigh, "You know, I have a ton to do to get ready for a very busy week at the mill. Did I tell you Dad's retiring after the first of the year? The paperwork makes my brain ache just thinking about it. And bookkeeping, that is a whole other story. There's a job opening, that's for sure. I've got to get over to Mom and Dad's right now, then I'm going to turn in early. For some odd reason I didn't get much sleep last night." Frank smiled one of his big winning smiles at Melody.

"I'll walk you to your pickup," Melody said and got up from the table. The two walked out the backdoor together.

"Well, fuck me," Sammy said out loud. Frank had just let them know he needed a bookkeeper. She wondered if his next move would be to offer the job to Melody in an effort to keep her in town. That Frank, he was sure a clever man.

Chapter Sixty-three

Sunday, October 19, 2014

Melody and Sammy

Sammy and Melody spent that Sunday afternoon taking turns napping on the couch and eating chicken soup.

While Melody napped Sammy let herself become totally, silently, absorbed in her drawings. There was no need for conversation between the sisters now that Sammy had laid out her plans for this evening's activities. Melody had agreed without argument but did share her worries about being caught and what they might be able to do to avoid that situation. Simple little details like wearing black and rubber gloves, parking whichever car they decided to use a couple blocks away from the funeral home rather than right out front, not turning the lights on in the building but using flashlights instead and not turning those on until fully inside with the door closed.

Sammy was glad for the input. She wished Sergeant Kell was working tonight; he could have stood guard, so to speak. He could even make excuses for them if someone came along and started asking questions. Sammy wasn't going to ask him for his help if he wasn't on the job. Overall she still wasn't certain she could fully trust him.

When Melody wasn't napping and Sammy was taking her turn on the couch, she sat in the big over-stuffed chair in the front room by the fire and worked on the last of the embroidery on her mother's favorite dress.

Tonight, around midnight, the two girls would sneak into the funeral home and turn their mother into ashes. Jesus, maybe they should just drive to the beach and throw the bones off a cliff into the ocean. No, that wouldn't be putting a loved one to rest in a respectful manner. Besides, what if some dog found one of the bones because they didn't all go in the ocean? What if... her mind turned over all the things that could go wrong with the cliff idea as well as the plans for tonight.

Melody thought about Frank as well. He wasn't the sort of man to lose his reason over a woman. He seemed okay albeit somewhat hurt when she walked him to his pickup. They had sat in his pickup rather than stand in the rain. He had kissed her hand and she had thanked him for a beautiful evening and a lovely, picture-perfect Sunday morning. Then as if the conversation in the kitchen hadn't just happened a few minutes earlier he reminded Melody that Wednesday night was Dairy Queen night and he would pick her up at 5:30 for dinner. It was as if nothing Sammy or she had said to him about leaving Sheridan for good had sunk in. That was a bit creepy. She didn't know how to address this so she had given him a quick kiss on the cheek and jumped out of the pickup and run into the house.

Sammy woke up just after 7:00 pm, just as Melody had finished her sewing. It had stopped raining. Sammy closed the sheets she had put up as curtains on the front room windows.

"It's dark now and I'm pretty sure no one's going to drop by at this hour. Let's start getting Mother ready to go," Sammy said to her sister.

"Okay, the dress is done and I've got just the thing to carry her in," said Melody. She got up out of the chair, went into the sewing room and returned with the small tan leather suit case which she placed on the floor in front of the fire place. "I believe this belonged to Mother," she said as she opened the well-worn case.

"What are all these newspaper clippings?" Sammy wanted to know.

Melody handed Sammy the yellowed article from their mother's hometown in Hamilton, Montana showing her as the lovely, young rodeo princess. Sammy's eyes lit up as she looked upon her mother's youthful face.

"There are a lot of articles in here I don't think we need to keep, well, unless you want to for some reason. There are tons of articles about the Uncle Joe Benton shooting, quite a few about what happened to Philip Mason and some others about that Montgomery guy who was found murdered in his trailer. And there are several about the trial of Bill Garrett. That story is a real heartbreaker. I've read them all." Melody sighed then continued.

"There's a few I think we should keep. They're rather short and should go in a family album or scrapbook so they don't get lost. There's a birth announcement for Mother. There's one for each of us too. These two here are the obituaries for Mother's parents. They died six months apart. Pretty sad, really." Melody handed the bits of old newspaper to her sister that she thought Sammy should read and put the others off to the side.

Sammy sat on the floor by the suitcase and in the firelight read each one she was handed.

Melody stood up and lit the candles on the mantel, the number of which seemed to grow with each trip to the store. She lit the big pink candle which sat on the coffee table and several others which now sat on the bookshelves. Then she took down the gold-trimmed white children's jewelry box from its spot above the fireplace. She opened it and took out the pictures of her mother as a child. "These should go in the keep pile we make into a family album. So should the baby bracelet. I'd like to have Mother's class ring, if it's okay with you. I think I'll get a chain and wear it around my neck with my class ring," Melody proposed to Sammy.

Sammy was now stirring the fire and throwing in the articles about the Montgomery murder, making a mental note to be sure and take Jesse Miller up on his invitation to come out to Prineville for a visit sometime. She stopped and looked in the little box. She knew that including any of the remaining jewelry in the cremation process wasn't a good idea from all the reading she had done online over the past week about how the process was done. She decided she wanted the horse scarf they had found when they had first started cleaning out Dad's bedroom. She told Melody.

"That leaves the broken heart locket." Melody gently took it from where her Mother had placed it so many years ago.

"Broken heart kind of says it all, doesn't it?" Sammy whispered as she carefully took it from Melody. "I think it is important to put it in the scrapbook as it does represent a part of Mother's life. It represents what shaped her and what she did after her rape. I understand how she made her choice to marry Dad and do her best to move forward with her life. To try to forget the past."

"Well, if anyone understood about forgetting their past and creating their life anew it would be you," Melody said to her sister in a kind and loving way.

Melody neatly folded her mother's blue dress, then laid the bottom of it in the open suitcase, leaving the top of the dress lying out. She pointed to what she had done and said, "We lay Mother here, then I'll put the rest of the dress on top of her. Sort of like we're tucking her into bed. I'll cut the stems off some of the carnations Frank bought me and lay those on top. Anything else you think should go in with Mother?"

Melody turned to see her sister throwing all the articles regarding the Uncle Joe Benton shooting into the fire.

"Hmmmm, can't think of anything off hand," Sammy said after thinking about it for a couple minutes. "I can't imagine she would want anything of Dad's, you know, like a hanky. Or anything from the farm here…" she was still looking distracted, lost in thought as she went into their dad's bedroom and came out with her mother's remains, still snuggly wrapped in Sergeant Terence Kell's black hoodie.

Sammy bent over and gingerly laid the bundle in the suitcase, then Melody covered it with the rest of the blue dress.

While Melody was getting the flowers ready, Sammy went into the sewing room and brought the two boxes of old photos they had found while cleaning the house and sat down next to the still-open suitcase.

Melody came back in with eight stemless white carnations and placed them on top of the blue dress. She stood back, looked at her handiwork and gave it a nod of approval. Sammy checked in the suitcase and nodded as well.

The sisters then looked over each picture from the two boxes, deciding which would go in the family scrapbook and which would not, making two different piles. Most of the photos were of people they didn't know, but they didn't burn any of them because they didn't want to get rid of something that might turn out to be something they would later realize they wanted.

At the bottom of one box they found their parents' marriage certificate. That was placed in the save pile. In the bottom of the second box they found a few old Christmas cards. Sammy opened each aging envelope as carefully as she could so as not to rip it. They were from their mother's parents. There were only three. Each one had a handwritten message inside. Small notes saying how much they loved and missed her and hoped she was happy. Those went into the keep pile as well.

"I know what we should do. We can each write Mother a short note and put those in on top of the flowers," Melody shared with Sammy. Sammy agreed and the two women set off searching around the house, getting paper and pens.

It didn't take long and both women had written a short note passing on love and wishes for a safe journey into the hereafter for their mother. Each one took a turn reading their note out loud then placing it in the suitcase. They didn't say a prayer or ask God to take their Mother to heaven as neither girl believed in such things.

Melody noted that here they were in the middle of October 2014 and it was around this time of year their parents had gotten married and arrived in Sheridan. Sammy noted that it was seven years later, this very same month, that their mother was murdered on this property, out in the barn.

That was the end to Emily Newberry Corbbet's memorial service as performed by her two daughters.

Melody closed the suitcase and announced, "Well, Mother's ready to go. Let's do this thing."

Melody and Sammy changed into dark clothes and soft-soled shoes. They stuffed rubber cleaning gloves in their back pockets and tested the batteries in their flashlights. Sammy made sure she was wearing a watch. They intentionally didn't bring their cell phones for fear a call would buzz in and make noise at the wrong time. Melody decided to bring a couple hairpins and a credit card in the event that the back door to the funeral home had gotten locked by some well-meaning visitor and she needed to pick the lock. Sammy stuck a screwdriver in her back pocket for the same reason.

They blew out the candles and turned out all the lights in the old farmhouse but one in the front room. It had started raining again and now the wind was blowing. When the women walked out the back door, they could see a fog moving in over the orchard.

"Damn it, Sammy! I'm scared!" Melody said once they were in the car, the suitcase containing their mother in Sammy's lap.

"Me too. Now don't give up, don't panic. Stay alert and drive like nothing's wrong."

They had decided to use Melody's car because it was more common in these parts and they didn't turn the headlights on when they pulled out of the driveway. They waited until they were on Rock Creek Road, heading toward the mill, before turning them on. Melody had been worried that Frank, in his effort to help keep the women safe, had told one of his night watchmen to stay on the lookout for odd comings and goings from the farm next door.

Melody turned her car north down the first side street they came to when they entered the little town of Sheridan. Up to this point they hadn't seen any other cars on the road. Most of the houses they passed were dark. Sammy rolled down her window to see if she could hear any dogs barking. Nothing there.

Melody turned east two blocks down, driving slowly, lights off. Then went for six blocks before Sammy waved at Melody to pull over in front of an old house she thought was vacant.

They carefully got out of the car and closed the doors, not making any noise, then they hurried down the middle of the street, crossed into the other side, went two blocks, then ducked into the back yard of the Stokes family home. Sammy held out her hand for Melody to wait. She listened and didn't hear anything except the rain on sidewalk and leaves blowing in the trees. She motioned for Melody to stop breathing so hard. Melody nodded her agreement but couldn't get herself under control so Sammy grabbed her by the arm and rushed her sister through to the back yard to the parking lot of the funeral home and up to the back door.

Sammy put on her gloves and tried the door. It came open with a click that she was positive could be heard all the way to Salem. She pushed her sister inside and closed the door all in one motion.

Both women breathed a sigh of relief in the complete blackness. Sammy lead Melody down a short hallway, turned left, and opened a door that went downstairs. Although their eyes had become accustomed to the dark while in the back yard, Sammy felt they couldn't see well enough to make it down the stairs. So she turned on her flashlight and shone it on the carpeted narrow stairway.

Sammy walked quickly and opened another door which led to a room with a conveyor belt and a glass window. On the wall next to the window were three very large buttons. Sammy hit the top button with the heel of her hand and light filled the room. The cremation machine on the other side of the wall gave forth a deep long *whoosh* sound.

Melody waved her hand at Sammy and pointed to the machine and then to her own ear, then shrugged, asking if anyone could hear the machine besides her in a made-up sign language.

Sammy mouthed the word *No* and shook her head. She then placed the small suitcase on the conveyor belt. She pointed to her watch and held up one finger. They now had to wait one hour for the crematorium to heat up to full power. It was only then that they would be able to hit the button for the conveyor belt to start rolling forward and the oven door to open up in the other room.

They sat down on the floor, turned off their flashlights to save batteries, and held each other's gloved hands. Each woman became lost in her own thoughts.

Sammy amused herself with visions of her upcoming art show. She imagined her art hanging on the walls of the gallery, people dressed in their trendy best Seattle fashions. Linda, wine glass in her hand, showing a few of her newest art lovers Sammy's "Haunted Orchard" drawings, then bringing them over to meet Sammy. She shakes their hands and answers how it was she came to be so inspired. "Well, it all started with this awful rape of my Mother…" no that wasn't going to work. *Rework that reply,* she told herself. Then she set herself to work out a seamless answer to any questions which might come her way, leaving out anything to do with Sheridan, Oregon.

Melody thought about how relaxing it had been to work on the embroidery for her Mother's dress. Maybe she would get out some of the old projects she had started when she was younger and work on them, just for something to do until she could go home to Glendale. Her mind wandered to Frank. She saw him standing in the driveway of her rundown ruined childhood home waving to her sadly as she drove away. She re-directed her thoughts to their recent lovemaking until her sister hit her arm and she looked up.

Sammy stood up and hit the middle button on the wall with her gloved hand. The conveyor belt started moving forward, loudly. Melody jumped up but there was nothing she could do about the noise. She hit Sammy on the arm and pointed at her ear. Sammy shrugged and pulled her finger across her neck like she was killing herself. Melody didn't understand what she was trying to say.

A part of the wall slid sideways under the window and the suitcase moved into the other room. The sideways door closed and the door to the oven opened as the suitcase touched it, then closed after the case was inside as soon as Sammy hit the middle button a second time.

"Phase two," Sammy stated out loud. Melody jumped back in surprise to hear her sister speak when they had agreed not to until they were back home. "Ya, I know, but after that batch of noise from the conveyor belt and the doors opening and closing, if someone heard that then we are truly fucked and us talking doesn't matter anymore."

"How long will this part take?" Melody asked, her nerves getting the best of her. Her stomach was starting to hurt.

"Only about forty-five minutes. If it was a whole person with a regular casket it would take around an hour and a half. A big fat person could take three hours. If you're huge, like over 400 pounds, then you won't fit in there at all and would have to be buried. At least that's what the article I read online said," Sammy stated in a matter of fact way.

"I might need a bathroom. My stomach is jumping up and down," Melody warned Sammy.

They turned on their flashlights and walked out into the hallway looking for a bathroom. It took going upstairs and into the public part of the funeral home before they found one. Sammy left Melody there and went into an area she had talked Josh into showing her. It was a display room with a couple sample coffins and three shelves of sample urns for cremated remains. She opened the cabinet doors below the shelves and found more urns and some less expensive decorated boxes. Some were made of wood and some were made of cardboard. She picked out a small, blue cardboard urn trimmed in gold, with white satin interior, for her Mother. She continued looking until she found a medium-sized dark brown wood box with inlaid mother of pearl on the top and sides. It had a little brass latch for a lock on the front. Inside was red velvet with a small decorative lock and key. She took this one as well.

After re-arranging the urns in the cabinet to hide the fact that anything had been taken Sammy returned to the bathroom to check on her sister. She found Melody doubled over, sitting on the toilet, breathing hard and gulping.

"What's wrong?!!" Sammy hissed at her sister.

"I think it's my nervous stomach acting up. With all the waffles, cinnamon rolls, cobbler, donuts, and cookies I've eaten in the last three weeks I'm surprised this hasn't happened sooner. But then I haven't ever been this scared in my life before, so who can say what's making me shit my brains out here in a funeral home I've broken into in the middle of the night!" Melody came back in a loud whisper in between moments of pain while her colon spasmed wildly.

Sammy put down the two urns on the counter next to the sink in the bathroom and checked her watch. "We've still got about thirty minutes to go on this phase. Then we have cool-down for an hour. We won't be making any noise again until I start the conveyor belt to bring Mother out of the cremation unit. Stay here. I'm going to check the front doors and windows to make sure no one is outside."

"No worries, I'm not leaving this bathroom anytime soon," Melody reassured her sister in a pained breathy whisper.

Sammy wandered around the office area of the funeral home, checked the door to ensure it was locked, peeked out the windows in a way that no one on the street could see her, then she went out the back door and listened for cars or footsteps. It was raining harder now, the wind making it appear to be going sideways rather than down. She returned to her sister after a short time.

"All's good out here, Mellie. How's it going in there?" Sammy asked from the doorway to the bathroom.

"I think the worst of it is over. I'm going to come out there and lie on that couch in the reception area until we need to go back into the basement," Melody answered meekly.

"Okay, don't flush the toilet. It will just make more noise," Sammy told her sister.

Melody came out of the bathroom and lay down on the big flowered sofa in the reception area of the funeral home. Sammy sat in one of the chairs, checking her watch every couple of minutes. Finally she stood up, checked her sister, who had fallen asleep, then went downstairs by herself to turn off the cremation unit. She hit the bottom button hard with the heel of her still-gloved hand. Instantly the jets in the oven turned off and the room went black. She was glad she had brought her flashlight. She turned it on and swept the room ensuring nothing was left down there. She checked the floor for footprints and found they had done a bit of tracking in of grass so she went upstairs, got some wet paper towels and wiped the prints.

"Sammy! Is everything okay?" Melody whispered when Sammy returned.

"Yep, all good, just wiping up some shoe prints. Now we wait an hour, run the conveyor belt back out, and sift through the ash with a poker to get out anything that might be left behind like hinges or snaps from the suitcase or the metal from the zipper on the hoodie. Then we have to break up the bones because they might still be holding their shape. It's hard to say how it will be for Mother, her bones having been in the ground for over twenty years," Sammy told her sister. She went into the bathroom and came out with the two boxes to show her.

"This cute little blue and gold one is for Mother. We can put her in here for transportation to Hamilton, Montana. I hope you're up for a road trip because I'm thinking we should leave first thing tomorrow. We would be back in plenty of time for the last harvest if we drive straight through. We can take turns: one drives, the other one sleeps. I'm going to take my camera and take some good pictures of Mother's home town. Her high school, rodeo grounds, anything left of the family ranch. I'll get a couple shots of her parents' gravesites as well." Sammy laid out her latest plans to Melody.

"I'm supposed to have dinner with Frank on Wednesday, but if we don't get back in time, I'll offer him a homemade spaghetti dinner with us when we return. I'll tell him you had to pop up to Seattle for a quick meeting and I went with you so you didn't have to drive alone," Melody confirmed. "The faster we get this job done the better. Now, how about we just gather Mother up when she comes out, hinges, snaps and all, and we worry about the rest at home. I've never wanted to get out of a place more than I do right this minute."

"Well, okay, you're right. The sooner we get out of here the better off we'll be. Let me look around for something to carry her and any hot bits back to the car," Sammy said as she wandered away to find just the right container and paper bags to put the other two urns in.

Chapter Sixty-four

Saturday, October 25th, 2014

Sammy

It had been a long day dealing with people coming out to Earl Corbbet's orchard for one last harvest. Sammy Corbbet was ready to get in her car and drive home to Seattle now, even though the plan had been to wait until Sunday morning. She told Melody she wanted to pack up and leave immediately.

Melody was concerned and let her sister know she should wait. "Jesus, Sammy. That's a long drive. I don't know about you but I'm pooped. Spend the night. We can have breakfast together in the morning then I'll help you pack up and you can be on your way."

The two women were standing in the kitchen of their dad's house. Sammy looked out the window to see Frank gathering up the tools he had brought out to the farm and loading his ladders onto his pickup.

"I hate it here and you know why. I have no reason to stay. You do, you have Frank out there in love with you now. In fact, I doubt if he'll let you leave at this point," Sammy said motioning toward the window. "Anyway, while you and Frank were out last night, I packed up all my clothes, my art supplies, and my drawings. Everything is in my Kia ready to roll. I'm even gassed up. I'll catch dinner on the road. Now give me a hug and kiss goodbye, sister dear, this chick is out of here." Sammy moved toward Melody with her arms out. The two women hugged for a long moment then kissed each other on the cheek.

Just then Frank walked into the kitchen. "Hey, what's this? You're not leaving, are you, Sammy?"

"Yep, this chick's got to fly! People to see, things to do! Be seeing you two crazy kids on the flip side!" Sammy said as she headed for the back door.

"I have a surprise for the two of you. I was going to save it for breakfast tomorrow but I guess I have to tell you both now," Frank said firmly.

Sammy stopped and turned around. "Okay, whatcha got?"

"I talked to my attorney who talked to your Mr. Peterman. I have arranged to buy your dad's property, orchard, barn, house, and all for the price of the back taxes owed. I hope to have the deal finalized before the end of the year. So, Sammy, there's no reason for you to go. Your home is safe, you can stay here forever," Frank informed the women.

"Frank?" was all Melody had managed to squeak out.

Sammy felt as if she was going to throw up or faint, she wasn't sure which. She forced her feet to move toward the back door. "That's a damned fucking shame, Frank," she said quietly while looking at her sister. "Goodbye, Melody. I'll text you when I get home." She turned and hurried as fast as she could to her car, jumped in, started the engine, and backed out of the driveway onto Rock Creek Road, her heart pounding in her throat. She sped out of town and onto the highway as if she was being chased by wild animals.

It took thirty full minutes for her to calm down and realize she was free and safe, no evil spirit or menacing phantom was after her. But it did occur to her that her sister would not be going back to her own life in Glendale. Melody would be staying in Sheridan as Frank's wife, forever tied to the town, just like their mother had been until her daughters had taken her back to Montana.

Sammy had time to think once on Interstate 5 heading north to Seattle. She thought about how she and Melody had made it out of West Valley Funeral Home that cold, windy, rainy night only a week ago completely undetected, carrying their mother's still-warm ashes in a small metal can. She snickered to herself as she remembered that they hadn't flushed the toilet after Melody's emergency poop attack. Barbara Stokes would be the one to find that. The image of that scene made Sammy laugh out loud in her car.

It was after 3:00 am when they got back to the house. Melody was barely holding it together and had to rush to the bathroom again once they arrived home.

So, while Melody hid and did what she had to do in the bathroom, Sammy had had to deal with the rest of the job. This entailed pouring the warm ashes out on some newspaper on the kitchen table, sorting through them for snaps or buckles or hinges, removing these items or any other metal. Then letting the ashes cool down completely before putting them into the small blue satin-covered cardboard box trimmed in gold piping. There were a few very small bones and teeth which had to be dealt with by putting them in the bottom of the box first and the rest of the ashes on top.

Once Melody had put herself to bed Sammy was able to take a very small glass bottle with a cork stopper and fill it with some of her mother's ashes for her to keep for herself. This she placed in the wood and mother-of-pearl urn she had stolen from the funeral home, along with the horse-print scarf, a piece of blue fabric from the hem of her mother's favorite dress, plus copies Sammy had made of the newspaper article of her mother's days as a rodeo princess, and a copy of the picture Joy Holiday had found of her mother at the Mother's Day brunch in May of 1987.

The family album she and Melody had started to put together hadn't gotten finished by the time she was to leave and Sammy knew it wouldn't be. She had told Melody she could keep it and add to it as notable family events happened. Sammy promised to send Melody any newspaper clippings of her art show, if in fact there turned out to be any, to add to the scrapbook.

Sammy's Kia drove along smoothly into Washington State. Again, Sammy felt herself unwind in degrees, the tension in her shoulders letting go. She rolled down her window just a bit so she could smell the river air.

The trip Sammy and Melody had taken to Montana had gone as well as the cremation of their mother. No one in Sheridan had really missed them, except Frank, who was easily made happy again with a spaghetti dinner he had asked the sisters to cook in the kitchen of his hilltop house. It was a large, modern home with floor-to-ceiling windows looking out on the deep green valley below where the little town of Sheridan had sat for over 100 years. Sammy couldn't imagine Frank being willing to live in her father's old dilapidated house or letting Melody live there now that Sammy was gone.

Sammy was glad she had been able to do one last thing before leaving Yamhill County for what she hoped to be the last time. She had taken her camera and driven up to the old pioneer cemetery on Willamina Mill road, where she had run from Philip Mason in fear. It was a perfect morning, dark, cloudy, wind blowing. She walked around taking pictures of anything she thought she could use to make into a drawing for her upcoming art show. She had half expected Mason to jump out from behind a tombstone and yell boo. The little outing hadn't been as cathartic as she had hoped but she was glad she had taken the time and pictures as she did come back with a few usable shots.

Sammy pulled up in front of her apartment building at 11:30 pm. She promised herself long hours of drawing and all the coffee and chocolates she wanted. She texted her sister she had made it home safely, then turned off her phone.

Chapter Sixty-five

Wednesday, December 24th, 2014

Melody

Melody stood before the full-length mirror in her pink night shirt looking at her profile with one hand on her hip and the other hand below her belly button. She tried to imagine herself with a large round tummy then smiled as she lovingly rubbed where she assumed her baby rested.

She figured she was nine weeks into her pregnancy. Melody was over the moon with happiness. How could such a wonderful thing have happened to her? She didn't know and she didn't care.

"Woman! Are you going to get dressed this morning or stay in bed all day?" came Frank's booming voice as he stomped up the stairs and into the master bedroom of his house. He found Melody with both hands on her lower abdomen admiring herself.

"Oh, look! A pretty girl in her night shirt! Where did she come from? I think I'll ask her to come live in my house and have my baby." Frank walked over and scooped Melody up in his arms, gently laid her on the big king-sized bed and kissed her sweetly on the mouth. She wrapped her arms around his neck and her legs around his waist in response.

"We are going to have to finish this later, Mellie. There is a bunch to do today. We need to pass out the Christmas bonus checks and the turkeys to the guys down at the mill this morning, then head over to Mom and Dad's," Frank informed her.

"I know but I don't feel so great in the mornings these days. I really would like to spend the day in bed. It won't be a complete washout. I can make some needed calls for the mill right here. I need to call Sammy, too, check on how she's doing and invite her to Christmas dinner one more time. Besides, it's Christmas Eve, aren't we going to your parent's house tomorrow for dinner? Why do we need to go today? The only real reason your mother wants to see me is to talk to me about the wedding. Weddings make me feel anxious and flustered and I already feel dizzy and nauseated. If she brings up the subject of flowers and the caterer I just might barf," Melody told Frank.

Frank propped himself up on one arm and put his head in his hand while he thought this idea over.

"Okay, this year only. Mom and Dad always passed out holiday checks and turkeys together to give the employees the feeling we are a family. It's good business and creates loyalty. It's tradition." Frank was serious now. "As a tradeoff here, you have to let me tell the men you're not with me this morning because you have morning sickness. They'll get a kick out of that bit of news and will want to know the date of the wedding. Give me a date, Mellie."

Melody thought for a moment. "What do you think of Valentine's Day?"

"I love it!!" Frank exclaimed as he jumped off the bed and finished getting dressed to go down to the mill. "I think the guys are going to love it, and most importantly I think my mom is going to be out of her mind with joy. Of course, any date would have suited her, pretty much.

"Can I ask you for one more favor? This can be my Christmas gift if you like. Tomorrow ask my mom for help with the wedding and... please, give her some tasks to work on. She always wanted a daughter and you are going to have to learn that role in our family now. Can you do this for me?" Frank asked looking at her directly.

"Yes, I'll do that. Your mother has been very welcoming to me. She always has and I am grateful, really, I am. I will do it tomorrow, for sure," Melody promised.

Frank was pleased as he ran downstairs to the kitchen, grabbed the scrambled eggs and toast he had made for Melody, and brought them up to her so she could have breakfast in bed on Christmas Eve morning. Before he left for the morning, he kissed her goodbye and told her that when he came home they'd drive to Salem and shop for baby things as she had asked to do the day before.

As soon as Melody heard Frank's pick-up drive away, she got out of bed and tiptoed across the thick light gray carpet to the black dresser, opened the bottom drawer and took out the blue leather album with *Family Memories* written in gold across the front. The smile slid from her face and she sighed heavily.

She laid the Corbbet family album down on the dark blue down comforter then she looked around the room. This was Frank's house. He'd had it built on property his family had owned for three generations when he married his first wife. Melody didn't know the woman; she wasn't from Yamhill County. What Melody had learned about her was that she had been Frank's trophy wife. According to Frank it cost him a small fortune just to keep her in shoes and handbags. She had picked all the colors and furniture for the house and it had to be the best, nothing was too good for her. Until Frank's money ran out, or so he told her, and she ran off with another man whom she assumed was twice as rich as Frank. She was so certain Frank had gone broke she didn't even ask for a divorce settlement. Besides, she had a bigger fish on her hook and needed to land him as fast as she could. Her second husband had been some con man from Texas who had lied to her about non-existent oil wells. He had thought they would be living on her divorce settlement. Once the money ran out from hocking her jewelry and designer handbags the Texan ran out on her, leaving her high and dry at some seedy motel outside Houston.

Frank said he had laughed all the way home from the attorney's office on that one. Later she would try to come back to Frank but Frank's attorney had hired a private investigator who had found out she'd been writing bad checks and had her picked up on outstanding warrants.

It was from this story about Frank and his first wife that Melody learned Frank could be just as ruthless as he was kind. Frank might appear to be some good ole boy running his daddy's lumber mill but it was best to not try to screw him over, ever.

Frank's second wife had also been a trophy wife. Tall, slender, long blond hair mostly from bleach jobs and hair extensions. She not only had to have her nails and toes done on a regular basis, she had had her lips plumped up, her boobs enlarged, and her tummy tucked.

Frank had let his second wife re-paint and re-furnish the entire house he had built while married to his first wife. As with his first wife, he never put his second wife's name on anything. Not the house, not on any of the cars, not on any bank accounts or credit cards. And this time not even on her jewelry or expensive handbags or shoes.

When this wife left him for a richer and much older man, she walked out the door with just the clothes on her back. But Frank did like the whites, grays, and blues his second wife had re-done the house in and kept it that way. Besides, no need to spend more money when he didn't see a good reason for it.

It was Frank's slight penny-pinching ways that had given Melody pause when it came to marrying him. Her father had been a tightwad because he didn't have any money. Frank was slow to spend his money because he saw no reason to pour gasoline out on the ground rather than use it as needed fuel for later, so to speak. She was glad she had some investments and her own bank accounts. These she hadn't told Frank about, at least not fully. She thought of these as insurance to be used in the event of... well, she wasn't sure what but just in case.

Frank now owned Earl Corbbet's old orchard. He had asked Melody if she cared what he did with the place and she had told him no, she did not care. The house was rented out to one of Frank's employees with five or six kids. The fruit trees were scheduled to be pulled out later in the winter so the area where the orchard had been could be used by Davison Mill for an extension of the pole yard and more parking for equipment, as needed. Melody didn't care if that section of the planet got swallowed up by the Earth or was paved over with cement. Whenever she visited there the place still gave her the creeps.

Melody looked at the eggs, toast, and orange juice Frank had put on the black nightstand beside the bed. She put on her robe and took her breakfast downstairs, eating a few bites and stirring it around to look like she had eaten her meal. *Like a child who's trying to show her parents she has done what they told her to do,* she thought. She put the plate in the sink then got into the stainless-steel refrigerator, pulled out a pint of caramel nut chocolate swirl ice cream, grabbed a spoon from the drawer, and headed back upstairs to bed.

Once she had gotten in bed and turned on the TV to some channel with a version of *A Christmas Carol* playing, she took a big bite of ice cream and opened the album to the first page. It held the birth announcement, birth certificate, and baby bracelet of her mother. The page after it held the three pictures of her mother at different stages of her childhood which she and Sammy had found in the little jewelry box.

The work on the album had started the day after Melody and Sammy had gotten back from their road trip to Hamilton, Montana where they had dropped off the little blue and gold urn of their mother's ashes. The trip had been successful in several ways. Once in Hamilton the sisters had driven to the local cemetery where Emily's parents had been buried. While at the gravesite, before they were able to sprinkle some of their mother's ashes (the rest they had planned to put out at the rodeo grounds and the high school, and the last bit out at what had been the old Newberry ranch), an old caretaker had shown up asking a lot of questions. When the girls explained what they planned to do the man offered to dig up a three-foot-deep spot between the two Newberry graves to place the small urn there for a small fee. The sisters agreed as long as they could stand there while he did it. They wanted to ensure it was actually done and not just something they paid for but never happened. The old man did as they asked. After twenty-seven years of being buried in a grave with her rapist back of the barn on the Corbbet orchard, Emily Louise Newberry Corbbet was put to rest between her mother and father, brought there by her own children. The girls then got back in Sammy's Kia and drove straight out of town not making one other stop until they needed gas. The round trip had taken three days, from when they left on Monday morning as planned out at the funeral home, to when they returned late that Wednesday evening.

Melody, with the help of Patty and Joy Holiday, had put the album together in a way that would have made any scrapbooker envious. Of course, they had left out the articles about the trial of William Garrett for the rape of their mother. But they had included the broken locket, which they taped down next to the marriage license and the picture of Earl with his arm around Emily, which Joy thought must have been taken when Emily first arrived to Sheridan but the sisters figured was taken after Melody was born.

The last harvest had gone off as well as could be expected. Lots of people showed up, some people wanted apples and pears, some wanted to look around the place, some thought it was an estate sale so Melody sold her father's bedroom set, her bedroom set, and Sammy's bedroom set. She'd had no idea furniture from the early '60s had come back in fashion and she got a good deal of money for them as well as for the kitchen table and chairs.

Frank had offered to handle the men that wanted to go in the barn to look for tools at rock bottom prices. That's when Melody had gotten a real look at the savvy business man Frank had grown up to be. She had also seen his sterner side when he saw a couple guys not watching what they were doing with one of the ladders and Frank had to bark orders at them to get them under control.

After the day was done and the last person had left the property and before Frank had told the sisters his big surprise of buying their dad's property, Frank had pulled $1,000 cash out of his pants pockets. Later Sammy told Melody she had gotten $1,000 from Jesse Miller, Jan's brother, for the old Chevy pickup.

Melody made sure Sammy took all the money. She was the one who had been put through so much, the one who had so much to lose, and the one who had had to orchestrate and carry out the actual cremation of their mother while Melody lay on the couch at the funeral home. It wasn't much but it was some cash in the event Sammy needed it for some unpredicted emergency.

Melody leaned back on the feather pillows covered in white Egyptian cotton and stretched out her legs while taking another bite of ice cream. She glanced over at the TV. Ebenezer Scrooge was falling into a grave as the Grim Reaper stood over him. She decided to call her sister.

"Hello?" Sammy answered the phone in a sleepy croaky voice.

"Good morning my sister. Merry Christmas, for what it's worth. Wanted to ensure you got your quilt from Mother that Joy Holiday pieced together for you. I mailed it last week. And I thought I'd give you one more chance to accept our offer to come to Frank's parents for Christmas dinner tomorrow," Melody said kindly to her sister. "Frank really wants you here with us."

"Oh, good morning, Mellie. Ya, I got the quilt just fine, came out nice. What time is it? Oh, 9:30! Why do you always call so early?" Sammy wanted to know.

"Well, Frank gets up at 6:00 every morning all bright-eyed and bushy-tailed and he makes sure I'm awake even if I don't get out of bed. At least he doesn't expect me to go in to work with him every morning while I have morning sickness but once that's over, I won't have any excuses, until the baby arrives."

"Did I tell you congratulations? I mean it. I'm happy for you. Oh, wait, ya. Linda's here, she's really happy for you too."

"Thanks, you guys, that is sweet. So, what about that Christmas dinner?"

"No fucking God-damned way! No offense intended. Frank is okay, I can be around him just fine even though he can be a little on the bossy side. But his folks, actually, anyone's folks, just can't be done. Besides, you know I don't do Christmas. Hell, you didn't do Christmas until like right now today. Now that I think about it, did we ever have Christmas as kids?"

"Hmmm, nooooo, I don't remember doing more than a few gifts and canned clam chowder for dinner. Oh, wait! Remember the year Dad put up that old fake silver tree in the window in the front room and left it there for two years?" Melody started laughing into her phone. She could hear Sammy laughing at the other end.

"Oh, my gawd! Yes!! Who finally took it down? Was it that poor woman Dad tried to date from the hardware store?" Sammy came back. Then both girls broke in to a hard, screaming laughter.

When the laughing died down Melody asked her sister, "Will you be my maid of honor?" in a somewhat sad tone.

"Ahhhh, shoot, Mellie. Do I have to come back to Sheridan? When is this thing? You aren't going to try to make me wear a pink dress, for God's sake!" Sammy moaned into her phone. Melody could hear Linda laughing in the background then Sammy say, "Stop it, it's not funny!" in a hushed voice.

"We set the date this morning, Valentine's Day. Even falls on a Saturday this year. Not totally certain about location. Hey, what about that country club in Salem where Frank's parents are members!" Melody perked up a bit. She looked over at the TV, Scrooge was running through town in his nightshirt grinning and singing with children following him.

"Whatever, Mellie. Gots to go, love you bunches. We'll talk later." Then Sammy hung up.

Melody looked out the big sliding glass doors that led out onto a small covered balcony deck with lounge chairs. It had started to snow. She suddenly felt very tired. She rolled over and curled up with one of the pillows and fell into a deep sleep.

She dreamed of running with Sammy down a very dark street in the rain carrying the cremated remains of their mother then quickly getting into her car, starting up the engine, and speeding away though the little town of Sheridan.

Then the scene changed to someplace she'd never seen before. The front room of a house, fire in the fireplace, a single stocking hung from the mantel. A Christmas tree lit up, presents wrapped with bright paper and bows underneath. Cheerful voices sing as an older woman plays the piano in the dining room. Emily Newberry, as a young teenager, takes a cookie from a plate on the table then kisses her father on the cheek as he reads the newspaper in his chair. Suddenly Emily looks up, straight at Melody as if she were in the room, and mouths the words, "Thank you."

THE END

About the Author

A fifth generation Oregonian, Gwen Barnard grew up in Portland and small towns on farms and private airports where her father ran skydiving centers. After raising her three children and retiring she was able to begin her lifelong dream of writing murder mysteries.

Upon the death of her father, who left her his rundown house and private airport on ten acres in Sheridan, Oregon, Gwen decided to weave a tale filled with covered-up murders and ghosts haunting the property. There may or may not be actual ghosts haunting the actual property.